CONAN—TRAPPED!

"And so, brave captain, farewell!" said Constantius. "I will remember you when, in an hour, Taramis lies in my arms."

Nailed to a tree, Conan clenched his mallet-like fists convulsively on the spike-heads. Knots and bunches of muscle started out of his massive arms as he bent his head forward and spat savagely at Constantius' face. The *voivode* laughed coolly, wiped the saliva from his gorget and reined his horse about.

"Remember me when the vultures are tearing at your living flesh," he called mockingly. "The desert scavengers are a particularly voracious breed. I have seen men hang for hours on a cross, eyeless, earless, and scalpless, before the sharp beaks had eaten their way into his vitals."

Without a backward glance he rode toward the city, a supple, erect figure, gleaming in his burnished armor, his stolid, bearded henchmen jogging beside him. A faint rising of dust from the worn trail marked their passing.

The man hanging on the cross was the one touch of sentient life in a landscape that seemed desolate and deserted in the late evening. Khauran, less than a mile away, might have been on the other side of the world, and existing in another age.

IN THE SAME SERIES

Shadow Kingdoms
People of the Dark
Beyond the Black River
Hour of the Dragon (forthcoming)

BEYOND THE BLACK RIVER

Robert E. Howard

COSMOS BOOKS

BEYOND THE BLACK RIVER

Published by
Dorchester Publishing Co., Inc.
200 Madison Ave.
New York, NY 10016
in collaboration with Wildside Press LLC

ISBN-10: 0-8439-5920-7
ISBN-13: 978-0-8439-5920-8

Printed in the United States of America.

CONTENTS

A WITCH SHALL BE BORN

Weird Tales, December 1934

1. The Blood-Red Crescent

Taramis, Queen of Khauran, awakened from a dream-haunted slumber to a silence that seemed more like the stillness of nighted catacombs than the normal quiet of a sleeping palace. She lay staring into the darkness, wondering why the candles in their golden candelabra had gone out. A flecking of stars marked a gold-barred casement that lent no illumination to the interior of the chamber. But as Taramis lay there, she became aware of a spot of radiance glowing in the darkness before her. She watched, puzzled. It grew and its intensity deepened as it expanded, a widening disk of lurid light hovering against the dark velvet hangings of the opposite wall. Taramis caught her breath, starting up to a sitting position. A dark object was visible in that circle of light — *a human head.*

In a sudden panic the queen opened her lips to cry out for her maids; then she checked herself. The glow was more lurid, the head more vividly limned. It was a woman's head, small, delicately molded, superbly poised, with a high-piled mass of lustrous black hair.

The face grew distinct as she stared — and it was the sight of this face which froze the cry in Taramis' throat. The features were her own! She might have been looking into a mirror which subtly altered her reflection, lending it a tigerish gleam of eye, a vindictive curl of lip.

"Ishtar!" gasped Taramis. "I am bewitched!"

Appallingly, the apparition spoke, and its voice was like honeyed venom.

"Bewitched? No, sweet sister! Here is no sorcery."

"Sister?" stammered the bewildered girl. "I have no sister."

"You never had a sister?" came the sweet, poisonously mocking voice. "Never a twin sister whose flesh was as soft as yours to caress or hurt?"

"Why, once I had a sister," answered Taramis, still convinced that she was in the grip of some sort of nightmare. "But she died."

The beautiful face in the disk was convulsed with the aspect of a fury; so hellish became its expression that Taramis, cowering back, half-expected to see snaky locks writhe hissing about the ivory brow.

"You lie!" The accusation was spat from between the snarling red lips. "She did not die! Fool! Oh, enough of this mummery! Look — and let your sight be blasted!"

Light ran suddenly along the hangings like flaming serpents, and incredibly the candles in the golden sticks flared up again. Taramis crouched on her velvet couch, her lithe legs flexed beneath her, staring wide-eyed at the pantherish figure which posed mockingly before her. It was as if she gazed upon another Taramis, identical with herself in every contour of feature and limb, yet animated by an alien and evil personality. The face of this stranger waif reflected the opposite of every characteristic the countenance of the queen denoted. Lust and mystery sparkled in her scintillant eyes, cruelty lurked in the curl of her full red lips. Each movement of her supple body was subtly suggestive. Her coiffure imitated that of the queen's, on her feet were gilded sandals such as Taramis wore in her boudoir. The sleeveless, low-necked silk tunic, girdled at the waist with a cloth-of-gold cincture, was a duplicate of the queen's night-garment.

"Who are you?" gasped Taramis, an icy chill she could not explain creeping along her spine. "Explain your presence before I call my ladies-in-waiting to summon the guard!"

"Scream until the roof-beams crack," callously answered the stranger. "Your sluts will not wake till dawn, though the palace spring into flames about them. Your guardsmen will not hear your squeals; they have been sent out of this wing of the palace."

"What!" exclaimed Taramis, stiffening with outraged majesty. "Who dared give my guardsmen such a command?"

"I did, sweet sister," sneered the other girl. "A little while ago, before I entered. They thought it was their darling adored queen. Ha! How beautifully I acted the part! With what imperious dignity, softened by womanly sweetness, did I address the great louts who knelt in their armor and plumed helmets!"

Taramis felt as if a stifling net of bewilderment were being drawn about her.

"Who are you?" she cried desperately. "What madness is this? Why do you come here?"

"Who am I?" There was the spite of a she-cobra's hiss in the soft response. The girl stepped to the edge of the couch, grasped the queen's white shoulders with fierce fingers, and bent to glare full into the startled eyes of Taramis. And under the spell of that hypnotic glare, the queen forgot to resent the unprecedented outrage of violent hands laid on regal flesh.

"Fool!" gritted the girl between her teeth. "Can you ask? Can you wonder? I am Salome!"

"Salome!" Taramis breathed the word, and the hairs prickled on her scalp as she realized the incredible, numbing truth of the statement. "I thought you died within the hour of your birth," she said feebly.

"So thought many," answered the woman who called herself Salome. "They carried me into the desert to die, damn them! I, a mewing, puling babe whose life was so young it was scarcely the flicker of a candle. And do you know why they bore me forth to die?"

"I—I have heard the story—" faltered Taramis.

Salome laughed fiercely, and slapped her bosom. The low-necked tunic left the upper parts of her firm breasts bare, and between them there shone a curious mark — a crescent, red as blood.

"The mark of the witch!" cried Taramis, recoiling.

"Aye!" Salome's laughter was dagger-edged with hate. "The curse of the kings of Khauran! Aye, they tell the tale in the marketplaces, with wagging beards and rolling eyes, the pious fools! They tell how the first queen of our line had traffic with a fiend of darkness and bore him a daughter who lives in foul legendry to this day. And thereafter in each century a girl baby was born into the Askhaurian dynasty, with a scarlet half-moon between her breasts, that signified her destiny.

"'Every century a witch shall be born.' So ran the ancient curse. And so it has come to pass. Some were slain at birth, as they sought to slay me. Some walked the earth as witches, proud daughters of Khauran, with the moon of Hell burning upon their ivory bosoms. Each was named Salome. I too am Salome. It was always Salome, the witch. It will always be Salome, the witch, even when the mountains of ice have roared down from the pole and ground the civilizations to ruin, and a new world has risen from the ashes and dust — even then there shall be Salomes to walk the earth, to trap men's hearts by their sorcery, to dance before the kings of the world, and see the heads of the wise men fall at their pleasure."

"But — but you —" stammered Taramis.

"I?" The scintillant eyes burned like dark fires of

mystery. "They carried me into the desert far from the city, and laid me naked on the hot sand, under the flaming sun. And then they rode away and left me for the jackals and the vultures and the desert wolves.

"But the life in me was stronger than the life in common folk, for it partakes of the essence of the forces that seethe in the black gulfs beyond mortal ken. The hours passed, and the sun slashed down like the molten flames of Hell, but I did not die — aye, something of that torment I remember, faintly and far away, as one remembers a dim, formless dream. Then there were camels, and yellow-skinned men who wore silk robes and spoke in a weird tongue. Strayed from the caravan road, they passed close by, and their leader saw me, and recognized the scarlet crescent on my bosom. He took me up and gave me life.

"He was a magician from far Khitai, returning to his native kingdom after a journey to Stygia. He took me with him to purple-towering Paikang, its minarets rising amid the vine-festooned jungles of bamboo, and there I grew to womanhood under his teaching. Age had steeped him deep in black wisdom, not weakened his powers of evil. Many things he taught me —"

She paused, smiling enigmatically, with wicked mystery gleaming in her dark eyes. Then she tossed her head.

"He drove me from him at last, saying that I was but a common witch in spite of his teachings, and not fit to command the mighty sorcery he would have taught me. He would have made me queen of the world and ruled the nations through me, he said, but I was only a harlot of darkness. But what of it? I could never endure to seclude myself in a golden tower, and spend the long hours staring into a crystal globe, mumbling over incantations written on serpent's skin in the blood of virgins, poring over musty volumes in forgotten languages.

"He said I was but an earthly sprite, knowing naught of the deeper gulfs of cosmic sorcery. Well, this world contains all I desire — power, and pomp, and glittering pageantry, handsome men and soft women for my paramours and my slaves. He had told me who I was, of the curse and my heritage. I have returned to take that to which I have as much right as you. Now it is mine by right of possession."

"What do you mean?" Taramis sprang up and faced her sister, stung out of her bewilderment and fright. "Do you imagine that by drugging a few of my maids and tricking a few of my guardsmen you have established a claim to the throne of Khauran? Do not forget that *I* am queen of Khauran! I shall give you a place of honor, as my sister, but —"

Salome laughed hatefully.

"How generous of you, dear, sweet sister! But before you begin putting me in my place — perhaps you will tell me whose soldiers camp in the plain outside the city walls?"

"They are the Shemitish mercenaries of Constantius, the Kothic *voivode* of the Free Companies."

"And what do they in Khauran?" cooed Salome.

Taramis felt that she was being subtly mocked, but she answered with an assumption of dignity which she scarcely felt.

"Constantius asked permission to pass along the borders of Khauran on his way to Turan. He himself is hostage for their good behavior as long as they are within my domains."

"And Constantius," pursued Salome. "Did he not ask your hand today?"

Taramis shot her a clouded glance of suspicion.

"How did you know that?"

An insolent shrug of the slim naked shoulders was the only reply.

"You refused, dear sister?"

"Certainly I refused!" exclaimed Taramis angrily. "Do you, an Askhaurian princess yourself, suppose that the queen of Khauran could treat such a proposal with anything but disdain? Wed a bloody-handed adventurer, a man exiled from his own kingdom because of his crimes, and the leader of organized plunderers and hired murderers?

"I should never have allowed him to bring his black-bearded slayers into Khauran. But he is virtually a prisoner in the south tower, guarded by my soldiers. Tomorrow I shall bid him order his troops to leave the kingdom. He himself shall be kept captive until they are over the border. Meantime, my soldiers man the walls of the city, and I have warned him that he will answer for any outrages perpetrated on the villagers or shepherds by his mercenaries."

"He is confined in the south tower?" asked Salome.

"That is what I said. Why do you ask?"

For answer Salome clapped her hands, and lifting her voice, with a gurgle of cruel mirth in it, called: "The queen grants you an audience, Falcon!"

A gold-arabesqued door opened and a tall figure entered the chamber, at the sight of which Taramis cried out in amazement and anger.

"Constantius! You dare enter my chamber!"

"As you see, your Majesty!" He bent his dark, hawk-like head in mock humility.

Constantius, whom men called Falcon, was tall, broad-shouldered, slim-waisted, lithe and strong as pliant steel. He was handsome in an aquiline, ruthless way. His face was burnt dark by the sun, and his hair, which grew far back from his high, narrow forehead, was black as a raven. His dark eyes were penetrating and alert, the hardness of his thin lips not softened by his thin black mustache. His boots were of Kordavan leather, his hose and doublet of plain, dark silk, tarnished with the wear of the camps and the stains of armor rust.

Twisting his mustache, he let his gaze travel up and down the shrinking queen with an effrontery that made her wince.

"By Ishtar, Taramis," he said silkily, "I find you

more alluring in your night-tunic than in your queenly robes. Truly, this is an auspicious night!"

Fear grew in the queen's dark eyes. She was no fool; she knew that Constantius would never dare this outrage unless he was sure of himself.

"You are mad!" she said. "If I am in your power in this chamber, you are no less in the power of my subjects, who will rend you to pieces if you touch me. Go at once, if you would live."

Both laughed mockingly, and Salome made an impatient gesture.

"Enough of this farce; let us on to the next act in the comedy. Listen, dear sister: it was I who sent Constantius here. When I decided to take the throne of Khauran, I cast about for a man to aid me, and chose the Falcon, because of his utter lack of all characteristics men call good."

"I am overwhelmed, princess," murmured Constantius sardonically, with a profound bow.

"I sent him to Khauran, and, once his men were camped in the plain outside, and he was in the palace, I entered the city by that small gate in the west wall — the fools guarding it thought it was you returning from some nocturnal adventure —"

"You hellcat!" Taramis' cheeks flamed and her resentment got the better of her regal reserve.

Salome smiled hardly.

"They were properly surprized and shocked, but admitted me without question. I entered the palace the same way, and gave the order to the surprized guards that sent them marching away, as well as the men who guarded Constantius in the south tower. Then I came here, attending to the ladies-in-waiting on the way."

Taramis' fingers clenched and she paled.

"Well, what next?" she asked in a shaky voice.

"Listen!" Salome inclined her head. Faintly through the casement there came the clank of marching men in armor; gruff voices shouted in an alien tongue, and cries of alarm mingled with the shouts.

"The people awaken and grow fearful," said Constantius sardonically. "You had better go and reassure them, Salome!"

"Call me Taramis," answered Salome. "We must become accustomed to it."

"What have you done?" cried Taramis. "What have you done?"

"I have gone to the gates and ordered the soldiers to open them," answered Salome. "They were astounded, but they obeyed. That is the Falcon's army you hear, marching into the city."

"You devil!" cried Taramis. "You have betrayed my people, in my guise! You have made me seem a traitor! Oh, I shall go to them —"

With a cruel laugh Salome caught her wrist and jerked her back. The magnificent suppleness of the queen was helpless against the vindictive strength that steeled Salome's slender limbs.

"You know how to reach the dungeons from the palace, Constantius?" said the witch-girl. "Good.

Take this spitfire and lock her into the strongest cell. The jailers are all sound in drugged sleep. I saw to that. Send a man to cut their throats before they can awaken. None must ever know what has occurred tonight. Thenceforward I am Taramis, and Taramis is a nameless prisoner in an unknown dungeon."

Constantius smiled with a glint of strong white teeth under his thin mustache.

"Very good; but you would not deny me a little — ah — amusement first?"

"Not I! Tame the scornful hussy as you will." With a wicked laugh Salome flung her sister into the Kothian's arms, and turned away through the door that opened into the outer corridor.

Fright widened Taramis' lovely eyes, her supple figure rigid and straining against Constantius' embrace. She forgot the men marching in the streets, forgot the outrage to her queenship, in the face of the menace to her womanhood. She forgot all sensations but terror and shame as she faced the complete cynicism of Constantius' burning, mocking eyes, felt his hard arms crushing her writhing body.

Salome, hurrying along the corridor outside, smiled spitefully as a scream of despair and agony rang shuddering through the palace.

2. The Tree of Death

The young soldier's hose and shirt were smeared with dried blood, wet with sweat and gray with dust.

Blood oozed from the deep gash in his thigh, from the cuts on his breast and shoulder. Perspiration glistened on his livid face and his fingers were knotted in the cover of the divan on which he lay. Yet his words reflected mental suffering that outweighed physical pain.

"She must be mad!" he repeated again and again, like one still stunned by some monstrous and incredible happening. "It's like a nightmare! Taramis, whom all Khauran loves, betraying her people to that devil from Koth! Oh, Ishtar, why was I not slain? Better die than live to see our queen turn traitor and harlot!"

"Lie still, Valerius," begged the girl who was washing and bandaging his wounds with trembling hands. "Oh, please lie still, darling! You will make your wounds worse. I dared not summon a leech —"

"No," muttered the wounded youth. "Constantius' blue-bearded devils will be searching the quarters for wounded Khaurani; they'll hang every man who has wounds to show he fought against them. Oh, Taramis, how could you betray the people who worshipped you?" In his fierce agony he writhed, weeping in rage and shame, and the terrified girl caught him in her arms, straining his tossing head against her bosom, imploring him to be quiet.

"Better death than the black shame that has come upon Khauran this day," he groaned. "Did you see it, Ivga?"

"No, Valerius." Her soft, nimble fingers were

again at work, gently cleansing and closing the gaping edges of his raw wounds. "I was awakened by the noise of fighting in the streets — I looked out a casement and saw the Shemites cutting down people; then presently I heard you calling me faintly from the alley door."

"I had reached the limits of my strength," he muttered. "I fell in the alley and could not rise. I knew they'd find me soon if I lay there — I killed three of the blue-bearded beasts, by Ishtar! They'll never swagger through Khauran's streets, by the gods! The fiends are tearing their hearts in Hell!"

The trembling girl crooned soothingly to him, as to a wounded child, and closed his panting lips with her own cool sweet mouth. But the fire that raged in his soul would not allow him to lie silent.

"I was not on the wall when the Shemites entered," he burst out. "I was asleep in the barracks, with the others not on duty. It was just before dawn when our captain entered, and his face was pale under his helmet. 'The Shemites are in the city,' he said. 'The queen came to the southern gate and gave orders that they should be admitted. She made the men come down from the walls, where they've been on guard since Constantius entered the kingdom. I don't understand it, and neither does anyone else, but I heard her give the order, and we obeyed as we always do. We are ordered to assemble in the square before the palace. Form ranks outside the barracks and march — leave your arms and armor here.

Ishtar knows what this means, but it is the queen's order.'

"Well, when we came to the square the Shemites were drawn up on foot opposite the palace, ten thousand of the blue-bearded devils, fully armed, and people's heads were thrust out of every window and door on the square. The streets leading into the square were thronged by bewildered folk. Taramis was standing on the steps of the palace, alone except for Constantius, who stood stroking his mustache like a great lean cat who has just devoured a sparrow. But fifty Shemites with bows in their hands were ranged below them.

"That's where the queen's guard should have been, but they were drawn up at the foot of the palace stair, as puzzled as we, though they had come fully armed, in spite of the queen's order.

"Taramis spoke to us then, and told us that she had reconsidered the proposal made her by Constantius — why, only yesterday she threw it in his teeth in open court! — and that she had decided to make him her royal consort. She did not explain why she had brought the Shemites into the city so treacherously. But she said that, as Constantius had control of a body of professional fighting-men, the army of Khauran would no longer be needed, and therefore she disbanded it, and ordered us to go quietly to our homes.

"Why, obedience to our queen is second nature to us, but we were struck dumb and found no word to answer. We broke ranks almost before we knew what we were doing, like men in a daze.

"But when the palace guard was ordered to disarm likewise and disband, the captain of the guard, Conan, interrupted. Men said he was off-duty the night before, and drunk. But he was wide awake now. He shouted to the guardsmen to stand as they were until they received an order from him — and such is his dominance of his men, that they obeyed in spite of the queen. He strode up to the palace steps and glared at Taramisand — then he roared: 'This is not the queen! This isn't Taramis! It's some devil in masquerade!'

"Then hell was to pay! I don't know just what happened. I think a Shemite struck Conan, and Conan killed him. The next instant the square was a battleground. The Shemites fell on the guardsmen, and their spears and arrows struck down many soldiers who had already disbanded.

"Some of us grabbed up such weapons as we could and fought back. We hardly knew what we were fighting for, but it was against Constantius and his devils — not against Taramis, I swear it! Constantius shouted to cut the traitors down. We were not traitors!" Despair and bewilderment shook his voice. The girl murmured pityingly, not understanding it all, but aching in sympathy with her lover's suffering.

"The people did not know which side to take. It was a madhouse of confusion and bewilderment. We who fought didn't have a chance, in no formation, without armor and only half-armed. The guards were fully armed and drawn up in a square, but there were only five hundred of them. They took a heavy toll before they were cut down, but there could be only one conclusion to such a battle. And while her people were being slaughtered before her, Taramis stood on the palace steps, with Constantius' arm about her waist, and laughed like a heartless, beautiful fiend! Gods, it's all mad — mad!

"I never saw a man fight as Conan fought. He put his back to the courtyard wall, and before they overpowered him the dead men were strewn in heaps thigh-deep about him. But at last they dragged him down, a hundred against one. When I saw him fall I dragged myself away feeling as if the world had burst under my very fingers. I heard Constantius call to his dogs to take the captain alive — stroking his mustache, with that hateful smile on his lips."

That smile was on the lips of Constantius at that very moment. He sat his horse among a cluster of his men — thick-bodied Shemites with curled blue-black beards and hooked noses; the low-swinging sun struck glints from their peaked helmets and the silvered scales of their corselets. Nearly a mile behind, the walls and towers of Khauran rose sheer out of the meadowlands.

By the side of the caravan road a heavy cross had been planted, and on this grim tree a man hung, nailed there by iron spikes through his hands and feet. Naked but for a loincloth, the man was almost a giant in stature, and his muscles stood out in thick corded ridges on limbs and body, which the sun had long ago burned brown. The perspiration of agony beaded his face and his mighty breast, but from under the tangled black mane that fell over his low, broad forehead, his blue eyes blazed with an unquenched fire. Blood oozed sluggishly from the lacerations in his hands and feet.

Constantius saluted him mockingly.

"I am sorry, captain," he said, "that I can not remain to ease your last hours, but I have duties to perform in yonder city — I must not keep our delicious queen waiting!" He laughed softly. "So I leave you to your own devices — and those beauties!" He pointed meaningly at the black shadows which swept incessantly back and forth, high above.

"Were it not for them, I imagine that a powerful brute like yourself should live on the cross for days. Do not cherish any illusions of rescue because I am leaving you unguarded. I have had it proclaimed that anyone seeking to take your body, living or dead, from the cross, will be flayed alive together with all the members of his family, in the public square. I am so firmly established in Khauran that my order is as good as a regiment of guardsmen. I am leaving no guard, because the vultures will not approach as long as anyone is near, and I do not wish them to feel any constraint. That is also why I brought you so far from the city. These desert vultures approach the walls no closer than this spot.

"And so, brave captain, farewell! I will remember you when, in an hour, Taramis lies in my arms."

Blood started afresh from the pierced palms as the victim's mallet-like fists clenched convulsively on the spike-heads. Knots and bunches of muscle started out of the massive arms, and Conan bent his head forward and spat savagely at Constantius' face. The *voivode* laughed coolly, wiped the saliva from his gorget and reined his horse about.

"Remember me when the vultures are tearing at your living flesh," he called mockingly. "The desert scavengers are a particularly voracious breed. I have seen men hang for hours on a cross, eyeless, earless, and scalpless, before the sharp beaks had eaten their way into his vitals."

Without a backward glance he rode toward the city, a supple, erect figure, gleaming in his burnished armor, his stolid, bearded henchmen jogging beside him. A faint rising of dust from the worn trail marked their passing.

The man hanging on the cross was the one touch of sentient life in a landscape that seemed desolate and deserted in the late evening. Khauran, less than a mile away, might have been on the other side of the world, and existing in another age.

Shaking the sweat out of his eyes, Conan stared blankly at the familiar terrain. On either side of the city, and beyond it, stretched the fertile meadowlands, with cattle browsing in the distance where fields and vineyards checkered the plain. The western and northern horizons were dotted with villages, miniature in the distance. A lesser distance to the southeast a silvery gleam marked the course of a river, and beyond that river sandy desert began abruptly to stretch away and away beyond the horizon. Conan stared at that expanse of empty waste shimmering tawnily in the late sunlight as a trapped hawk stares at the open sky. A revulsion shook him when he glanced at the gleaming towers of Khauran. The city had betrayed him — trapped him into circumstances that left him hanging to a wooden cross like a hare nailed to a tree.

A red lust for vengeance swept away the thought. Curses ebbed fitfully from the man's lips. All his universe contracted, focused, became incorporated in the four iron spikes that held him from life and freedom. His great muscles quivered, knotting like iron cables. With the sweat starting out on his graying skin, he sought to gain leverage, to tear the nails from the wood. It was useless. They had been driven deep. Then he tried to tear his hands off the spikes, and it was not the knifing, abysmal agony that finally caused him to cease his efforts, but the futility of it. The spike-heads were broad and heavy; he could not drag them through the wounds. A surge of helplessness shook the giant, for the first time in his life. He hung motionless, his head resting on his breast, shutting his eyes against the aching glare of the sun.

A beat of wings caused him to look, just as a feathered shadow shot down out of the sky. A keen beak, stabbing at his eyes, cut his cheek, and he jerked his head aside, shutting his eyes involuntarily. He shouted, a croaking, desperate shout of menace, and the vultures swerved away and retreated, frightened by the sound. They resumed their wary circling above his head. Blood trickled over Conan's mouth, and he licked his lips involuntarily, spat at the salty taste.

Thirst assailed him savagely. He had drunk deeply of wine the night before, and no water had touched his lips since before the battle in the square, that dawn. And killing was thirsty, salt-sweaty work. He glared at the distant river as a man in Hell glares through the opened grille. He thought of gushing freshets of white water he had breasted, laved to the shoulders in liquid jade. He remembered great horns of foaming ale, jacks of sparkling wine gulped carelessly or spilled on the tavern floor. He bit his lip to keep from bellowing in intolerable anguish as a tortured animal bellows.

The sun sank, a lurid ball in a fiery sea of blood. Against a crimson rampart that banded the horizon the towers of the city floated unreal as a dream. The very sky was tinged with blood to his misted glare. He licked his blackened lips and stared with bloodshot eyes at the distant river. It too seemed crimson like blood, and the shadows crawling up from the east seemed black as ebony.

In his dulled ears sounded the louder beat of wings. Lifting his head he watched with the burning glare of a wolf the shadows wheeling above him. He knew that his shouts would frighten them away no longer. One dipped — dipped — lower and lower. Conan drew his head back as far as he could, waiting with terrible patience. The vulture swept in with a swift roar of wings. Its beak flashed down, ripping the skin on Conan's chin as he jerked his head aside; then before the bird could flash away, Conan's head lunged forward on his mighty neck muscles, and his teeth, snapping like those of a wolf, locked on the bare, wattled neck.

Instantly the vulture exploded into squawking, flapping hysteria. Its thrashing wings blinded the man, and its talons ripped his chest. But grimly he hung on, the muscles starting out in lumps on his jaws. And the scavenger's neck-bones crunched between those powerful teeth. With a spasmodic flutter the bird hung limp. Conan let go, spat blood from his mouth. The other vultures, terrified by the fate of their companion, were in full flight to a distant tree, where they perched like black demons in conclave.

Ferocious triumph surged through Conan's numbed brain. Life beat strongly and savagely through his veins. He could still deal death; he still lived. Every twinge of sensation, even of agony, was a negation of death.

"By Mitra!" Either a voice spoke, or he suffered

from hallucination. "In all my life I have never seen such a thing!"

Shaking the sweat and blood from his eyes, Conan saw four horsemen sitting their steeds in the twilight and staring up at him. Three were lean, white-robed hawks, Zuagir tribesmen without a doubt, nomads from beyond the river. The other was dressed like them in a white, girdled *khalat* and a flowing headdress which, banded about the temples with a triple circlet of braided camelhair, fell to his shoulders. But he was not a Shemite. The dusk was not so thick, nor Conan's hawk-like sight so clouded, that he could not perceive the man's facial characteristics.

He was as tall as Conan, though not so heavy-limbed. His shoulders were broad and his supple figure was hard as steel and whalebone. A short black beard did not altogether mask the aggressive jut of his lean jaw, and gray eyes cold and piercing as a sword gleamed from the shadow of the *kafieh*. Quieting his restless steed with a quick, sure hand, this man spoke: "By Mitra, I should know this man!"

"Aye!" It was the guttural accents of a Zuagir. "It is the Cimmerian who was captain of the queen's guard!"

"She must be casting off all her old favorites," muttered the rider. "Who'd have ever thought it of Queen Taramis? I'd rather have had a long, bloody war. It would have given us desert folk a chance to plunder. As it is we've come this close to the walls and found only this nag" — he glanced at a fine gelding led by one of the nomads — "and this dying dog."

Conan lifted his bloody head.

"If I could come down from this beam I'd make a dying dog out of you, you Zaporoskan thief!" he rasped through blackened lips.

"Mitra, the knave knows me!" exclaimed the other. "How, knave, do you know me?"

"There's only one of your breed in these parts," muttered Conan. "You are Olgerd Vladislav, the outlaw chief."

"Aye! And once a hetman of the kozaki of the Zaporoskan River, as you have guessed. Would you like to live?"

"Only a fool would ask that question," panted Conan.

"I am a hard man," said Olgerd, "and toughness is the only quality I respect in a man. I shall judge if you are a man, or only a dog after all, fit only to lie here and die."

"If we cut him down we may be seen from the walls," objected one of the nomads.

Olgerd shook his head.

"The dusk is too deep. Here, take this ax, Djebal, and cut down the cross at the base."

"If it falls forward it will crush him," objected Djebal. "I can cut it so it will fall backward, but then the shock of the fall may crack his skull and tear loose all his entrails."

"If he's worthy to ride with me he'll survive it," answered Olgerd imperturbably. "If not, then he doesn't deserve to live. Cut!"

The first impact of the battle-ax against the wood and its accompanying vibrations sent lances of agony through Conan's swollen feet and hands. Again and again the blade fell, and each stroke reverberated on his bruised brain, setting his tortured nerves aquiver. But he set his teeth and made no sound. The ax cut through, the cross reeled on its splintered base and toppled backward. Conan made his whole body a solid knot of iron-hard muscle, jammed his head back hard against the wood and held it rigid there. The beam struck the ground heavily and rebounded slightly. The impact tore his wounds and dazed him for an instant. He fought the rushing tide of blackness, sick and dizzy, but realized that the iron muscles that sheathed his vitals had saved him from permanent injury.

And he had made no sound, though blood oozed from his nostrils and his belly-muscles quivered with nausea. With a grunt of approval Djebal bent over him with a pair of pincers used to draw horseshoe nails, and gripped the head of the spike in Conan's right hand, tearing the skin to get a grip on the deeply embedded head. The pincers were small for that work. Djebal sweated and tugged, swearing and wrestling with the stubborn iron, working it back and forth — in swollen flesh as well as in wood. Blood started, oozing over the Cimmerian's fingers. He lay so still he might have been dead, except for the spasmodic rise and fall of his great chest. The spike gave way, and Djebal held up the bloodstained thing with a grunt of satisfaction, then flung it away and bent over the other.

The process was repeated, and then Djebal turned his attention to Conan's skewered feet. But the Cimmerian, struggling up to a sitting posture, wrenched the pincers from his fingers and sent him staggering backward with a violent shove. Conan's hands were swollen to almost twice their normal size. His fingers felt like misshapen thumbs, and closing his hands was an agony that brought blood streaming from under his grinding teeth. But somehow, clutching the pincers clumsily with both hands, he managed to wrench out first one spike and then the other. They were not driven so deeply into the wood as the others had been.

He rose stiffly and stood upright on his swollen, lacerated feet, swaying drunkenly, the icy sweat dripping from his face and body. Cramps assailed him and he clamped his jaws against the desire to retch.

Olgerd, watching him impersonally, motioned him toward the stolen horse. Conan stumbled toward it, and every step was a stabbing, throbbing hell that flecked his lips with bloody foam. One misshapen, groping hand fell clumsily on the saddlebow, a bloody foot somehow found the stirrup. Setting his teeth, he swung up, and he almost fainted in midair; but he came down in the saddle — and as he did so, Olgerd struck the horse sharply with his whip. The startled beast reared, and the man in the saddle swayed and slumped like a sack of sand, almost unseated. Conan had wrapped a rein about each hand, holding it in place with a clamping thumb. Drunkenly he exerted the strength of his knotted biceps, wrenching the horse down; it screamed, its jaw almost dislocated.

One of the Shemites lifted a water-flask questioningly.

Olgerd shook his head.

"Let him wait until we get to camp. It's only ten miles. If he's fit to live in the desert he'll live that long without a drink."

The group rode like swift ghosts toward the river; among them Conan swayed like a drunken man in the saddle, bloodshot eyes glazed, foam drying on his blackened lips.

3. A Letter to Nemedia

The savant Astreas, traveling in the East in his never-tiring search for knowledge, wrote a letter to his friend and fellow-philosopher Alcemides, in his native Nemedia, which constitutes the entire knowledge of the Western nations concerning the events of that period in the East, always a hazy, half-mythical region in the minds of the Western folk.

Astreas wrote, in part: "You can scarcely conceive, my dear old friend, of the conditions now existing in this tiny kingdom since Queen Taramis admitted Constantius and his mercenaries, an event which I briefly described in my last, hurried letter. Seven months have passed since then, during which time it seems as though the devil himself had been loosed in this unfortunate realm. Taramis seems to have gone quite mad; whereas formerly she was famed for her virtue, justice and tranquility, she is now notorious for qualities precisely opposite to those just enumerated. Her private life is a scandal — or perhaps 'private' is not the correct term, since the queen makes no attempt to conceal the debauchery of her court. She constantly indulges in the most infamous revelries, in which the unfortunate ladies of the court are forced to join, young married women as well as virgins.

"She herself has not bothered to marry her paramour, Constantius, who sits on the throne beside her and reigns as her royal consort, and his officers follow his example, and do not hesitate to debauch any woman they desire, regardless of her rank or station. The wretched kingdom groans under exorbitant taxation, the farms are stripped to the bone, and the merchants go in rags which are all that is left them by the tax-gatherers. Nay, they are lucky if they escape with a whole skin.

"I sense your incredulity, good Alcemides; you will fear that I exaggerate conditions in Khauran. Such conditions would be unthinkable in any of the Western countries, admittedly. But you must realize the vast difference that exists between West and East, especially this part of the East. In the first place, Khauran is a kingdom of no great size, one of the many principalities which at one time formed the eastern part of the empire of Koth, and which later regained the independence which was theirs at a still earlier age. This part of the world is made up of these tiny realms, diminutive in comparison with the great kingdoms of the West, or the great sultanates of the farther East, but important in their control of the caravan routes, and in the wealth concentrated in them.

"Khauran is the most southeasterly of these principalities, bordering on the very deserts of eastern Shem. The city of Khauran is the only city of any magnitude in the realm, and stands within sight of the river which separates the grasslands from the sandy desert, like a watchtower to guard the fertile meadows behind it. The land is so rich that it yields three and four crops a year, and the plains north and west of the city are dotted with villages. To one accustomed to the great plantations and stock-farms of the West, it is strange to see these tiny fields and vineyards; yet wealth in grain and fruit pours from them as from a horn of plenty. The villagers are agriculturists, nothing else. Of a mixed, aboriginal race, they are unwarlike, unable to protect themselves, and forbidden the possession of arms. Dependent wholly upon the soldiers of the city for protection, they are helpless under the present conditions. So the savage revolt of the rural sections, which would be a certainty in any Western nation, is here impossible.

"They toil supinely under the iron hand of Constantius, and his black-bearded Shemites ride incessantly through the fields, with whips in their hands, like the slave drivers of the black serfs who toil in the plantations of southern Zingara.

"Nor do the people of the city fare any better. Their wealth is stripped from them, their fairest daughters taken to glut the insatiable lust of Constantius and his mercenaries. These men are utterly without mercy or compassion, possessed of all the characteristics our armies learned to abhor in our wars against the Shemitish allies of Argos — inhuman cruelty, lust, and wild-beast ferocity. The people of the city are Khauran's ruling caste, predominantly Hyborian, and valorous and warlike. But the treachery of their queen delivered them into the hands of their oppressors. The Shemites are the only armed force in Khauran, and the most hellish punishment is inflicted on any Khauran found possessing weapons. A systematic persecution to destroy the young Khaurani men able to bear arms has been savagely pursued. Many have ruthlessly been slaughtered, others sold as slaves to the Turanians. Thousands have fled the kingdom and either entered the service of other rulers, or become outlaws, lurking in numerous bands along the borders.

"At present there is some possibility of invasion from the desert, which is inhabited by tribes of Shemitish nomads. The mercenaries of Constantius are men from the Shemitish cities of the west, Pelishtim, Anakim, Akkharim, and are ardently hated by the Zuagirs and other wandering tribes. As you know, good Alcemides, the countries of these barbarians are divided into the western meadowlands which stretch to the distant ocean, and in which rise the cities of the town-dwellers, and the eastern deserts, where the lean nomads hold sway; there is incessant warfare between the dwellers of the cities and the dwellers of the desert.

"The Zuagirs have fought with and raided Khauran for centuries, without success, but they resent its conquest by their western kin. It is rumored that their natural antagonism is being fomented by the man who was formerly the captain of the queen's guard, and who, somehow escaping the hate of Constantius, who actually had him upon the cross, fled to the nomads. He is called Conan, and is himself a barbarian, one of those gloomy Cimmerians whose ferocity our soldiers have more than once learned to their bitter cost. It is rumored that he has become the right-hand man of Olgerd Vladislav, the *kozak* adventurer who wandered down from the northern steppes and made himself chief of a band of Zuagirs. There are also rumors that this band has increased vastly in the last few months, and that Olgerd, incited no doubt by this Cimmerian, is even considering a raid on Khauran.

"It can not be anything more than a raid, as the Zuagirs are without siege-machines, or the knowledge of investing a city, and it has been proven repeatedly in the past that the nomads in their loose formation, or rather lack of formation, are no match in hand-to-hand fighting for the well-disciplined, fully-armed warriors of the Shemitish cities. The natives of Khauran would perhaps welcome this conquest, since the nomads could deal with them no more harshly than their present masters, and even total extermination would be preferable to the suffering they have to endure. But they are so cowed and helpless that they could give no aid to the invaders.

"Their plight is most wretched. Taramis, apparently possessed of a demon, stops at nothing. She has abolished the worship of Ishtar, and turned the temple into a shrine of idolatry. She has destroyed the ivory image of the goddess which these eastern Hyborians worship (and which, inferior as it is to the true religion of Mitra which we Western nations recognize, is still superior to the devil worship of the Shemites) and filled the temple of Ishtar with obscene images of every imaginable sort — gods and goddesses of the night, portrayed in all the salacious and perverse poses and with all the revolting characteristics that a degenerate brain could conceive. Many of these images are to be identified as foul deities of the Shemites, the Turanians, the Vendhyans, and the Khitans, but others are reminiscent of a hideous and half-remembered antiquity, vile shapes forgotten except in the most obscure legends. Where the queen gained the knowledge of them I dare not even hazard a guess.

"She has instituted human sacrifice, and since her mating with Constantius, no less than five hundred men, women and children have been immolated. Some of these have died on the altar she has set up in the temple, herself wielding the sacrificial dagger, but most have met a more horrible doom.

"Taramis has placed some sort of monster in a crypt in the temple. What it is, and whence it came, none knows. But shortly after she had crushed the desperate revolt of her soldiers against Constantius, she spent a night alone in the desecrated temple, alone except for a dozen bound captives, and the shuddering people saw thick, foul-smelling smoke curling up from the dome, heard all night the frenetic chanting of the queen, and the agonized cries of her tortured captives; and toward dawn another voice mingled with these sounds — a strident, inhuman croaking that froze the blood of all who heard.

"In the full dawn Taramis reeled drunkenly from the temple, her eyes blazing with demoniac triumph. The captives were never seen again, nor the croaking voice heard. But there is a room in the temple into which none ever goes but the queen, driving a human sacrifice before her. And this victim is never seen again. All know that in that grim chamber lurks some monster from the black night of ages, which devours the shrieking humans Taramis delivers up to it.

"I can no longer think of her as a mortal woman, but as a rabid she-fiend, crouching in her blood-fouled lair amongst the bones and fragments of her victims, with taloned, crimsoned fingers. That the gods allow her to pursue her awful course unchecked almost shakes my faith in divine justice.

"When I compare her present conduct with her deportment when first I came to Khauran, seven months ago, I am confused with bewilderment, and almost inclined to the belief held by many of the people — that a demon has possessed the body of Taramis. A young soldier, Valerius, had another belief. He believed that a witch had assumed a form identical with that of Khauran's adored ruler. He believed that Taramis had been spirited away in the night, and confined in some dungeon, and that this being ruling in her place was but a female sorcerer. He swore that he would find the real queen, if she still lived, but I greatly fear that he himself has fallen victim to the cruelty of Constantius. He was implicated in the revolt of the palace guards, escaped and remained in hiding for some time, stubbornly refusing to seek safety abroad, and it was during this time that I encountered him and he told me his beliefs.

"But he has disappeared, as so many have, whose fate one dares not conjecture, and I fear he has been apprehended by the spies of Constantius.

"But I must conclude this letter and slip it out of the city by means of a swift carrier pigeon, which will carry it to the post whence I purchased it, on the borders of Koth. By rider and camel-train it will eventually come to you. I must haste, before dawn. It is late, and the stars gleam whitely on the gardened roofs of Khauran. A shuddering silence envelops the city, in which I hear the throb of a sullen drum from the distant temple. I doubt not that Taramis is there, concocting more deviltry."

But the savant was incorrect in his conjecture concerning the whereabouts of the woman he called Taramis. The girl whom the world knew as queen of Khauran stood in a dungeon, lighted only by a flickering torch which played on her features, etching the diabolical cruelty of her beautiful countenance.

On the bare stone floor before her crouched a figure whose nakedness was scarcely covered with tattered rags.

This figure Salome touched contemptuously with the upturned toe of her gilded sandal, and smiled vindictively as her victim shrank away.

"You do not love my caresses, sweet sister?"

Taramis was still beautiful, in spite of her rags and the imprisonment and abuse of seven weary months. She did not reply to her sister's taunts, but bent her head as one grown accustomed to mockery.

This resignation did not please Salome. She bit her red lip, and stood tapping the toe of her shoe against the flags as she frowned down at the passive figure. Salome was clad in the barbaric splendor of a woman of Shushan. Jewels glittered in the torchlight on her gilded sandals, on her gold breastplates and the slender chains that held them in place. Gold anklets clashed as she moved, jeweled bracelets weighted her bare arms. Her tall coiffure was that of a Shemitish woman, and jade pendants hung from gold hoops in her ears, flashing and sparkling with each impatient movement of her haughty head. A gem-crusted girdle supported a silk skirt so transparent that it was in the nature of a cynical mockery of convention.

Suspended from her shoulders and trailing down her back hung a darkly scarlet cloak, and this was thrown carelessly over the crook of one arm and the bundle that arm supported.

Salome stooped suddenly and with her free hand grasped her sister's disheveled hair and forced back the girl's head to stare into her eyes. Taramis met that tigerish glare without flinching.

"You are not so ready with your tears as formerly, sweet sister," muttered the witch-girl.

"You shall wring no more tears from me," answered Taramis. "Too often you have reveled in the spectacle of the queen of Khauran sobbing for mercy on her knees. I know that you have spared me only to torment me; that is why you have limited your tortures to such torments as neither slay nor permanently disfigure. But I fear you no longer; you have strained out the last vestige of hope, fright and shame from me. Slay me and be done with it, for I have shed my last tear for your enjoyment, you she-devil from Hell!"

"You flatter yourself, my dear sister," purred

Salome. "So far it is only your handsome body that I have caused to suffer, only your pride and self-esteem that I have crushed. You forget that, unlike myself, you are capable of mental torment. I have observed this when I have regaled you with narratives concerning the comedies I have enacted with some of your stupid subjects. But this time I have brought more vivid proof of these farces. Did you know that Krallides, your faithful councillor, had come skulking back from Turan and been captured?"

Taramis turned pale.

"What — what have you done to him?"

For answer Salome drew the mysterious bundle from under her cloak. She shook off the silken swathings and held it up — the head of a young man, the features frozen in a convulsion as if death had come in the midst of inhuman agony.

Taramis cried out as if a blade had pierced her heart.

"Oh, Ishtar! Krallides!"

"Aye! He was seeking to stir up the people against me, poor fool, telling them that Conan spoke the truth when he said I was not Taramis. How would the people rise against the Falcon's Shemites? With sticks and pebbles? Bah! Dogs are eating his headless body in the marketplace, and this foul carrion shall be cast into the sewer to rot.

"How, sister!" She paused, smiling down at her victim. "Have you discovered that you still have unshed tears? Good! I reserved the mental torment for the last. Hereafter I shall show you many such sights as — this!"

Standing there in the torchlight with the severed head in her hand she did not look like anything ever born by a human woman, in spite of her awful beauty. Taramis did not look up. She lay face down on the slimy floor, her slim body shaken in sobs of agony, beating her clenched hands against the stones. Salome sauntered toward the door, her anklets clashing at each step, her ear-pendants winking in the torch-glare.

A few moments later she emerged from a door under a sullen arch that let into a court which in turn opened upon a winding alley. A man standing there turned toward her — a giant Shemite, with somber eyes and shoulders like a bull, his great black beard falling over his mighty, silver-mailed breast.

"She wept?" His rumble was like that of a bull, deep, low-pitched and stormy. He was the general of the mercenaries, one of the few even of Constantius' associates who knew the secret of the queens of Khauran.

"Aye, Khumbanigash. There are whole sections of her sensibilities that I have not touched. When one sense is dulled by continual laceration, I will discover a newer, more poignant pang. — Here, dog!" A trembling, shambling figure in rags, filth and matted hair approached, one of the beggars that slept in the alleys and open courts. Salome tossed the head to him. "Here, deaf one; cast that in the nearest sewer. — Make the sign with your hands, Khumbanigash. He can not hear."

The general complied, and the tousled head bobbed, as the man turned painfully away.

"Why do you keep up this farce?" rumbled Khumbanigash. "You are so firmly established on the throne that nothing can unseat you. What if the Khaurani fools learn the truth? They can do nothing. Proclaim yourself in your true identity! Show them their beloved ex-queen — and cut off her head in the public square!"

"Not yet, good Khumbanigash —"

The arched door slammed on the hard accents of Salome, the stormy reverbations of Khumbanigash. The mute beggar crouched in the courtyard, and there was none to see that the hands which held the severed head were quivering strongly — brown, sinewy hands, strangely incongruous with the bent body and filthy tatters.

"I knew it!" It was a fierce, vibrant whisper, scarcely audible. "She lives! Oh, Krallides, your martyrdom was not in vain! They have her locked in that dungeon! Oh, Ishtar, if you love true men, aid me now!"

4. Wolves of the Desert

Olgerd Vladislav filled his jeweled goblet with crimson wine from a golden jug and thrust the vessel across the ebony table to Conan the Cimmerian.

Olgerd's apparel would have satisfied the vanity of any Zaporoskan hetman.

His *khalat* was of white silk, with pearls sewn on the bosom. Girdled at the waist with a Bakhauriot belt, its skirts were drawn back to reveal his wide silken breeches, tucked into short boots of soft green leather, adorned with gold thread. On his head was a green silk turban, wound about a spired helmet chased with gold. His only weapon was a broad curved Cherkees knife in an ivory sheath girdled high on his left hip, *kozak* fashion. Throwing himself back in his gilded chair with its carven eagles, Olgerd spread his booted legs before him, and gulped down the sparkling wine noisily.

To his splendor the huge Cimmerian opposite him offered a strong contrast, with his square-cut black mane, brown scarred countenance and burning blue eyes. He was clad in black mesh-mail, and the only glitter about him was the broad gold buckle of the belt which supported his sword in its worn leather scabbard.

They were alone in the silk-walled tent, which was hung with gilt-worked tapestries and littered with rich carpets and velvet cushions, the loot of the caravans. From outside came a low, incessant murmur, the sound that always accompanies a great throng of men, in camp or otherwise. An occasional gust of desert wind rattled the palm leaves.

"Today in the shadow, tomorrow in the sun," quoth Olgerd, loosening his crimson girdle a trifle and reaching again for the wine jug. "That's the way of life. Once I was a hetman on the Zaporoska; now I'm a desert chief. Seven months ago you were hanging on a cross outside Khauran. Now you're lieutenant to the most powerful raider between Turan and the western meadows. You should be thankful to me!"

"For recognizing my usefulness?" Conan laughed and lifted the jug. "When you allow the elevation of a man, one can be sure that you'll profit by his advancement. I've earned everything I've won, with my blood and sweat." He glanced at the scars on the insides of his palms. There were scars, too, on his body, scars that had not been there seven months ago.

"You fight like a regiment of devils," conceded Olgerd. "But don't get to thinking that you've had anything to do with the recruits who've swarmed in to join us. It was our success at raiding, guided by my wit, that brought them in. These nomads are always looking for a successful leader to follow, and they have more faith in a foreigner than in one of their own race.

"There's no limit to what we may accomplish! We have eleven thousand men now. In another year we may have three times that number. We've contented ourselves, so far, with raids on the Turanian outposts and the city-states to the west. With thirty or forty thousand men we'll raid no longer. We'll invade and conquer and establish ourselves as rulers. I'll be emperor of all Shem yet, and you'll be my vizier, so long as you carry out my orders unquestioningly. In the meantime, I think we'll ride eastward and storm that Turanian outpost at Vezek, where the caravans pay toll."

Conan shook his head. "I think not."

Olgerd glared, his quick temper irritated.

"What do you mean, *you* think not? *I* do the thinking for this army!"

"There are enough men in this band now for my purpose," answered the Cimmerian. "I'm sick of waiting. I have a score to settle."

"Oh!" Olgerd scowled, and gulped wine, then grinned. "Still thinking of that cross, eh? Well, I like a good hater. But that can wait."

"You told me once you'd aid me in taking Khauran," said Conan.

"Yes, but that was before I began to see the full possibilities of our power," answered Olgerd. "I was only thinking of the loot in the city. I don't want to waste our strength unprofitably. Khauran is too strong a nut for us to crack now. Maybe in a year —"

"Within the week," answered Conan, and the *kozak* stared at the certainty in his voice.

"Listen," said Olgerd, "even if I were willing to throw away men on such a hare-brained attempt — what could you expect? Do you think these wolves could besiege and take a city like Khauran?"

"There'll be no siege," answered the Cimmerian.

"I know how to draw Constantius out into the plain."

"And what then?" cried Olgerd with an oath. "In the arrow-play our horsemen would have the worst of it, for the armor of the *asshuri* is the better, and when it came to sword-strokes their close-marshaled ranks of trained swordsmen would cleave through our loose lines and scatter our men like chaff before the wind."

"Not if there were three thousand desperate Hyborian horsemen fighting in a solid wedge such as I could teach them," answered Conan.

"And where would you secure three thousand Hyborians?" asked Olgerd with vast sarcasm. "Will you conjure them out of the air?"

"I *have* them," answered the Cimmerian imperturbably. "Three thousand men of Khauran camp at the oasis of Akrel awaiting my orders."

"*What?*" Olgerd glared like a startled wolf.

"Aye. Men who had fled from the tyranny of Constantius. Most of them have been living the lives of outlaws in the deserts east of Khauran, and are gaunt and hard and desperate as man-eating tigers. One of them will be a match for any three squat mercenaries. It takes oppression and hardship to stiffen men's guts and put the fire of Hell into their thews. They were broken up into small bands; all they needed was a leader. They believed the word I sent them by my riders, and assembled at the oasis and put themselves at my disposal."

"All this without my knowledge?" A feral light began to gleam in Olgerd's eyes. He hitched at his weapon-girdle.

"It was *I* they wished to follow, not *you.*"

"And what did you tell these outcasts to gain their allegiance?" There was a dangerous ring in Olgerd's voice.

"I told them that I'd use this horde of desert wolves to help them destroy Constantius and give Khauran back into the hands of its citizens."

"You fool!" whispered Olgerd. "Do you deem yourself chief already?"

The men were on their feet, facing each other across the ebony board, devil-lights dancing in Olgerd's cold gray eyes, a grim smile on the Cimmerian's hard lips.

"I'll have you torn between four palm trees," said the *kozak* calmly.

"Call the men and bid them do it!" challenged Conan. "See if they obey you!"

Baring his teeth in a snarl, Olgerd lifted his hand — then paused. There was something about the confidence in the Cimmerian's dark face that shook him. His eyes began to burn like those of a wolf.

"You scum of the western hills," he muttered, "have you dared seek to undermine my power?"

"I didn't have to," answered Conan. "You lied when you said I had nothing to do with bringing in the new recruits. I had everything to do with it. They took your orders, but they fought for me. There is not room for two chiefs of the Zuagirs. They know I am the stronger man. I understand them better than you, and they, me; because I am a barbarian too."

"And what will they say when you ask them to fight for the Khaurani?" asked Olgerd sardonically.

"They'll follow me. I'll promise them a camel-train of gold from the palace. Khauran will be willing to pay that as a guerdon for getting rid of Constantius. After that, I'll lead them against the Turanians as you have planned. They want loot, and they'd as soon fight Constantius for it as anybody."

In Olgerd's eyes grew a recognition of defeat. In his red dreams of empire he had missed what was going on about him. Happenings and events that had seemed meaningless before now flashed into his mind, with their true significance, bringing a realization that Conan spoke no idle boast. The giant black-mailed figure before him was the real chief of the Zuagirs.

"Not if you die!" muttered Olgerd, and his hand flickered toward his hilt. But quick as the stroke of a great cat Conan's arm shot across the table and his fingers locked on Olgerd's forearm. There was a snap of breaking bones, and for a tense instant the scene held: the men facing each other as motionless as images, perspiration starting out on Olgerd's forehead. Conan laughed, never easing his grip on the broken arm.

"Are you fit to live, Olgerd?"

His smile did not alter as the corded muscles rippled in knotting ridges along his forearm and his fingers ground into the *kozak's* quivering flesh. There was the sound of broken bones grating together and Olgerd's face turned the color of ashes; blood oozed from his lip where his teeth sank, but he uttered no sound.

With a laugh Conan released him and drew back, and the *kozak* swayed, caught the table edge with his good hand to steady himself.

"I give you life, Olgerd, as you gave it to me," said Conan tranquilly, "though it was for your own ends that you took me down from the cross. It was a bitter test you gave me then; you couldn't have endured it; neither could anyone, but a western barbarian.

"Take your horse and go. It's tied behind the tent, and food and water are in the saddlebags. None will see your going, but go quickly. There's no room for a fallen chief on the desert. If the warriors see you, maimed and deposed, they'll never let you leave the camp alive."

Olgerd did not reply. Slowly, without a word, he he turned and stalked across the tent, through the flapped opening. Unspeaking he climbed into the saddle of the great white stallion that stood tethered there in the shade of a spreading palm tree; and unspeaking, with his broken arm thrust in the bosom of his *khalat,* he reined the steed about and rode eastward into the open desert, out of the life of the people of the Zuagir.

Inside the tent Conan emptied the wine-jug and smacked his lips with relish. Tossing the empty vessel into a corner, he braced his belt and strode out through the front opening, halting for a moment to let his gaze sweep over the lines of camel-hair tents that stretched before him, and the white-robed figures that moved among them, arguing, singing, mending bridles or whetting tulwars.

He lifted his voice in a thunder that carried to the farthest confines of the encampment: "*Aie,* you dogs, sharpen your ears and listen! Gather around here. I have a tale to tell you."

5. The Voice From the Crystal

In a chamber in a tower near the city wall a group of men listened attentively to the words of one of their number. They were young men, but hard and sinewy, with the bearing that comes only to men rendered desperate by adversity. They were clad in mail shirts and worn leather; swords hung at their girdles.

"I knew that Conan spoke the truth when he said it was not Taramis!" the speaker exclaimed. "For months I have haunted the outskirts of the palace, playing the part of a deaf beggar. At last I learned what I had believed — that our queen was a prisoner in the dungeons that adjoin the palace. I watched my opportunity and captured a Shemitish jailer — knocked him senseless as he left the courtyard late one night — dragged him into a cellar near by and questioned him. Before he died he told me what I have just told you, and what we have suspected all along — that the woman ruling Khauran is a witch: Salome. Taramis, he said, is imprisoned in the lowest dungeon.

"This invasion of the Zuagirs gives us the opportunity we sought. What Conan means to do, I can not say. Perhaps he merely wishes vengeance on Constantius. Perhaps he intends sacking the city and destroying it. He is a barbarian and no one can understand their minds.

"But this is what we must do: rescue Taramis while the battle rages! Constantius will march out into the plain to give battle. Even now his men are mounting. He will do this because there is not sufficient food in the city to stand a siege. Conan burst out of the desert so suddenly that there was no time to bring in supplies. And the Cimmerian is equipped for a siege. Scouts have reported that the Zuagirs have siege engines, built, undoubtedly, according to the instructions of Conan, who learned all the arts of war among the Western nations.

"Constantius does not desire a long siege; so he will march with his warriors into the plain, where he expects to scatter Conan's forces at one stroke. He will leave only a few hundred men in the city, and they will be on the walls and in the towers commanding the gates.

"The prison will be left all but unguarded. When we have freed Taramis our next actions will depend upon circumstances. If Conan wins, we must show Taramis to the people and bid them rise — they will! Oh, they will! With their bare hands they are enough to overpower the Shemites left in the city and close the gates against both the mercenaries and the nomads. Neither must get within the walls! Then we will parley with Conan. He was always loyal to Taramis. If he knows the truth, and she appeals to him, I believe he will spare the city. If, which is more probable, Constantius prevails, and Conan is routed, we must steal out of the city with the queen and seek safety in flight.

"Is all clear?"

They replied with one voice.

"Then let us loosen our blades in our scabbards, commend our souls to Ishtar, and start for the prison, for the mercenaries are already marching through the southern gate."

This was true. The dawnlight glinted on peaked helmets pouring in a steady stream through the broad arch, on the bright housings of the chargers. This would be a battle of horsemen, such as is possible only in the lands of the East. The riders flowed through the gates like a river of steel — somber figures in black and silver mail, with their curled beards and hooked noses, and their inexorable eyes in which glimmered the fatality of their race — the utter lack of doubt or of mercy.

The streets and the walls were lined with throngs of people who watched silently these warriors of an alien race riding forth to defend their native city. There was no sound; dully, expressionless they watched, those gaunt people in shabby garments, their caps in their hands.

In a tower that overlooked the broad street that led to the southern gate, Salome lolled on a velvet couch cynically watching Constantius as he settled his broad sword-belt about his lean hips and drew on his gauntlets. They were alone in the chamber. Outside, the rhythmical clank of harness and shuffle of horses' hoofs welled up through the gold-barred casements.

"Before nightfall," quoth Constantius, giving a twirl to his thin mustache, "you'll have some captives to feed to your temple-devil. Does it not grow weary of soft, city-bred flesh? Perhaps it would relish the harder thews of a desert man."

"Take care you do not fall prey to a fiercer beast than Thaug," warned the girl. "Do not forget who it is that leads these desert animals."

"I am not likely to forget," he answered. "That is one reason why I am advancing to meet him. The dog has fought in the West and knows the art of siege. My scouts had some trouble in approaching his columns, for his outriders have eyes like hawks; but they did get close enough to see the engines he is dragging on ox-cart wheels drawn by camels — catapults, rams, ballistas, mangonelsby — Ishtar! he must have had ten thousand men working day and night for a month. Where he got the material for their construction is more than I can understand. Perhaps he has a treaty with the Turanians, and gets supplies from them.

"Anyway, they won't do him any good. I've fought these desert wolves before — an exchange of arrows for awhile, in which the armor of my warriors protects them — then a charge and my squadrons sweep through the loose swarms of the nomads, wheel and sweep back through, scattering them to the four winds. I'll ride back through the south gate before sunset, with hundreds of naked captives staggering at my horse's tail. We'll hold a fête tonight, in the great square. My soldiers delight in flaying their enemies alive — we will have a wholesale skinning, and make these weak-kneed townsfolk watch. As for Conan, it will afford me intense pleasure, if we take him alive, to impale him on the palace steps."

"Skin as many as you like," answered Salome indifferently. "I would like a dress made of human hide. But at least a hundred captives you must give to me — for the altar, and for Thaug."

"It shall be done," answered Constantius, with his gauntleted hand brushing back the thin hair from his high bald forehead, burned dark by the sun. "For victory and the fair honor of Taramis!" he said sardonically, and, taking his vizored helmet under his arm, he lifted a hand in salute, and strode clanking from the chamber. His voice drifted back, harshly lifted in orders to his officers.

Salome leaned back on the couch, yawned, stretched herself like a great supple cat, and called: "Zang!"

A cat-footed priest, with features like yellowed parchment stretched over a skull, entered noiselessly.

Salome turned to an ivory pedestal on which stood two crystal globes, and taking from it the smaller, she handed the glistening sphere to the priest.

"Ride with Constantius," she said. "Give me the news of the battle. Go!"

The skull-faced man bowed low, and hiding the globe under his dark mantle, hurried from the chamber.

Outside in the city there was no sound, except the clank of hoofs and after a while the clang of a closing gate. Salome mounted a wide marble stair that led to the flat, canopied, marble-battlemented roof. She was above all other buildings of the city. The streets were deserted, the great square in front of the palace was empty. In normal times folk shunned the grim temple which rose on the opposite side of that square, but now the town looked like a dead city. Only on the southern wall and the roofs that overlooked it was there any sign of life. There the people massed thickly. They made no demonstration, did not know whether to hope for the victory or defeat of Constantius. Victory meant further misery under his intolerable rule; defeat probably meant the sack of the city and red massacre. No word had come from Conan. They did not know what to expect at his hands. They remembered that he was a barbarian.

The squadrons of the mercenaries were moving out into the plain. In the distance, just this side of the river, other dark masses were moving, barely recognizable as men on horses. Objects dotted the farther bank; Conan had not brought his siege engines across the river, apparently fearing an attack in the midst of the crossing. But he had crossed with his full force of horsemen. The sun rose and struck glints of fire from the dark multitudes. The squadrons from the city broke into a gallop; a deep roar reached the ears of the people on the wall.

The rolling masses merged, intermingled; at that distance it was a tangled confusion in which no details stood out. Charge and countercharge were not to be identified. Clouds of dust rose from the plains, under the stamping hoofs, veiling the action. Through these swirling clouds masses of riders loomed, appearing and disappearing, and spears flashed.

Salome shrugged her shoulders and descended the stair. The palace lay silent. All the slaves were on the wall, gazing vainly southward with the citizens.

She entered the chamber where she had talked with Constantius, and approached the pedestal, noting that the crystal globe was clouded, shot with bloody streaks of crimson. She bent over the ball, swearing under her breath.

"Zang!" she called. "Zang!"

Mists swirled in the sphere, resolving themselves into billowing dust clouds through which black figures rushed unrecognizably; steel glinted like lightning in the murk. Then the face of Zang leaped into startling distinctness; it was as if the wide eyes gazed up at Salome. Blood trickled from a gash in the skull-like head, the skin was gray with sweat-runneled dust. The lips parted, writhing; to other ears than Salome's it would have seemed that the face in the crystal contorted silently. But sound to her came as plainly from those ashen lips as if the priest had been in the same room with her, instead of miles away, shouting into the smaller crystal. Only the gods of darkness knew what unseen, magic filaments linked together those shimmering spheres.

"Salome!" shrieked the bloody head. *"Salome!"*

"I hear!" she cried. "Speak! How goes the battle?"

"Doom is upon us!" screamed the skull-like apparition. "Khauran is lost! *Aie*, my horse is down and I can not win clear! Men are falling around me! They are dying like flies, in their silvered mail!"

"Stop yammering and tell me what happened!" she cried harshly.

"We rode at the desert-dogs and they came on to meet us!" yowled the priest. "Arrows flew in clouds between the hosts, and the nomads wavered. Constantius ordered the charge. In even ranks we thundered upon them.

"Then the masses of their horde opened to right and left, and through the cleft rushed three thousand Hyborian horsemen whose presence we had not even suspected. Men of Khauran, mad with hate! Big men in full armor on massive horses! In a solid wedge of steel they smote us like a thunderbolt. They split our ranks asunder before we knew what was upon us, and then the desert-men swarmed on us from either flank.

"They have ripped our ranks apart, broken and scattered us! It is a trick of that devil Conan! The siege engines are false — mere frames of palm trunks and painted silk, that fooled our scouts who saw them from afar. A trick to draw us out to our doom! Our warriors flee! Khumbanigash is down — Conan slew him. I do not see Constantius. The Khaurani rage through our milling masses like blood-mad lions, and the desert-men feather us with arrows. I — ahhh!"

There was a flicker as of lightning, or trenchant steel, a burst of bright blood — then abruptly the image vanished, like a bursting bubble, and Salome was staring into an empty crystal ball that mirrored only her own furious features.

She stood perfectly still for a few moments, erect and staring into space. Then she clapped her hands and another skull-like priest entered, as silent and immobile as the first.

"Constantius is beaten," she said swiftly. "We are doomed. Conan will be crashing at our gates within the hour. If he catches me, I have no illusions as to what I can expect. But first I am going to make sure that my cursed sister never ascends the throne again. Follow me! Come what may, we shall give Thaug a feast."

As she descended the stairs and galleries of the palace, she heard a faint rising echo from the distant walls. The people there had begun to realize that the battle was going against Constantius. Through the dust clouds masses of horsemen were visible, racing toward the city.

Palace and prison were connected by a long closed gallery, whose vaulted roof rose on gloomy arches. Hurrying along this, the false queen and her slave passed through a heavy door at the other end that let them into the dim-lit recesses of the prison. They had emerged into a wide, arched corridor at a point near where a stone stair descended into the darkness. Salome recoiled suddenly, swearing. In the gloom of the hall lay a motionless form — a Shemitish jailer, his short beard tilted toward the roof as his head hung on a half-severed neck. As panting voices from below reached the girl's ears, she shrank back into the black shadow of an arch, pushing the priest behind her, her hand groping in her girdle.

6. The Vulture's Wings

It was the smoky light of a torch which roused Taramis, queen of Khauran, from the slumber in which she sought forgetfulness. Lifting herself on her hand she raked back her tangled hair and blinked up, expecting to meet the mocking countenance of Salome, malign with new torments. Instead a cry of pity and horror reached her ears.

"Taramis! Oh, my queen!"

The sound was so strange to her ears that she thought she was still dreaming. Behind the torch she could make out figures now, the glint of steel, then five countenances bent toward her, not swarthy and hook-nosed, but lean, aquiline faces, browned by the sun. She crouched in her tatters, staring wildly.

One of the figures sprang forward and fell on one knee before her, arms stretched appealingly toward her.

"Oh, Taramis! Thank Ishtar we have found you! Do you not remember me, Valerius? Once with your own lips you praised me, after the battle of Korveka!"

"Valerius!" she stammered. Suddenly tears welled into her eyes. "Oh, I dream! It is some magic of Salome's, to torment me!"

"No!" The cry rang with exultation. "It is your own true vassals come to rescue you! Yet we must hasten. Constantius fights in the plain against Conan, who has brought the Zuagirs across the river, but three hundred Shemites yet hold the city. We slew the jailer and took his keys, and have seen no other guards. But we must be gone. Come!"

The queen's legs gave way, not from weakness but

from the reaction. Valerius lifted her like a child, and with the torchbearer hurrying before them, they left the dungeon and went up a slimy stone stair. It seemed to mount endlessly, but presently they emerged into a corridor.

They were passing a dark arch when the torch was suddenly struck out, and the bearer cried out in fierce, brief agony. A burst of blue fire glared in the dark corridor, in which the furious face of Salome was limned momentarily, with a beast-like figure crouching beside her — then the eyes of the watchers were blinded by that blaze.

Valerius tried to stagger along the corridor with the queen; dazedly he heard the sound of murderous blows driven deep in flesh, accompanied by gasps of death and a bestial grunting. Then the queen was torn brutally from his arms, and a savage blow on his helmet dashed him to the floor.

Grimly he crawled to his feet, shaking his head in an effort to rid himself of the blue flame which seemed still to dance devilishly before him. When his blinded sight cleared, he found himself alone in the corridor — alone except for the dead. His four companions lay in their blood, heads and bosoms cleft and gashed. Blinded and dazed in that hell-born glare, they had died without an opportunity of defending themselves. The queen was gone.

With a bitter curse Valerius caught up his sword, tearing his cleft helmet from his head to clatter on the flags; blood ran down his cheek from a cut in his scalp.

Reeling, frantic with indecision, he heard a voice calling his name in desperate urgency: "Valerius! *Valerius!*"

He staggered in the direction of the voice, and rounded a corner just in time to have his arms filled with a soft, supple figure which flung itself frantically at him.

"Ivga! Are you mad!"

"I had to come!" she sobbed. "I followed you — hid in an arch of the outer court. A moment ago I saw *her* emerge with a brute who carried a woman in his arms. I knew it was Taramis, and that you had failed! Oh, you are hurt!"

"A scratch!" He put aside her clinging hands. "Quick, Ivga, tell me which way they went!"

"They fled across the square toward the temple."

He paled. "Ishtar! Oh, the fiend! She means to give Taramis to the devil she worships! Quick, Ivga! Run to the south wall where the people watch the battle! Tell them that their real queen has been found — that the impostor has dragged her to the temple! Go!"

Sobbing, the girl sped away, her light sandals pattering on the cobblestones, and Valerius raced across the court, plunged into the street, dashed into the square upon which it debouched, and raced for the great structure that rose on the opposite side.

His flying feet spurned the marble as he darted up

the broad stair and through the pillared portico. Evidently their prisoner had given them some trouble. Taramis, sensing the doom intended for her, was fighting against it with all the strength of her splendid young body. Once she had broken away from the brutish priest, only to be dragged down again.

The group was halfway down the broad nave, at the other end of which stood the grim altar and beyond that the great metal door, obscenely carven, through which many had gone, but from which only Salome had ever emerged. Taramis' breath came in panting gasps; her tattered garment had been torn from her in the struggle. She writhed in the grasp of her apish captor like a white, naked nymph in the arms of a satyr. Salome watched cynically, though impatiently, moving toward the carven door, and from the dusk that lurked along the lofty walls the obscene gods and gargoyles leered down, as if imbued with salacious life.

Choking with fury, Valerius rushed down the great hall, sword in hand. At a sharp cry from Salome, the skull-faced priest looked up, then released Taramis, drew a heavy knife, already smeared with blood, and ran at the oncoming Khaurani.

But cutting down men blinded by the devil's-flame loosed by Salome was different from fighting a wiry young Hyborian afire with hate and rage.

Up went the dripping knife, but before it could fall Valerius' keen narrow blade slashed through the air, and the fist that held the knife jumped from its wrist in a shower of blood. Valerius, berserk, slashed again and yet again before the crumpling figure could fall. The blade licked through flesh and bone. The skull-like head fell one way, the half-sundered torso the other.

Valerius whirled on his toes, quick and fierce as a jungle-cat, glaring about for Salome. She must have exhausted her fire-dust in the prison. She was bending over Taramis, grasping her sister's black locks in one hand, in the other lifting a dagger. Then with a fierce cry Valerius' sword was sheathed in her breast with such fury that the point sprang out between her shoulders. With an awful shriek the witch sank down, writhing in convulsions, grasping at the naked blade as it was withdrawn, smoking and dripping. Her eyes were unhuman; with a more than human vitality she clung to the life that ebbed through the wound that split the crimson crescent on her ivory bosom. She groveled on the floor, clawing and biting at the naked stones in her agony.

Sickened at the sight, Valerius stooped and lifted the half-fainting queen. Turning his back on the twisting figure upon the floor, he ran toward the door, stumbling in his haste. He staggered out upon the portico, halted at the head of the steps. The square thronged with people. Some had come at Ivga's incoherent cries; others had deserted the walls in fear of the onsweeping hordes out of the desert, fleeing unreasoningly toward the center of the city. Dumb resignation had vanished. The throng seethed and milled, yelling and screaming. About the road there sounded somewhere the splintering of stone and timbers.

A band of grim Shemites cleft the crowd — the guards of the northern gates, hurrying toward the south gate to reinforce their comrades there. They reined up short at sight of the youth on the steps, holding the limp, naked figure in his arms. The heads of the throng turned toward the temple; the crowd gaped, anew bewilderment added to their swirling confusion.

"Here is your queen!" yelled Valerius, straining to make himself understood above the clamor. The people gave back a bewildered roar. They did not understand, and Valerius sought in vain to lift his voice above their bedlam. The Shemites rode toward the temple steps, beating a way through the crowd with their spears.

Then a new, grisly element introduced itself into the frenzy. Out of the gloom of the temple behind Valerius wavered a slim white figure, laced with crimson. The people screamed; there in the arms of Valerius hung the woman they thought their queen; yet there in the temple door staggered another figure, like a reflection of the other. Their brains reeled. Valerius felt his blood congeal as he stared at the swaying witch-girl. His sword had transfixed her, sundered her heart. She should be dead; by all laws of nature she should be dead. Yet there she swayed, on her feet, clinging horribly to life.

"Thaug!" she screamed, reeling in the doorway. *"Thaug!"* As in answer to that frightful invocation there boomed a thunderous croaking from within the temple, the snapping of wood and metal.

"That is the queen!" roared the captain of the Shemites, lifting his bow. "Shoot down the man and other woman!"

But the roar of a roused hunting-pack rose from the people; they had guessed the truth at last, understood Valerius' frenzied appeals, knew that the girl who hung limply in his arms was their true queen. With a soul-shaking yell they surged on the Shemites, tearing and smiting with tooth and nail and naked hands, with the desperation of hard-pent fury loosed at last. Above them Salome swayed and tumbled down the marble stair, dead at last.

Arrows flickered about him as Valerius ran back between the pillars of the portico, shielding the body of the queen with his own. Shooting and slashing ruthlessly the mounted Shemites were holding their own with the maddened crowd. Valerius darted to the temple door — with one foot on the threshold he recoiled, crying out in horror and despair.

Out of the gloom at the other end of the great hall a vast dark form heaved up — came rushing toward him in gigantic frog-like hops. He saw the gleam of great unearthly eyes, the shimmer of fangs or talons. He fell back from the door, and then the whir of a shaft past his ear warned him that death was also behind him. He wheeled desperately. Four or five

Shemites had cut their way through the throng and were spurring their horses up the steps, their bows lifted to shoot him down. He sprang behind a pillar, on which the arrows splintered. Taramis had fainted. She hung like a dead woman in his arms.

Before the Shemites could loose again, the doorway was blocked by a gigantic shape. With affrighted yells the mercenaries wheeled and began beating a frantic way through the throng, which crushed back in sudden, galvanized horror, trampling one another in their stampede.

But the monster seemed to be watching Valerius and the girl. Squeezing its vast, unstable bulk through the door, it bounded toward him, as he ran down the steps. He felt it looming behind him, a giant shadowy thing, like a travesty of nature cut out of the heart of night, a black shapelessness in which only the staring eyes and gleaming fangs were distinct.

There came a sudden thunder of hoofs; a rout of Shemites, bloody and battered, streamed across the square from the south, plowing blindly through the packed throng. Behind them swept a horde of horsemen yelling in a familiar tongue, waving red swords — the exiles, returned! With them rode fifty black-bearded desert-riders, and at their head a giant figure in black mail.

"Conan!" shrieked Valerius. "*Conan!*"

The giant yelled a command. Without checking their headlong pace, the desert men lifted their bows, drew and loosed. A cloud of arrows sang across the square, over the seething heads of the multitudes, and sank feather-deep in the black monster. It halted, wavered, reared, a black blot against the marble pillars. Again the sharp cloud sang, and yet again, and the horror collapsed and rolled down the steps, as dead as the witch who had summoned it out of the night of ages.

Conan drew rein beside the portico, leaped off. Valerius had laid the queen on the marble, sinking beside her in utter exhaustion. The people surged about, crowding in. The Cimmerian cursed them back, lifted her dark head, pillowed it against his mailed shoulder.

"By Crom, what is this? The real Taramis! But who is that yonder?"

"The demon who wore her shape," panted Valerius.

Conan swore heartily. Ripping a cloak from the shoulders of a soldier, he wrapped it about the naked queen. Her long dark lashes quivered on her cheeks; her eyes opened, stared up unbelievingly into the Cimmerian's scarred face.

"Conan!" Her soft fingers caught at him. "Do I dream? *She* told me you were dead —"

"Scarcely!" He grinned hardly. "You do not dream. You are queen of Khauran again. I broke Constantius, out there by the river. Most of his dogs never lived to reach the walls, for I gave orders that no prisoners be taken — except Constantius. The city guard closed the gate in our faces, but we burst it in with rams swung from our saddles. I left all my wolves outside, except this fifty. I didn't trust them in here, and these Khaurani lads were enough for the gate guards."

"It has been a nightmare!" she whimpered. "Oh, my poor people! You must help me try to repay them for all they have suffered, Conan, henceforth councilor as well as captain!"

Conan laughed, but shook his head. Rising, he set the queen upon her feet, and beckoned to a number of his Khaurani horsemen who had not continued the pursuit of the fleeing Shemites. They sprang from their horses, eager to do the bidding of their new-found queen.

"No, lass, that's over with. I'm chief of the Zuagirs now, and must lead them to plunder the Turanians, as I promised. This lad, Valerius, will make you a better captain than I. I wasn't made to dwell among marble walls, anyway. But I must leave you now, and complete what I've begun. Shemites still live in Khauran."

As Valerius started to follow Taramis across the square toward the palace, through a lane opened by the wildly cheering multitude, he felt a soft hand slipped timidly into his sinewy fingers and turned to receive the slender body of Ivga in his arms. He crushed her to him and drank her kisses with the gratitude of a weary fighter who has attained rest at last through tribulation and storm.

But not all men seek rest and peace; some are born with the spirit of the storm in their blood, restless harbingers of violence and bloodshed, knowing no other path. . . .

The sun was rising. The ancient caravan road was thronged with white-robed horsemen, in a wavering line that stretched from the walls of Khauran to a spot far out in the plain. Conan the Cimmerian sat at the head of the column, near the jagged end of a wooden beam that stuck up out of the ground. Near that stump rose a heavy cross, and on that cross a man hung by spikes through his hands and feet.

"Seven months ago, Constantius," said Conan, "it was I who hung there, and you who sat here."

Constantius did not reply; he licked his gray lips and his eyes were glassy with pain and fear. Muscles writhed like cords along his lean body.

"You are more fit to inflict torture than to endure it," said Conan tranquilly. "I hung there on a cross as you are hanging, and I lived, thanks to circumstances and a stamina peculiar to barbarians. But you civilized men are soft; your lives are not nailed to your spines as are ours. Your fortitude consists mainly in inflicting torment, not in enduring it. You will be dead before sundown. And so, Falcon of the desert, I leave you to the companionship of another bird of the desert."

He gestured toward the vultures whose shadows swept across the sands as they wheeled overhead.

From the lips of Constantius came an inhuman cry of despair and horror.

Conan lifted his reins and rode toward the river that shone like silver in the morning sun. Behind him the white-clad riders struck into a trot; the gaze of each, as he passed a certain spot, turned impersonally and with the desert man's lack of compassion, toward the cross and the gaunt figure that hung there, black against the sunrise. Their horses' hoofs beat out a knell in the dust. Lower and lower swept the wings of the hungry vultures.

THE GRISLY HORROR

Weird Tales, February 1935

1. The Horror in the Pines

The silence of the pine woods lay like a brooding cloak about the soul of Bristol McGrath. The black shadows seemed fixed, immovable as the weight of superstition that overhung this forgotten back country. Vague ancestral dreads stirred at the back of McGrath's mind; for he was born in the pine woods, and sixteen years of roaming about the world had not erased their shadows. The fearsome tales at which he had shuddered as a child whispered again in his consciousness; tales of black shapes stalking the midnight glades. . . .

Cursing these childish memories, McGrath quickened his pace. The dim trail wound tortuously between dense walls of giant trees. No wonder he had been unable to hire anyone in the distant river village to drive him to the Ballville estate. The road was impassable for a vehicle, choked with rotting stumps and new growth. Ahead of him it bent sharply.

McGrath halted short, frozen to immobility. The silence had been broken at last, in such a way as to bring a chill tingling to the backs of his hands. For the sound had been the unmistakable groan of a human being in agony. Only for an instant was McGrath motionless. Then he was gliding about the bend of the trail with the noiseless slouch of a hunting panther.

A blue snub-nosed revolver had appeared as if by magic in his right hand. His left involuntarily clenched in his pocket on the bit of paper that was responsible for his presence in that grim forest. That paper was a frantic and mysterious appeal for aid; it was signed by McGrath's worst enemy, and contained the name of a woman long dead.

McGrath rounded the bend in the trail, every nerve tense and alert, expecting anything — except what he actually saw. His startled eyes hung on the grisly object for an instant, and then swept the forest walls. Nothing stirred there. A dozen feet back from the trail visibility vanished in a ghoulish twilight, where *anything* might lurk unseen. McGrath dropped to his knee beside the figure that lay in the trail before him.

It was a man, spread-eagled, hands and feet bound to four pegs driven deeply in the hard-packed earth; a black-bearded, hook-nosed, swarthy man. "Ahmed!" muttered McGrath. "Ballville's Arab servant! God!"

For it was not the binding cords that brought the glaze to the Arab's eyes. A weaker man than McGrath might have sickened at the mutilations which keen knives had wrought on the man's body. McGrath recognized the work of an expert in the art of torture. Yet a spark of life still throbbed in the tough frame of the Arab. McGrath's gray eyes grew bleaker as he noted the position of the victim's body, and his mind flew back to another, grimmer jungle, and a half-flayed black man pegged out on a path as a warning to the white man who dared invade a forbidden land.

He cut the cords, shifted the dying man to a more comfortable position. It was all he could do. He saw the delirium ebb momentarily in the bloodshot eyes, saw recognition glimmer there. Clots of bloody foam splashed the matted beard. The lips writhed soundlessly, and McGrath glimpsed the bloody stump of a severed tongue.

The black-nailed fingers began scrabbling in the dust. They shook, clawing erratically, but with purpose. McGrath bent close, tense with interest, and saw crooked lines grow under the quivering fingers. With the last effort of an iron will, the Arab was tracing a message in the characters of his own language. McGrath recognized the name: "Richard Ballville"; it was followed by "danger," and the hand waved weakly up the trail; then — and McGrath stiffened convulsively — "*Constance*". One final effort of the dragging finger traced "John De Al —" Suddenly the bloody frame was convulsed by one last sharp agony; the lean, sinewy hand knotted spasmodically and then fell limp.

Ahmed ibn Suleyman was beyond vengeance or mercy.

McGrath rose, dusting his hands, aware of the tense stillness of the grim woods around him; aware of a faint rustling in their depths that was not caused by any breeze. He looked down at the mangled figure with involuntary pity, though he knew well the foulness of the Arab's heart, a black evil that had matched that of Ahmed's master, Richard Ballville. Well, it seemed that master and man had at last met their match in human fiendishness. But who, or *what*? For a hundred years the Ballvilles had ruled supreme over this back country, first over their wide plantations and hundreds of slaves, and later over the submissive descendants of those slaves. Richard, the last of the Ballvilles, had exercised as much authority over the pinelands as any of his autocratic ancestors. Yet from this country where men had bowed to the Ballvilles for a century, had come that frenzied cry of fear, a telegram that McGrath clenched in his coat pocket.

Stillness succeeded the rustling, more sinister than any sound. McGrath knew he was watched; knew that the spot where Ahmed's body lay was the invisible deadline that had been drawn for him. He believed that he would be allowed to turn and retrace his steps unmolested to the distant village. He knew that if he continued on his way, death would strike him suddenly and unseen. Turning, he strode back the way he had come.

He made the turn and kept straight on until he had passed another crook in the trail. Then he halted, listened. All was silent. Quickly he drew the paper from his pocket, smoothed out the wrinkles and read, again, in the cramped scrawl of the man he hated most on earth:

> Bristol:
>
> If you still love Constance Brand, for God's sake forget your hate and come to Ballville Manor as quickly as the devil can drive you.
>
> RICHARD BALLVILLE.

That was all. It reached him by telegraph in that Far Western city where McGrath had resided since his return from Africa. He would have ignored it, but for the mention of Constance Brand. That name had sent a choking, agonizing pulse of amazement through his soul, had sent him racing toward the land of his birth by train and plane, as if, indeed, the devil were on his heels. It was the name of one he thought dead for three years; the name of the only woman Bristol McGrath had ever loved.

Replacing the telegram, he left the trail and headed westward, pushing his powerful frame between the thick-set trees. His feet made little sound on the matted pine needles. His progress was all but noiseless. Not for nothing had he spent his boyhood in the country of the big pines.

Three hundred yards from the old road he came

upon that which he sought — an ancient trail paralleling the road. Choked with young growth, it was little more than a trace through the thick pines. He knew that it ran to the back of the Ballville mansion; did not believe the secret watchers would be guarding it. For how could they know he remembered it?

He hurried south along it, his ears whetted for any sound. Sight alone could not be trusted in that forest. The mansion, he knew, was not far away, now. He was passing through what had once been fields, in the days of Richard's grandfather, running almost up to the spacious lawns that girdled the Manor. But for half a century they had been abandoned to the advance of the forest.

But now he glimpsed the Manor, a hint of solid bulk among the pine tops ahead of him. And almost simultaneously his heart shot into his throat as a scream of human anguish knifed the stillness. He could not tell whether it was a man or a woman who screamed, and his thought that it might be a woman winged his feet in his reckless dash toward the building that loomed starkly up just beyond the straggling fringe of trees.

The young pines had even invaded the once generous lawns. The whole place wore an aspect of decay. Behind the Manor, the barns and outhouses which once housed slave families were crumbling in ruin. The mansion itself seemed to totter above the litter, a creaky giant, rat-gnawed and rotting, ready to collapse at any untoward event. With the stealthy tread of a tiger Bristol McGrath approached a window on the side of the house. From that window sounds were issuing that were an affront to the tree-filtered sunlight and a crawling horror to the brain.

Nerving himself for what he might see, he peered within.

2. Black Torture

He was looking into a great dusty chamber which might have served as a ballroom in antebellum days; its lofty ceiling was hung with cobwebs, its rich oak panels showed dark and stained. But there was a fire in the great fireplace — a small fire, just large enough to heat to a white glow the slender steel rods thrust into it.

But it was only later that Bristol McGrath saw the fire and the things that glowed on the hearth. His eyes were gripped like a spell on the master of the Manor; and once again he looked on a dying man.

A heavy beam had been nailed to the paneled wall, and from it jutted a rude crosspiece. From this cross-piece Richard Ballville hung by cords about his wrists. His toes barely touched the floor, tantalizingly, inviting him to stretch his frame continually in an effort to relieve the agonizing strain on his arms. The cords had cut deeply into his wrists; blood trickled down his arms; his hands were black and swollen almost to bursting. He was naked except for his trousers, and McGrath saw that already the white-hot irons had been horribly employed. There was reason enough for the deathly pallor of the man, the cold beads of agony upon his skin. Only his fierce vitality had allowed him thus long to survive the ghastly burns on his limbs and body.

On his breast had been burned a curious symbol — a cold hand laid itself on McGrath's spine. For he recognized that symbol, and once again his memory raced away across the world and the years to a black, grim, hideous jungle where drums bellowed in fire-shot darkness and naked priests of an abhorred cult traced a frightful symbol in quivering human flesh.

Between the fireplace and the dying man squatted a thick-set black man, clad only in ragged, muddy trousers. His back was toward the window, presenting an impressive pair of shoulders. His bullet-head was set squarely between those gigantic shoulders, like that of a frog, and he appeared to be avidly watching the face of the man on the crosspiece.

Richard Ballville's bloodshot eyes were like those of a tortured animal, but they were fully sane and conscious; they blazed with desperate vitality. He lifted his head painfully and his gaze swept the room. Outside the window McGrath instinctively shrank back. He did not know whether Ballville saw him or not. The man showed no sign to betray the presence of the watcher to the bestial black who scrutinized him. Then the brute turned his head toward the fire, reaching a long ape-like arm toward a glowing iron — and Ballville's eyes blazed with a fierce and urgent meaning the watcher could not mistake. McGrath did not need the agonized motion of the tortured head that accompanied the look. With a tigerish bound he was over the windowsill and in the room, even as the startled black shot erect, whirling with apish agility.

McGrath had not drawn his gun. He dared not risk a shot that might bring other foes upon him. There was a butcher-knife in the belt that held up the ragged, muddy trousers. It seemed to leap like a living thing into the hand of the black as he turned. But in McGrath's hand gleamed a curved Afghan dagger that had served him well in many a bygone battle.

Knowing the advantage of instant and relentless attack, he did not pause. His feet scarcely touched the floor inside before they were hurling him at the astounded black man.

An inarticulate cry burst from the thick red lips. The eyes rolled wildly, the butcher-knife went back and hissed forward with the swiftness of a striking cobra that would have disemboweled a man whose thews were less steely than those of Bristol McGrath.

But the black was involuntarily stumbling backward as he struck, and that instinctive action slowed his stroke just enough for McGrath to avoid it with a lightning-like twist of his torso. The long blade hissed under his armpit, slicing cloth and skin — and simultaneously the Afghan dagger ripped through the black, bull throat.

There was no cry, but only a choking gurgle as the man fell, spouting blood. McGrath had sprung free as a wolf springs after delivering the death-stroke. Without emotion he surveyed his handiwork. The black man was already dead, his head half-severed from his body. That slicing sidewise lunge that slew in silence, severing the throat to the spinal column, was a favorite stroke of the hairy hillmen that haunt the crags overhanging the Khyber Pass. Less than a dozen white men have ever mastered it. Bristol McGrath was one.

McGrath turned to Richard Ballville. Foam dripped on the seared, naked breast, and blood trickled from the lips. McGrath feared that Ballville had suffered the same mutilation that had rendered Ahmed speechless; but it was only suffering and shock that numbed Ballville's tongue. McGrath cut his cords and eased him down on a worn old divan near by. Ballville's lean, muscle-corded body quivered like taut steel strings under McGrath's hands. He gagged, finding his voice.

"I knew you'd come!" he gasped, writhing at the contact of the divan against his seared flesh. "I've hated you for years, but I knew —"

McGrath's voice was harsh as the rasp of steel. "What did you mean by your mention of Constance Brand? She is dead."

A ghastly smile twisted the thin lips.

"No, she's not dead! But she soon will be, if you don't hurry. Quick! Brandy! There on the table — that beast didn't drink it all."

McGrath held the bottle to his lips; Ballville drank avidly. McGrath wondered at the man's iron nerve. That he was in ghastly agony was obvious. He should be screaming in a delirium of pain. Yet he held to sanity and spoke lucidly, though his voice was a laboring croak.

"I haven't much time," he choked. "Don't interrupt. Save your curses till later. We both loved Constance Brand. She loved you. Three years ago she disappeared. Her garments were found on the bank of a river. Her body was never recovered. You went to Africa to drown your sorrow; I retired to the estate of my ancestors and became a recluse.

"What you didn't know — what the world didn't know — was that Constance Brand came with me! No, she didn't drown. That ruse was my idea. For three years Constance Brand has lived in this house!" He achieved a ghastly laugh. "Oh, don't look so stunned, Bristol. She didn't come of her own free will. She loved you too much. I kidnapped her, brought her here by force — Bristol!" His voice rose to a frantic shriek. "If you kill me you'll never learn where she is!"

The frenzied hands that had locked on his corded throat relaxed and sanity returned to the red eyes of Bristol McGrath.

"Go on," he whispered in a voice not even he recognized.

"I couldn't help it," gasped the dying man. "She was the only woman I ever loved — oh, don't sneer, Bristol. The others didn't count. I brought her here where I was king. She couldn't escape, couldn't get word to the outside world. No one lives in this section except nigger descendants of the slaves owned by my family. My word is — *was* — their only law.

"I swear I didn't harm her. I only kept her prisoner, trying to force her to marry me. I didn't want her any other way. I was mad, but I couldn't help it. I come of a race of autocrats who took what they wanted, recognized no law but their own desires. You know that. You understand it. You come of the same breed yourself.

"Constance hates me, if that's any consolation to you, damn you. She's strong, too. I thought I could break her spirit. But I couldn't, not without the whip, and I couldn't bear to use that." He grinned hideously at the wild growl that rose unbidden to McGrath's lips. The big man's eyes were coals of fire; his hard hands knotted into iron mallets.

A spasm racked Ballville, and blood started from his lips. His grin faded and he hurried on.

"All went well until the foul fiend inspired me to send for John De Albor. I met him in Vienna, years ago. He's from East Africa — a devil in human form! He saw Constance — lusted for her as only a man of his type can. When I finally realized that, I tried to kill him. Then I found that he was stronger than I; that he'd made himself master of the niggers — *my* niggers, to whom my word had always been law. He taught them his devilish cult —"

"Voodoo," muttered McGrath involuntarily.

"No! Voodoo is infantile beside this black fiendishness. Look at the symbol on my breast, where De Albor burned it with a white-hot iron. You have been in Africa. You understand the brand of Zambebwei.

"De Albor turned my Negroes against me. I tried to escape with Constance and Ahmed. My own blacks hemmed me in. I did smuggle a telegram through to the village by a man who remained faithful to me — they suspected him and tortured him until he admitted it. John De Albor brought me his head.

"Before the final break I hid Constance in a place where no one will ever find her, except you. De Albor tortured Ahmed until he told that I had sent for a friend of the girl's, to aid us. Then De Albor sent his men up the road with what was left of Ahmed, as a warning to you if you came. It was this morning that they seized us; I hid Constance last night. Not even Ahmed knew where. De Albor tortured me to make me tell —" the dying man's hands clenched and a fierce passionate light blazed in his eyes. McGrath knew that not all the torments of all the hells could ever have wrung that secret from Ballville's iron lips.

"It was the least you could do," he said, his voice harsh with conflicting emotions. "I've lived in Hell for three years because of you — and Constance has.

You deserve to die. If you weren't dying already I'd kill you myself."

"Damn you, do you think I want your forgiveness?" gasped the dying man. "I'm glad you suffered. If Constance didn't need your help, I'd like to see you dying as I'm dying — and I'll be waiting for you in Hell. But enough of this. De Albor left me awhile to go up the road and assure himself that Ahmed was dead. This beast got to swilling my brandy and decided to torture me some himself.

"Now listen — Constance is hidden in Lost Cave. No man on earth knows of its existence except you and me — not even the Negroes. Long ago I put an iron door in the entrance, and I killed the man who did the work; so the secret is safe. There's no key. You've got to open it by working certain knobs."

It was more and more difficult for the man to enunciate intelligibly. Sweat dripped from his face, and the cords of his arms quivered.

"Run your fingers over the edge of the door until you find three knobs that form a triangle. You can't see them; you'll have to feel. Press each one in counter-clockwise motion, three times, around and around. Then pull on the bar. The door will open. Take Constance and fight your way out. If you see they're going to get you, shoot her! Don't let her fall into the hands of that black beast —"

The voice rose to a shriek, foam spattered from the livid writhing lips, and Richard Ballville heaved himself almost upright, then toppled limply back.

The iron will that had animated the broken body had snapped at last, as a taut wire snaps.

McGrath looked down at the still form, his brain a maelstrom of seething emotions, then wheeled, glaring, every nerve atingle, his pistol springing into his hand.

3. The Black Priest

A man stood in the doorway that opened upon the great outer hall — a tall man in a strange alien garb. He wore a turban and a silk coat belted with a gay-hued girdle. Turkish slippers were on his feet. His skin was not much darker than McGrath's, his features distinctly oriental in spite of the heavy glasses he wore.

"Who the devil are you?" demanded McGrath, covering him.

"Ali ibn Suleyman, *effendi,*" answered the other in faultless Arabic. "I came to this place of devils at the urging of my brother, Ahmed ibn Suleyman, whose soul may the Prophet ease. In New Orleans the letter came to me. I hastened here. And lo, stealing through the woods, I saw black men dragging my brother's corpse to the river. I came on, seeking his master."

McGrath mutely indicated the dead man. The Arab bowed his head in stately reverence.

"My brother loved him," he said. "I would have vengeance for my brother and my brother's master.

Effendi, let me go with you."

"All right." McGrath was afire with impatience. He knew the fanatical clan-loyalty of the Arabs, knew that Ahmed's one decent trait had been a fierce devotion for the scoundrel he served. "Follow me."

With a last glance at the master of the Manor and the black body sprawling like a human sacrifice before him, McGrath left the chamber of torture. Just so, he reflected, one of Ballville's warrior-king ancestors might have lain in some dim past age, with a slaughtered slave at his feet to serve his spirit in the land of ghosts.

With the Arab at his heels, McGrath emerged into the girdling pines that slumbered in the still heat of the noon. Faintly to his ears a distant pulse of sound was borne by a vagrant drift of breeze. It sounded like the throb of a faraway drum.

"Come on!" McGrath strode through the cluster of outhouses and plunged into the woods that rose behind them. Here, too, had once stretched the fields that built the wealth of the aristocratic Ballvilles; but for many years they had been abandoned. Paths straggled aimlessly through the ragged growth, until presently the growing denseness of the trees told the invaders that they were in forest that had never known the woodsman's ax. McGrath looked for a path. Impressions received in childhood are always enduring. Memory remains, overlaid by later things, but unerring through the years. McGrath found the path he sought, a dim trace, twisting through the trees.

They were forced to walk single file; the branches scraped their clothing, their feet sank into the carpet of pine needles. The land trended gradually lower. Pines gave way to cypresses, choked with underbrush. Scummy pools of stagnant water glimmered under the trees. Bullfrogs croaked, mosquitoes sang with maddening insistence about them. Again the distant drum throbbed across the pinelands.

McGrath shook the sweat out of his eyes. That drum roused memories well fitted to these somber surroundings. His thoughts reverted to the hideous scar seared on Richard Ballville's naked breast. Ballville had supposed that he, McGrath, knew its meaning; but he did not. That it portended black horror and madness he knew, but its full significance he did not know. Only once before had he seen that symbol, in the horror-haunted country of Zambebwei, into which few white men had ever ventured, and from which only one white man had ever escaped alive. Bristol McGrath was that man, and he had only penetrated the fringe of that abysmal land of jungle and black swamp. He had not been able to plunge deep enough into that forbidden realm either to prove or to disprove the ghastly tales men whispered of an ancient cult surviving a prehistoric age, of the worship of a monstrosity whose mold violated an accepted law of nature. Little enough he had seen; but what he had seen had filled him with shuddering horror that sometimes returned now in crimson nightmares.

No word had passed between the men since they had left the Manor, McGrath plunged on through the vegetation that choked the path. A fat, blunt-tailed moccasin slithered from under his feet and vanished. Water could not be far away; a few more steps revealed it. They stood on the edge of a dank, slimy marsh from which rose a miasma of rotting vegetable matter. Cypresses shadowed it. The path ended at its edge. The swamp stretched away and away, lost to sight swiftly in twilight dimness.

What now, *effendi*?" asked Ali. "Are we to swim this morass?"

"It's full of bottomless quagmires," answered McGrath. "It would be suicide for a man to plunge into it. Not even the piney woods niggers have ever tried to cross it. But there *is* a way to get to the hill that rises in the middle of it. You can just barely glimpse it, among the branches of the cypresses, see? Years ago, when Ballville and I were boys — and friends — we discovered an old, old Indian path, a secret, submerged road that led to that hill. There's a cave in the hill, and a woman is imprisoned in that cave. I'm going to it. Do you want to follow me, or to wait for me here? The path is a dangerous one."

"I will go, *effendi*," answered the Arab.

McGrath nodded in appreciation, and began to scan the trees about him. Presently he found what he was looking for — a faint blaze on a huge cypress, an old mark, almost imperceptible. Confidently then, he stepped into the marsh beside the tree. He himself had made that mark, long ago. Scummy water rose over his shoe soles, but no higher. He stood on a flat rock, or rather on a heap of rocks, the topmost of which was just below the stagnant surface. Locating a certain gnarled cypress far out in the shadow of the marsh, he began walking directly toward it, spacing his strides carefully, each carrying him to a rock-step invisible below the murky water. Ali ibn Suleyman followed him, imitating his motions.

Through the swamp they went, following the marked trees that were their guideposts. McGrath wondered anew at the motives that had impelled the ancient builders of the trail to bring these huge rocks from afar and sink them like piles into the slush. The work must have been stupendous, requiring no mean engineering skill. Why had the Indians built this broken road to Lost Island? Surely that isle and the cave in it had some religious significance to the red men; or perhaps it was their refuge against some stronger foe.

The going was slow; a misstep meant a plunge into marshy ooze, into unstable mire that might swallow a man alive. The island grew out of the trees ahead of them — a small knoll, girdled by a vegetation-choked beach. Through the foliage was visible the rocky wall that rose sheer from the beach to a height of fifty or sixty feet. It was almost like a granite block rising from a flat sandy rim. The pinnacle was almost bare of growth.

McGrath was pale, his breath coming in quick gasps. As they stepped upon the beach-like strip, Ali, with a glance of commiseration, drew a flask from his pocket.

"Drink a little brandy, *effendi*," he urged, touching the mouth to his own lips, oriental-fashion. "It will aid you."

McGrath knew that Ali thought his evident agitation was a result of exhaustion. But he was scarcely aware of his recent exertions. It was the emotions that raged within him — the thought of Constance Brand, whose beautiful form had haunted his troubled dreams for three dreary years. He gulped deeply of the liquor, scarcely tasting it, and handed back the flask.

"Come on!"

The pounding of his own heart was suffocating, drowning the distant drum, as he thrust through the choking vegetation at the foot of the cliff. On the gray rock above the green mask appeared a curious carven symbol, as he had seen it years ago, when its discovery led him and Richard Ballville to the hidden cavern. He tore aside the clinging vines and fronds, and his breath sucked in at the sight of a heavy iron door set in the narrow mouth that opened in the granite wall.

McGrath's fingers were trembling as they swept over the metal, and behind him he could hear Ali breathing heavily. Some of the white man's excitement had imparted itself to the Arab. McGrath's hands found the three knobs, forming the apices of a triangle — mere protuberances, not apparent to the sight. Controlling his jumping nerves, he pressed them as Ballville had instructed him, and felt each give slightly at the third pressure. Then, holding his breath, he grasped the bar that was welded in the middle of the door, and pulled. Smoothly, on oiled hinges, the massive portal swung open.

They looked into a wide tunnel that ended in another door, this a grille of steel bars. The tunnel was not dark; it was clean and roomy, and the ceiling had been pierced to allow light to enter, the holes covered with screens to keep out insects and reptiles. But through the grille he glimpsed something that sent him racing along the tunnel, his heart almost bursting through his ribs. Ali was close at his heels.

The grille-door was not locked. It swung outward under his fingers. He stood motionless, almost stunned with the impact of his emotions.

His eyes were dazzled by a gleam of gold; a sunbeam slanted down through the pierced rock roof and struck mellow fire from the glorious profusion of golden hair that flowed over the white arm that pillowed the beautiful head on the carved oak table.

"*Constance!*" It was a cry of hunger and yearning that burst from his livid lips.

Echoing the cry, the girl started up, staring wildly, her hands at her temples, her lambent hair rippling over her shoulders. To his dizzy gaze she seemed to float in an aureole of golden light.

"Bristol! Bristol McGrath!" she echoed his call with a haunting, incredulous cry. Then she was in his arms, her white arms clutching him in a frantic embrace, as if she feared he was but a phantom that might vanish from her.

For the moment the world ceased to exist for Bristol McGrath. He might have been blind, deaf and dumb to the universe at large. His dazed brain was cognizant only of the woman in his arms, his senses drunken with the softness and fragrance of her, his soul stunned with the overwhelming realization of a dream he had thought dead and vanished forever.

When he could think consecutively again, he shook himself like a man coming out of a trance, and stared stupidly around him. He was in a wide chamber, cut in the solid rock. Like the tunnel, it was illumined from above, and the air was fresh and clean. There were chairs, tables and a hammock, carpets on the rocky floor, cans of food and a water cooler. Ballville had not failed to provide for his captive's comfort. McGrath glanced around at the Arab, and saw him beyond the grille. Considerately he had not intruded upon their reunion.

"Three years!" the girl was sobbing. "Three years I've waited. I knew you'd come! I knew it! But we must be careful, my darling. Richard will kill you if he finds you — kill us both!"

"He's beyond killing anyone," answered McGrath. "But just the same, we've got to get out of here."

Her eyes flared with new terror.

"Yes! John De Albor! Ballville was afraid of him. That's why he locked me in here. He said he'd sent for you. I was afraid for you —"

"Ali!" McGrath called. "Come in here. We're getting out of here now, and we'd better take some water and food with us. We may have to hide in the swamps for —"

Abruptly Constance shrieked, tore herself from her lover's arms. And McGrath, frozen by the sudden, awful fear in her wide eyes, felt the dull jolting impact of a savage blow at the base of his skull. Consciousness did not leave him, but a strange paralysis gripped him. He dropped like an empty sack on the stone floor and lay there like a dead man, helplessly staring up at the scene which tinged his brain with madness — Constance struggling frenziedly in the grasp of the man he had known as Ali ibn Suleyman, now terribly transformed.

The man had thrown off his turban and glasses. And in the murky whites of his eyes, McGrath read the truth with its grisly implications — the man was not an Arab. He was a negroid mixed breed. Yet some of his blood must have been Arab, for there was a slightly Semitic cast to his countenance, and this cast, together with his oriental garb and his perfect acting of his part, had made him seem genuine.

But now all this was discarded and the negroid strain was uppermost; even his voice, which had enunciated the sonorous Arabic, was now the throaty gutturals of the Negro.

"You've killed him!" the girl sobbed hysterically, striving vainly to break away from the cruel fingers that prisoned her white wrists.

"He's not dead yet," laughed the octoroon. "The fool quaffed drugged brandy — a drug found only in the Zambebwei jungles. It lies inactive in the system until made effective by a sharp blow on a nerve center."

"Please do something for him!" she begged.

The fellow laughed brutally.

"Why should I? He has served his purpose. Let him lie there until the swamp insects have picked his bones. I should like to watch that — but we will be far away before nightfall." His eyes blazed with the bestial gratification of possession. The sight of this white beauty struggling in his grasp seemed to rouse all the jungle lust in the man. McGrath's wrath and agony found expression only in his bloodshot eyes. He could not move hand or foot.

"It was well I returned alone to the Manor," laughed the octoroon. "I stole up to the window while this fool talked with Richard Ballville. The thought came to me to let him lead me to the place where you were hidden. It had never occurred to me that there was a hiding-place in the swamp. I had the Arab's coat, slippers and turban; I had thought I might use them sometime. The glasses helped, too. It was not difficult to make an Arab out of myself. This man had never seen John De Albor. I was born in East Africa and grew up a slave in the house of an Arab — before I ran away and wandered to the land of Zambebwei.

"But enough. We must go. The drum has been muttering all day. The blacks are restless. I promised them a sacrifice to Zemba. I was going to use the Arab, but by the time I had tortured out of him the information I desired, he was no longer fit for a sacrifice. Well, let them bang their silly drum. They'd like to have *you* for the Bride of Zemba, but they don't know I've found you. I have a motor-boat hidden on the river five miles from here —"

"You fool!" shrieked Constance, struggling passionately. "Do you think you can carry a white girl down the river, like a slave?"

"I have a drug which will make you like a dead woman," he said. "You will lie in the bottom of the boat, covered by sacks. When I board the steamer that shall bear us from these shores, you will go into my cabin in a large, well-ventilated trunk. You will know nothing of the discomforts of the voyage. You will awake in Africa —"

He was fumbling in his shirt, necessarily releasing her with one hand. With a frenzied scream and a desperate wrench, she tore loose and sped out through the tunnel. John De Albor plunged after her, bellowing. A red haze floated before McGrath's maddened eyes. The girl would plunge to her death in the swamps, unless she remembered the guide-marks — perhaps it was death she sought, in preference to the fate planned for her by the fiendish Negro.

They had vanished from his sight, out of the tunnel; but suddenly Constance screamed again, with a new poignancy. To McGrath's ears came an excited jabbering of Negro gutturals. De Albor's accents were lifted in angry protest. Constance was sobbing hysterically. The voices were moving away. McGrath got a vague glimpse of a group of figures through the masking vegetation as they moved across the line of the tunnel mouth. He saw Constance being dragged along by half a dozen giant blacks, typical pineland dwellers, and after them came John De Albor, his hands eloquent in dissension. That glimpse only, through the fronds, and then the tunnel mouth gaped empty and the sound of splashing water faded away through the marsh.

4. The Black God's Hunger

In the brooding silence of the cavern Bristol McGrath lay staring blankly upward, his soul a seething hell. Fool, fool, to be taken in so easily! Yet, how could he have known? He'd never seen De Albor; he had supposed he was a full-blooded Negro. Ballville had called him a black beast, but he must have been referring to his soul. De Albor, but for the betraying murk of his eyes, might pass anywhere for a white man.

The presence of those black men meant but one thing: they had followed him and De Albor, had seized Constance as she rushed from the cave. De Albor's evident fear bore a hideous implication; he had said the blacks wanted to sacrifice Constance — now she was in their hands.

"God!" The word burst from McGrath's lips, startling in the stillness, startling to the speaker. He was electrified; a few moments before he had been dumb. But now he discovered he could move his lips, his tongue. Life was stealing back through his dead limbs; they stung as if with returning circulation. Frantically he encouraged that sluggish flow. Laboriously he worked his extremities, his fingers, hands, wrists and finally, with a surge of wild triumph, his arms and legs. Perhaps De Albor's hellish drug had lost some of its power through age. Perhaps McGrath's unusual stamina threw off the effects as another man could not have done.

The tunnel door had not been closed, and McGrath knew why: they did not want to shut out the insects which would soon dispose of a helpless body; already the pests were streaming through the door, a noisome horde.

McGrath rose at last, staggering drunkenly, but with his vitality surging more strongly each second. When he tottered from the cave, no living thing met his glare. Hours had passed since the Negroes had departed with their prey. He strained his ears for the drum. It was silent. The stillness rose like an invisible black mist around him. Stumblingly he splashed along the rock-trail that led to hard ground. Had the blacks taken their captive back to the death-haunted Manor, or deeper into the pinelands?

Their tracks were thick in the mud: half a dozen pairs of bare, splay feet, the slender prints of Constance's shoes, the marks of De Albor's Turkish slippers. He followed them with increasing difficulty as the ground grew higher and harder.

He would have missed the spot where they turned off the dim trail but for the fluttering of a bit of silk in the faint breeze. Constance had brushed against a tree-trunk there, and the rough bark had shredded off a fragment of her dress. The band had been headed east, toward the Manor. At the spot where the bit of cloth hung, they had turned sharply southward. The matted pine needles showed no tracks, but disarranged vines and branches bent aside marked their progress, until McGrath, following these signs, came out upon another trail leading southward.

Here and there were marshy spots, and these showed the prints of feet, bare and shod. McGrath hastened along the trail, pistol in hand, in full possession of his faculties at last. His face was grim and pale, De Albor had not had an opportunity to disarm him after striking that treacherous blow. Both the octoroon and the blacks of the pinelands believed him to be lying helpless back in Lost Cave. That, at least, was to his advantage.

He kept straining his ears in vain for the drum he

had heard earlier in the day. The silence did not reassure him. In a voodoo sacrifice drums would be thundering, but he knew he was dealing with something even more ancient and abhorrent than voodoo.

Voodoo was comparatively a young religion, after all, born in the hills of Haiti. Behind the froth of voodooism rose the grim religions of Africa, like granite cliffs glimpsed through a mask of green fronds. Voodooism was a mewling infant beside the black, immemorial colossus that had reared its terrible shape in the older land through uncounted ages. Zambebwei! The very name sent a shudder through him, symbolic of horror and fear. It was more than the name of a country and the mysterious tribe that inhabited that country; it signified something fearfully old and evil, something that had survived its natural epoch — a religion of the Night, and a deity whose name was Death and Horror.

He had seen no Negro cabins. He knew these were farther to the east and south, most of them, huddling along the banks of the river and the tributary creeks. It was the instinct of the black man to build his habitation by a river, as he had built by the Congo, the Nile and the Niger since Time's first gray dawn. Zambebwei! The word beat like a throb of a tom-tom through the brain of Bristol McGrath. The soul of the black man had not changed, through the slumberous centuries. Change might come in the clangor of city streets, in the raw rhythms of Harlem; but the swamps of the Mississippi do not differ enough from the swamps of the Congo to work any great transmutation in the spirit of a race that was old before the first white king wove the thatch of his wattled hut-palace.

Following that winding path through the twilight dimness of the big pines, McGrath did not find it in his soul to marvel that black slimy tentacles from the depths of Africa had stretched across the world to breed nightmares in an alien land. Certain natural conditions produce certain effects, breed certain pestilences of body or mind, regardless of their geographical situation. The river-haunted pinelands were as abysmal in their way as were the reeking African jungles.

The trend of the trail was away from the river. The land sloped very gradually upward, and all signs of marsh vanished.

The trail widened, showing signs of frequent use. McGrath became nervous. At any moment he might meet someone. He took to the thick woods alongside the trail, and forced his way onward, each movement sounding cannon-loud to his whetted ears. Sweating with nervous tension, he came presently upon a smaller path, which meandered in the general direction he wished to go. The pinelands were crisscrossed by such paths.

He followed it with greater ease and stealth, and presently, coming to a crook in it, saw it join the main trail. Near the point of junction stood a small log cabin, and between him and the cabin squatted a big black man. This man was hidden behind the bole of a huge pine beside the narrow path, and peering around it toward the cabin. Obviously he was spying on someone, and it was quickly apparent who this was, as John De Albor came to the door and stared despairingly down the wide trail. The black watcher stiffened and lifted his fingers to his mouth as if to sound a far-carrying whistle, but De Albor shrugged his shoulders helplessly and turned back into the cabin again. The Negro relaxed, though he did not alter his vigilance.

What this portended, McGrath did not know, nor did he pause to speculate. At the sight of De Albor a red mist turned the sunlight to blood, in which the black body before him floated like an ebony goblin.

A panther stealing upon its kill would have made as much noise as McGrath made in his glide down the path toward the squatting black. He was aware of no personal animosity toward the man, who was but an obstacle in his path of vengeance. Intent on the cabin, the black man did not hear that stealthy approach. Oblivious to all else, he did not move or turn — until the pistol butt descended on his woolly skull with an impact that stretched him senseless among the pine needles.

McGrath crouched above his motionless victim, listening. There was no sound nearby — but suddenly, far away, there rose a long-drawn shriek that shuddered and died away. The blood congealed in McGrath's veins. Once before he had heard that sound — in the low forest-covered hills that fringe the borders of forbidden Zambebwei; his black boys had turned the color of ashes and fallen on their faces. What it was he did not know; and the explanation offered by the shuddering natives had been too monstrous to be accepted by a rational mind. They called it the voice of the god of Zambebwei.

Stung to action, McGrath rushed down the path and hurled himself against the back door of the cabin. He did not know how many blacks were inside; he did not care. He was berserk with grief and fury.

The door crashed inward under the impact. He lit on his feet inside, crouching, gun leveled hip-high, lips asnarl.

But only one man faced him — John De Albor, who sprang to his feet with a startled cry. The gun dropped from McGrath's fingers. Neither lead nor steel could glut his hate now. It must be with naked hands, turning back the pages of civilization to the red dawn days of the primordial.

With a growl that was less like the cry of a man than the grunt of a charging lion, McGrath's fierce hands locked about the octoroon's throat. De Albor was borne backward by the hurtling impact, and the men crashed together over a camp cot, smashing it to ruins. And as they tumbled on the dirt floor, McGrath set himself to kill his enemy with his bare fingers.

The octoroon was a tall man, rangy and strong.

But against the berserk white man he had no chance. He was hurled about like a sack of straw, battered and smashed savagely against the floor, and the iron fingers that were crushing his throat sank deeper and deeper until his tongue protruded from his gaping blue lips and his eyes were starting from his head. With death no more than a hand's breadth from the octoroon, some measure of sanity returned to McGrath.

He shook his head like a dazed bull; eased his terrible grip a trifle, and snarled: "Where is the girl? Quick, before I kill you!"

De Albor retched and fought for breath, ashen-faced. "The blacks!" he gasped. "They have taken her to be the Bride of Zemba! I could not prevent them. They demand a sacrifice. I offered them you, but they said you were paralyzed and would die anyway — they were cleverer than I thought. They followed me back to the Manor from the spot where we left the Arab in the road — followed us from the Manor to the island.

"They are out of hand — mad with blood-lust. But even I, who know black men as none else knows them, I had forgotten that not even a priest of Zambebwei can control them when the fire of worship runs in their veins. I am their priest and master — yet when I sought to save the girl, they forced me into this cabin and set a man to watch me until the sacrifice is over. You must have killed him; he would never have let you enter here."

With a chill grimness, McGrath picked up his pistol.

"You came here as Richard Ballville's friend," he said unemotionally. "To get possession of Constance Brand, you made devil-worshippers out of the black people. You deserve death for that. When the European authorities that govern Africa catch a priest of Zambebwei, they hang him. You have admitted that you are a priest. Your life is forfeit on that score, too. But it is because of your hellish teachings that Constance Brand is to die, and it's for that reason that I'm going to blow out your brains."

John De Albor shriveled. "She is not dead yet," he gasped, great drops of perspiration dripping from his ashy face. "She will not die until the moon is high above the pines. It is full tonight, the Moon of Zambebwei. Don't kill me. Only I can save her. I know I failed before. But if I go to them, appear to them suddenly and without warning, they'll think it is because of supernatural powers that I was able to escape from the hut without being seen by the watchman. That will renew my prestige.

"You can't save her. You might shoot a few blacks, but there would still be scores left to kill you — and her. But I have a plan — yes, I am a priest of Zambebwei. When I was a boy I ran away from my Arab master and wandered far until I came to the land of Zambebwei. There I grew to manhood and became a priest, dwelling there until the white blood in me drew me out in the world again to learn the ways of the white men. When I came to America I brought a *Zemba* with me — I can not tell you how. . . .

"Let me save Constance Brand!" He was clawing at McGrath, shaking as if with an ague. "I love her, even as you love her. I will play fair with you both, I swear it! Let me save her! We can fight for her later, and I'll kill you if I can."

The frankness of that statement swayed McGrath more than anything else the octoroon could have said. It was a desperate gamble — but after all, Constance would be no worse off with John De Albor alive than she was already. She would be dead before midnight unless something was done swiftly.

"Where is the place of sacrifice?" asked McGrath.

"Three miles away, in an open glade," answered De Albor. "South on the trail that runs past my cabin. All the blacks are gathered there except my guard and some others who are watching the trail below the cabin. They are scattered out along it, the nearest out of sight of my cabin, but within sound of the loud, shrill whistle with which these people signal one another.

"This is my plan. You wait here in my cabin, or in the woods, as you choose. I'll avoid the watchers on the trail, and appear suddenly before the blacks at the House of Zemba. A sudden appearance will impress them deeply, as I said. I know I can not persuade them to abandon their plan, but I will make them postpone the sacrifice until just before dawn. And before that time I will manage to steal the girl and flee with her. I'll return to your hiding-place, and we'll fight our way out together."

McGrath laughed. "Do you think I'm an utter fool? You'd send your blacks to murder me, while you carried Constance away as you planned. I'm going with you. I'll hide at the edge of the clearing, to help you if you need help. And if you make a false move, I'll get you, if I don't get anybody else."

The octoroon's murky eyes glittered, but he nodded acquiescence.

"Help me bring your guard into the cabin," said McGrath. "He'll be coming to soon. We'll tie and gag him and leave him here."

The sun was setting and twilight was stealing over the pinelands as McGrath and his strange companion stole through the shadowy woods. They had circled to the west to avoid the watchers on the trail, and were now following on the many narrow footpaths which traced their way through the forest. Silence reigned ahead of them, and McGrath mentioned this.

"Zemba is a god of silence," muttered De Albor. "From sunset to sunrise on the night of the full moon, no drum is beaten. If a dog barks, it must be slain; if a baby cries, it must be killed. Silence locks the jaws of the people until Zemba roars. Only *his* voice is lifted on the night of the Moon of Zemba."

McGrath shuddered. The foul deity was an intangible spirit, of course, embodied only in legend; but De Albor spoke of it as a living thing.

A few stars were blinking out, and shadows crept through the thick woods, blurring the trunks of the trees that melted together in darkness. McGrath knew they could not be far from the House of Zemba. He sensed the close presence of a throng of people, though he heard nothing.

De Albor, ahead of him, halted suddenly, crouching. McGrath stopped, trying to pierce the surrounding mask of interlacing branches.

"What is it?" muttered the white man, reaching for his pistol.

De Albor shook his head, straightening. McGrath could not see the stone in his hand, caught up from the earth as he stooped.

"Do you hear something?" demanded McGrath.

De Albor motioned him to lean forward, as if to whisper in his ear. Caught off his guard, McGrath bent toward him — even so he divined the treacherous African's intention, but it was too late. The stone in De Albor's hand crashed sickeningly against the white man's temple. McGrath went down like a slaughtered ox, and De Albor sped away down the path to vanish like a ghost in the gloom.

5. The Voice of Zemba

In the darkness of the woodland path McGrath stirred at last, and staggered groggily to his feet. That desperate blow might have crushed the skull of a man whose physique and vitality were not that of a bull. His head throbbed and there was dried blood on his temple; but his strongest sensation was burning scorn at himself for having again fallen victim to John De Albor. And yet, who would have suspected that move? He knew De Albor would kill him if he could, but he had not expected an attack *before* the rescue of Constance. The fellow was dangerous and unpredictable as a cobra. Had his pleas to be allowed to attempt Constance's rescue been but a ruse to escape death at the hands of McGrath?

McGrath stared dizzily at the stars that gleamed through the ebon branches, and sighed with relief to see that the moon had not yet risen. The pinewoods were black as only pinelands can be, with a darkness that was almost tangible, like a substance that could be cut with a knife.

McGrath had reason to be grateful for his rugged constitution. Twice that day had John De Albor outwitted him, and twice the white man's iron frame had survived the attack. His gun was in his scabbard, his knife in its sheath. De Albor had not paused to search, had not paused for a second stroke to make sure. Perhaps there had been a tinge of panic in the

African's actions.

Well, this did not change matters a great deal. He believed that De Albor would make an effort to save the girl. And McGrath intended to be on hand, whether to play a lone hand, or to aid the octoroon. This was no time to hold grudges, with the girl's life at stake. He groped down the path, spurred by a rising glow in the east.

He came upon the glade almost before he knew it. The moon hung in the low branches, blood-red, high enough to illumine it and the throng of black people who squatted in a vast semicircle about it, facing the moon. Their rolling eyes gleamed milkily in the shadows, their features were grotesque masks. None spoke. No head turned toward the bushes behind which he crouched.

He had vaguely expected blazing fires, a blood-stained altar, drums and the chant of maddened worshippers; that would be voodoo. But this was not voodoo, and there was a vast gulf between the two cults. There were no fires, no altars. But the breath hissed through his locked teeth. In a far land he had sought in vain for the rituals of Zambebwei; now he looked upon them within forty miles of the spot where he was born.

In the center of the glade the ground rose slightly to a flat level. On this stood a heavy iron-bound stake that was indeed but the sharpened trunk of a good-sized pine driven deep into the ground. And there was something living chained to that stake —

something which caused McGrath to catch his breath in horrified unbelief.

He was looking upon a god of Zambebwei. Stories had told of such creatures, wild tales drifting down from the borders of the forbidden country, repeated by shivering natives about jungle fires, passed along until they reached the ears of skeptical white traders. McGrath had never really believed the stories, though he had gone searching for the being they described. For they spoke of a beast that was a blasphemy against nature — a beast that sought food strange to its natural species.

The thing chained to the stake was an ape, but such an ape as the world at large never dreamed of, even in nightmares. Its shaggy gray hair was shot with silver that shone in the rising moon; it looked gigantic as it squatted ghoulishly on its haunches. Upright, on its bent, gnarled legs, it would be as tall as a man, and much broader and thicker. But its prehensile fingers were armed with talons like those of a tiger — not the heavy blunt nails of the natural anthropoid, but the cruel scimitar-curved claws of the great carnivora. Its face was like that of a gorilla, low browed, flaring-nostriled, chinless; but when it snarled, its wide flat nose wrinkled like that of a great cat, and the cavernous mouth disclosed saber-like fangs, the fangs of a beast of prey. This was Zemba, the creature sacred to the people of the land of Zambebwei — a monstrosity, a violation of an accepted law of nature — a carnivorous ape. Men had laughed at the story, hunters and zoologists and traders.

But now McGrath knew that such creatures dwelt in black Zambebwei and were worshipped, as primitive man is prone to worship an obscenity or perversion of nature. Or a survival of past eons: that was what the flesh-eating apes of Zambebwei were — survivors of a forgotten epoch, remnants of a vanished prehistoric age, when nature was experimenting with matter, and life took many monstrous forms.

The sight of the monstrosity filled McGrath with revulsion; it was abysmal, a reminder of that brutish and horror-shadowed past out of which mankind crawled so painfully, eons ago. This thing was an affront to sanity; it belonged in the dust of oblivion with the dinosaur, the mastodon, and the saber-toothed tiger.

It looked massive beyond the stature of modern beasts — shaped on the plan of another age, when all things were cast in a mightier mold. He wondered if the revolver at his hip would have any effect on it; wondered by what dark and subtle means John De Albor had brought the monster from Zambebwei to the pinelands.

But something was happening in the glade, heralded by the shaking of the brute's chain as it thrust forward its nightmare-head.

From the shadows of the trees came a file of black men and women, young, naked except for a mantle of monkey-skins and parrot-feathers thrown over the shoulders of each. More regalia brought by John De Albor, undoubtedly. They formed a semicircle at a safe distance from the chained brute, and sank to their knees, bending their heads to the ground before him. Thrice this motion was repeated. Then, rising, they formed two lines, men and women facing one another, and began to dance; at least it might by courtesy be called a dance. They hardly moved their feet at all, but all other parts of their bodies were in constant motion, twisting, rotating, writhing. The measured, rhythmical movements had no connection at all with the voodoo dances McGrath had witnessed. This dance was disquietingly archaic in its suggestion, though even more depraved and bestial — naked primitive passions framed in a cynical debauchery of motion.

No sound came from the dancers, or from the votaries squatting about the ring of trees. But the ape, apparently infuriated by the continued movements, lifted his head and sent into the night the frightful shriek McGrath had heard once before that day — he had heard it in the hills that border black Zambebwei. The brute plunged to the end of his heavy chain, foaming and gnashing his fangs, and the dancers fled like spume blown before a gust of wind. They scattered in all directions — and then McGrath started up in his covert, barely stifling a cry.

From the deep shadows had come a figure, gleaming tawnily in contrast to the black forms about it. It was John De Albor, naked except for a mantle of bright feathers, and on his head a circlet of gold that might have been forged in Atlantis. In his hand he bore a gold wand that was the scepter of the high priests of Zambebwei.

Behind him came a pitiful figure, at the sight of which the moon-lit forest reeled to McGrath's sight.

Constance had been drugged. Her face was that of a sleepwalker; she seemed not aware of her peril, or the fact that she was naked. She walked like a robot, mechanically responding to the urge of the cord tied about her white neck. The other end of that cord was in John De Albor's hand, and he half-led, half-dragged her toward the horror that squatted in the center of the glade. De Albor's face was ashy in the moonlight that now flooded the glade with molten silver. Sweat beaded his skin. His eyes gleamed with fear and ruthless determination. And in a staggering instant McGrath knew that the man had failed, that he had been unable to save Constance, and that now, to save his own life from his suspicious followers, he himself was dragging the girl to the gory sacrifice.

No vocal sound came from the votaries, but hissing intake of breath sucked through thick lips, and the rows of black bodies swayed like reeds in the wind. The great ape leaped up, his face a slavering devil's mask; he howled with frightful eagerness, gnashing his great fangs that yearned to sink into that soft white flesh, and the hot blood beneath. He surged against his chain, and the stout post quivered. McGrath, in the bushes, stood frozen, paralyzed by the imminence of horror. And then John De Albor stepped behind the unresisting girl and gave her a powerful push that sent her reeling forward to pitch headlong on the ground under the monster's talons.

And simultaneously McGrath moved. His move was instinctive rather than conscious. His .44 jumped into his hand and spoke, and the great ape screamed like a man death-stricken and reeled, clapping misshapen hands to its head.

An instant the throng crouched frozen, white eyes bulging, jaws hanging slack. Then before any could move, the ape, blood gushing from his head, wheeled, seized the chain in both hands and snapped it with a wrench that twisted the heavy links apart as if they had been paper.

John De Albor stood directly before the mad brute, paralyzed in his tracks. Zemba roared and leaped, and the African went down under him, disemboweled by the razor-like talons, his head crushed to a crimson pulp by a sweep of the great paw.

Ravening, the monster charged among the votaries, clawing and ripping and smiting, screaming intolerably. Zambebwei spoke, and death was in his bellowing. Screaming, howling, fighting, the black people scrambled over one another in their mad flight. Men and women went down under those shearing talons, were dismembered by those gnashing fangs. It was a red drama of the primitive —

destruction amuck and ariot, the primordial embodied in fangs and talons, gone mad and plunging in slaughter. Blood and brains deluged the earth, black bodies and limbs and fragments of bodies littered the moonlighted glade in ghastly heaps before the last of the howling wretches found refuge among the trees. The sounds of their blundering, panic-stricken flight drifted back.

McGrath had leaped from his covert almost as soon as he had fired. Unnoticed by the terrified Negroes, and himself scarcely cognizant of the slaughter raging him, he raced across the glade toward the pitiful figure that lay limply beside the iron-bound stake.

"Constance!" he cried, gathering her to his breast.

Languidly she opened her cloudy eyes. He held her close, heedless of the screams and devastation surging about them. Slowly recognition grew in those lovely eyes.

"Bristol!" she murmured, incoherently. Then she screamed, clung to him, sobbing hysterically. "Bristol! They told me you were dead! The blacks! The horrible blacks! They're going to kill me! They were going to kill De Albor too, but he promised to sacrifice —"

"Don't, girl, don't!" He subdued her frantic tremblings. "It's all right, now —" Abruptly he looked up into the grinning bloodstained face of nightmare and death. The great ape had ceased to rend his dead victims and was slinking toward the living pair in the center of the glade. Blood oozed from the wound in its sloping skull that had maddened it.

McGrath sprang toward it, shielding the prostrate girl; his pistol spurted flame, pouring a stream of lead into the mighty breast as the beast charged.

On it came, and his confidence waned. Bullet after bullet he sent crashing into its vitals, but it did not halt. Now he dashed the empty gun full into the gargoyle face without effect, and with a lurch and a roll it had him in its grasp. As the giant arms closed crushingly about him, he abandoned all hope, but following his fighting instinct to the last, he drove his dagger hilt-deep in the shaggy belly.

But even as he struck, he felt a shudder run through the gigantic frame. The great arms fell away — and then he was hurled to the ground in the last death throe of the monster, and the thing was swaying, its face a death mask. Dead on its feet, it crumpled, toppled to the ground, quivered and lay still. Not even a man-eating ape of Zambebwei could survive that close-range volley of mushrooming lead.

As the man staggered up, Constance rose and reeled into his arms, crying hysterically.

"It's all right *now,* Constance," he panted, crushing her to him. "The Zemba's dead; De Albor's dead; Ballville's dead; the Negroes have run away. There's nothing to prevent us leaving now. The Moon of Zambebwei was the end for them. But it's the beginning of life for us."

JEWELS OF GWAHLUR

Weird Tales, March 1935

1. Paths of Intrigue

The cliffs rose sheer from the jungle, towering ramparts of stone that glinted jade-blue and dull crimson in the rising sun, and curved away and away to east and west above the waving emerald ocean of fronds and leaves. It looked insurmountable, that giant palisade with its sheer curtains of solid rock in which bits of quartz winked dazzlingly in the sunlight. But the man, who was working his tedious way upward was already halfway to the top.

He came from a race of hillmen, accustomed to scaling forbidding crags, and he was a man of unusual strength and agility. His only garment was a pair of short red silk breeks, and his sandals were slung to his back, out of his way, as were his sword and dagger.

The man was powerfully built, supple as a panther. His skin was bronzed by the sun, his square-cut black mane confined by a silver band about his temples. His iron muscles, quick eyes and sure feet served him well here, for it was a climb to test these qualities to the utmost. A hundred and fifty feet below him waved the jungle. An equal distance above him the rim of the cliffs was etched against the morning sky.

He labored like one driven by the necessity of haste; yet he was forced to move at a snail's pace, clinging like a fly on a wall. His groping hands and feet found niches and knobs, precarious holds at best, and sometimes he virtually hung by his finger-nails. Yet upward he went, clawing, squirming, fighting for every foot. At times he paused to rest his aching muscles, and, shaking the sweat out of his eyes, twisted his head to stare searchingly out over the jungle, combing the green expanse for any trace of human life or motion.

Now the summit was not far above him, and he observed, only a few feet above his head, a break in the sheer stone of the cliff. An instant later he had reached it — a small cavern, just below the edge of the rim. As his head rose above the lip of its floor, he grunted. He clung there, his elbows hooked over the lip. The cave was so tiny that it was little more than a niche cut in the stone, but it held an occupant. A shriveled brown mummy, cross-legged, arms folded on the withered breast upon which the shrunken head was sunk, sat in the little cavern. The limbs were bound in place with rawhide thongs which had become mere rotted wisps. If the form had ever been clothed, the ravages of time had long ago reduced the garments to dust. But thrust between the crossed arms and the shrunken breast there was a roll of parchment, yellowed with age to the color of old ivory.

The climber stretched forth a long arm and wrenched away this cylinder. Without investigation he thrust it into his girdle and hauled himself up until he was standing in the opening of the niche. A spring upward and he caught the rim of the cliffs and pulled himself up and over almost with the same motion.

There he halted, panting, and stared downward.

It was like looking into the interior of a vast bowl, rimmed by a circular stone wall. The floor of the bowl was covered with trees and denser vegetation, though nowhere did the growth duplicate the jungle denseness of the outer forest. The cliffs marched around it without a break and of uniform height. It was a freak of nature, not to be paralleled, perhaps, in the whole world: a vast, natural amphitheater, a circular bit of forested plain, three or four miles in diameter, cut off from the rest of world, and confined within the ring of those palisaded cliffs.

But the man on the cliffs did not devote his thoughts to marveling at the topographical phenomenon. With tense eagerness he searched the treetops below him, and exhaled a gusty sigh when he caught the glint of marble domes amidst the twinkling green. It was no myth, then; below him lay the fabulous and deserted palace of Alkmeenon.

Conan the Cimmerian, late of the Barachan Isles, of the Black Coast, and of many other climes where life ran wild, had come to the kingdom of Keshan following the lure of a fabled treasure that outshone the hoard of the Turanian kings.

Keshan was a barbaric kingdom lying in the eastern hinterlands of Kush where the broad grasslands merge with the forests that roll up from the south. The people were a mixed race, a dusky nobility ruling a population that was largely pure Negro. The rulers — princes and high priests — claimed descent from a white race which, in a mythical age, had ruled a kingdom whose capital city was Alkmeenon. Conflicting legends sought to explain the reason for that race's eventual downfall, and the abandonment of the city by the survivors. Equally nebulous were the tales of the Teeth of Gwahlur, the treasure of Alkmeenon. But these misty legends had been enough to bring Conan to Keshan, over vast distances of plain, river-laced jungle, and mountains.

He had found Keshan, which in itself was considered mythical by many northern and western nations, and he had heard enough to confirm the rumors of the treasure that men called the Teeth of Gwahlur. But its hiding-place he could not learn, and he was confronted with the necessity of explaining his presence in Keshan. Unattached strangers were not welcome there.

But he was not nonplussed. With cool assurance he made his offer to the stately, plumed, suspicious grandees of the barbarically magnificent court. He was a professional fighting-man. In search of employment (he said) he had come to Keshan. For a price he would train the armies of Keshan and lead them against Punt, their hereditary enemy, whose recent successes in the field had aroused the fury of Keshan's irascible king.

This proposition was not so audacious it might seem. Conan's fame had preceded him, even into distant Keshan; his exploits as a chief of the black corsairs, those wolves of the southern coasts, had made his name known, admired and feared throughout the black kingdoms. He did not refuse tests devised by the dusky lords. Skirmishes along the borders were incessant, affording the Cimmerian plenty of opportunities to demonstrate his ability at hand-to-hand fighting. His reckless ferocity impressed the lords of Keshan, already aware of his reputation as a leader of men, and the prospects seemed favorable. All Conan secretly desired was employment to give him legitimate excuse for remaining in Keshan long enough to locate the hiding-place of the Teeth of Gwahlur. Then there came an interruption. Thutmekri came to Keshan at the head of an embassy from Zembabwei.

Thutmekri was a Stygian, an adventurer and a rogue whose wits had recommended him to the twin kings of the great hybrid trading kingdom which lay many days' march to the east. He and the Cimmerian knew each other of old, and without love. Thutmekri likewise had a proposition to make to the king of Keshan, and it also concerned the conquest of

Punt — which kingdom, incidentally, lying east of Keshan, had recently expelled the Zembabwan traders and burned their fortresses.

His offer outweighed even the prestige of Conan. He pledged himself to invade Punt from the east with a host of black spearmen, Shemitish archers, and mercenary swordsman, and to aid the king of Keshan to annex the hostile kingdom. The benevolent kings of Zembabwei desired only a monopoly of the trade of Keshan and her tributaries — and, as a pledge of good faith, some of the Teeth of Gwahlur. These would be put to no base usage, Thutmekri hastened to explain to the suspicious chieftains; they would be placed in the temple of Zembabwei beside the squat gold idols of Dagon and Derketo, sacred guests in the holy shrine of the kingdom, to seal the covenant between Keshan and Zembabwei. This statement brought a savage grin to Conan's hard lips.

The Cimmerian made no attempt to match wits and intrigue with Thutmekri and his Shemitish partner, Zargheba. He knew that if Thutmekri won his point, he would insist on the instant banishment of his rival. There was but one thing for Conan to do: find the jewels before the king of Keshan made up his mind, and flee with them. But by this time he was certain that they were not hidden in Keshia, the royal city, which was a swarm of thatched huts crowding about a mud wall that enclosed a palace of stone and mud and bamboo.

While he fumed with nervous impatience, the

high priest Gorulga announced that before any decision could be reached, the will of the gods must be ascertained concerning the proposed alliance with Zembabwei and the pledge of objects long held holy and inviolate. The oracle of Alkmeenon must be consulted.

This was an awesome thing, and it caused tongues to wag excitedly in palace and beehive hut. Not for a century had the priests visited the silent city. The oracle, men said, was the Princess Yelaya, the last ruler of Alkmeenon, who had died in the full bloom of her youth and beauty, and whose body had miraculously remained unblemished throughout the ages. Of old, priests had made their way into the haunted city, and she had taught them wisdom. The last priest to seek the oracle had been a wicked man, who had sought to steal for himself the curiously cut jewels that men called the Teeth of Gwahlur. But some doom had come upon him in the deserted palace, from which his acolytes, fleeing, had told tales of horror that had for a hundred year frightened the priests from the city and the oracle.

But Gorulga, the present high priest, as one confident in his knowledge of his own integrity, announced that he would go with a handful of followers to revive the ancient custom. And in the excitement tongues buzzed indiscreetly, and Conan caught the clue for which he had sought for weeks — the overheard whisper of a lesser priest that sent the Cimmerian stealing out of Keshia the night before the dawn when the priests were to start.

Riding as hard as he dared for a night and a day and a night, he came in the early dawn to the cliffs of Alkmeenon, which stood in the southwestern corner of the kingdom, amidst uninhabited jungle which was taboo to common men. None but the priests dared approach the haunted vale within a distance of many miles. And not even a priest had entered Alkmeenon for a hundred years.

No man had ever climbed these cliffs, legends said, and none but the priests knew the secret entrance into the valley. Conan did not waste time looking for it. Steeps that balked these black people, horsemen and dwellers of plain and level forest, were not impossible for a man born in the rugged hills of Cimmeria.

Now on the summit of the cliffs he looked down into the circular valley and wondered what plague, war, or superstition had driven the members of that ancient white race forth from their stronghold to mingle with and be absorbs by the black tribes that hemmed them in.

This valley had been their citadel. There the palace stood, and there only the royal family and their court dwelt. The real city stood outside the cliffs. Those waving masses of green jungle vegetation hid its ruins. But the domes that glistened in the leaves below him were the unbroken pinnacles of the royal palace of Alkmeenon which had defied the corroding ages.

Swinging a leg over the rim he went down swiftly. The inner side of the cliffs was more broken, not quite so sheer. In less than half the time it had taken him to ascend the outer side, he dropped to the swarded valley floor.

With one hand on his sword, he looked alertly about him. There was no reason to suppose men lied when they said that Alkmeenon was empty and deserted, haunted only by the ghosts of the dead past. But it was Conan's nature to be suspicious and wary. The silence was primordial; not even a leaf quivered on a branch. When he bent to peer under the trees, he saw nothing but the marching rows of trunks, receding and receding into the blue gloom of the deep woods.

Nevertheless he went warily, sword in hand, his restless eyes combing the shadows from side to side, his springy tread making no sound on the sward. All about him he saw signs of an ancient civilization; marble fountains, voiceless and crumbling, stood in circles of slender trees whose patterns were too symmetrical to have been a chance of nature. Forest-growth and underbrush had invaded the evenly planned groves, but their outlines were still visible. Broad pavements ran away under the trees, broken, and with grass growing through the wide cracks. He glimpsed walls with ornamental copings, lattices of carven stone that might once have served as the walls of pleasure pavilions.

Ahead of him, through the trees, the domes

gleamed and the bulk of the structure supporting them became more apparent as he advanced. Presently, pushing through a screen of vine-tangled branches, he came into a comparatively open space where the trees straggled, unencumbered by undergrowth, and saw before him the wide, pillared portico of the palace.

As he mounted the broad marble steps, he noted that the building was in a far better state of preservation than the lesser structures he had glimpsed. The thick walls and massive pillars seemed too powerful to crumble before the assault of time and the elements. The same enchanted quiet brooded over all. The catlike pad of his sandaled feet seemed startlingly loud in the stillness.

Somewhere in this palace lay the effigy or image which had in times past served as oracle for the priests of Keshan. And somewhere in the palace, unless that indiscreet priest had babbled a lie, was hidden the treasure of the forgotten kings of Alkmeenon.

Conan passed into a broad, lofty hall, lined with tall columns, between which arches gaped, their doors long rotted away. He traversed this in a twilight dimness, and at the other end passed through great double-valved bronze doors which stood partly open, as they might have stood for centuries. He emerged into a vast domed chamber which must have served as audience hall for the kings of Alkmeenon.

It was octagonal in shape, and the great dome up to which the lofty ceiling curved obviously was cunningly pierced, for the chamber was much better lighted than the hall which led to it. At the farther side of the great room there rose a dais with broad lapis lazuli steps leading up to it, and on that dais there stood a massive chair with ornate arms and a high back which once doubtless supported a cloth-of-gold canopy. Conan grunted explosively and his eyes lit. The golden throne of Alkmeenon, named in immemorial legendry! He weighed it with a practised eye. It represented a fortune in itself, if he were but able to bear it away. Its richness fired his imagination concerning the treasure itself, and made him burn with eagerness. His fingers itched to plunge among the gems he had heard described by storytellers in the market squares of Keshia, who repeated tales handed down from mouth to mouth through the centuries — jewels not to be duplicated in the world, rubies, emeralds, diamonds, bloodstones, opals, sapphires, the loot of the ancient world.

He had expected to find the oracle-effigy seated on the throne, but since it was not, it was probably placed in some other part of the palace, if indeed, such a thing really existed. But since he had turned his face toward Keshan, so many myths had proved to be realities that he did not doubt that he would find some kind of image or god.

Behind the throne there was a narrow arched doorway which doubtless had been masked by hangings in the days of Alkmeenon's life. He glanced through it and saw that it let into an alcove, empty, and with a narrow corridor leading off from it at right angles. Turning away from it, he spied another arch to the left of the dais, and it, unlike the others, was furnished with a door. Nor was it any common door. The portal was of the same rich metal as the throne, and carved with many curious arabesques.

At his touch it swung open so readily that its hinges might recently have been oiled. Inside he halted, staring.

He was in a square chamber of no great dimensions, whose marble walls rose to an ornate ceiling, inlaid with gold. Gold friezes ran about the base and the top of the walls, and there was no door other than the one through which he had entered. But he noted these details mechanically. His whole attention was centered on the shape which lay on an ivory dais before him.

He had expected an image, probably carved with the skill of a forgotten art. But no art could mimic the perfection of the figure that lay before him.

It was no effigy of stone or metal or ivory. It was the actual body of a woman, and by what dark art the ancients had preserved that form unblemished for so many ages Conan could not even guess. The very garments she wore were intact — and Conan scowled at that, a vague uneasiness stirring at the back of his mind. The arts that preserved the body should not have affected the garments. Yet there they were — gold breast-plates set with concentric circles of small gems, gilded sandals, and a short silken skirt upheld by a jeweled girdle. Neither cloth nor metal showed any signs of decay.

Yelaya was coldly beautiful, even in death. Her body was like alabaster, slender yet voluptuous; a great crimson jewel gleamed against the darkly piled foam of her hair.

Conan stood frowning down at her, and then tapped the dais with his sword. Possibilities of a hollow containing the treasure occurred to him, but the dais rang solid. He turned and paced the chamber in some indecision. Where should he search first, in the limited time at his disposal? The priest he had overheard babbling to a courtesan had said the treasure was hidden in the palace. But that included a space of considerable vastness. He wondered if he should hide himself until the priests had come and gone, and then renew the search. But there was a strong chance that they might take the jewels with them when they returned to Keshia. For he was convinced that Thutmekri had corrupted Gorulga.

Conan could predict Thutmekri's plans, from his knowledge of the man. He knew that it had been Thutmekri who had proposed the conquest of Punt to the kings of Zembabwei, which conquest was but one move toward their real goal — the capture of the Teeth of Gwahlur. Those wary kings would demand proof that the treasure really existed before they made any move. The jewels Thutmekri asked as a pledge would furnish that proof.

With positive evidence of the treasure's reality, kings of Zembabwei would move. Punt would be invaded simultaneously from the east and the west, but the Zembabwans would see to it that the Keshani did most of the fighting, and then, when both Punt and Keshan were exhausted from the struggle, the Zembabwans would crush both races, loot Keshan and take the treasure by force, if they had to destroy every building and torture every living human in the kingdom.

But there was always another possibility: if Thutmekri could get his hands on the hoard, it would be characteristic of the man to cheat his employers, steal the jewels for himself and decamp, leaving the Zembabwan emissaries holding the sack.

Conan believed that this consulting of the oracle was but a ruse to persuade the king of Keshan to accede to Thutmekri's wishes — for he never for a moment doubted that Gorulga was as subtle and devious as all the rest mixed up in this grand swindle. Conan had not approached the high priest himself, because in the game of bribery he would have no chance against Thutmekri, and to attempt it would be to play directly into the Stygian's hands. Gorulga could denounce the Cimmerian to the people, establish a reputation for integrity, and rid Thutmekri of his rival at one stroke. He wondered how Thutmekri had corrupted the high priest, and just what could be offered as a bribe to a man who had the greatest treasure in the world under his fingers.

At any rate he was sure that the oracle would be made to say that the gods willed it that Keshan should follow Thutmekri's wishes, and he was sure, too, that it would drop a few pointed remarks concerning himself. After that Keshia would be too hot for the Cimmerian, nor had Conan had any intention of returning when he rode away in the night.

The oracle chamber held no clue for him. He went forth into the great throne-room and laid his hands on the throne. It was heavy, but he could tilt it up. The floor beneath, a thick marble dais, was solid. Again he sought the alcove. His mind clung to a secret crypt near the oracle. Painstakingly he began to tap along the walls, and presently his taps rang hollow at a spot opposite the mouth of the narrow corridor. Looking more closely he saw that the crack between the marble panel at that point and the next was wider than usual. He inserted a dagger-point and pried.

Silently the panel swung open, revealing a niche in the wall, but nothing else. He swore feelingly. The aperture was empty, and it did not look as if it had ever served as a crypt for treasure. Leaning into the niche he saw a system of tiny holes in the wall, about on a level with a man's mouth. He peered through, and grunted understandingly. That was the wall that formed the partition between the alcove and the oracle chamber. Those holes had not been visible in the chamber. Conan grinned. This explained the mystery of the oracle, but it was a bit cruder than he had expected. Gorulga would plant either himself or some trusted minion in that niche, to talk through the holes, and the credulous acolytes, black men all, would accept it as the veritable voice of Yelaya.

Remembering something, the Cimmerian drew forth the roll of parchment he had taken from the mummy and unfolded it carefully, as it seemed ready to fall to pieces with age. He scowled over the dim characters with which it was covered. In his roaming about the world the giant adventurer had picked up a wide smattering of knowledge, particularly including the speaking and reading of many alien tongues. Many a sheltered scholar would have been astonished at the Cimmerian's linguistic abilities, for he had experienced many adventures where knowledge of a strange language had meant the difference between life and death.

These characters were puzzling, at once familiar and unintelligible, and presently he discovered the reason. They were the characters of archaic Pelishtim, which possessed many points of difference from the modem script, with which he was familiar, and which, three centuries ago, had been modified by conquest by a nomad tribe. This older, purer script baffled him. He made out a recurrent phrase, however, which he recognized as a proper name: Bît-Yakin. He gathered that it was the name of the writer.

Scowling, his lips unconsciously moving as he

struggled with the task, he blundered through the manuscript, finding much of it untranslatable and most of the rest of it obscure.

He gathered that the writer, the mysterious Bît-Yakin, had come from afar with his servants, and entered the valley of Alkmeenon. Much that followed was meaningless, interspersed as it was with unfamiliar phrases and characters. Such as he could translate seemed to indicate the passing of a very long period of time. The name of Yelaya was repeated frequently, and toward the last part of the manuscript it became apparent that Bît-Yakin knew that death was upon him. With a slight start Conan realized that the mummy in the cavern must be the remains of the writer of the manuscript, the mysterious Pelishtim, Bît-Yakin. The man had died, as he had prophesied, and his servants, obviously, had placed him in that open crypt, high up on the cliffs, according to his instructions before his death.

It was strange that Bît-Yakin was not mentioned in any of the legends of Alkmeenon. Obviously he had come to the valley after it had been deserted by the original inhabitants — the manuscript indicated as much — but it seemed peculiar that the priests who came in the old days to consult the oracle had not seen the man or his servants. Conan felt sure that the mummy and this parchment were more than a hundred years old. Bît-Yakin had dwelt in the valley when the priests came of old to bow before dead Yelaya. Yet concerning him the legends were silent, telling only of a deserted city, haunted only by the dead.

Why had the man dwelt in this desolate spot, and to what unknown destination had his servants departed after disposing of their master's corpse?

Conan shrugged his shoulders and thrust the parchment back into his girdle — he started violently, the skin on the backs of his hands tingling. Startlingly, shockingly in the slumberous stillness, there had boomed the deep strident clangor of a great gong!

He wheeled, crouching like a great cat, sword in hand, glaring down the narrow corridor from which the sound had seemed to come. Had the priests of Keshia arrived? This was improbable, he knew; they would not have had time to reach the valley. But that gong was indisputable evidence of human presence.

Conan was basically a direct-actionist. Such subtlety as he possessed had been acquired through contact with the more devious races. When taken offguard by some unexpected occurrence, he reverted instinctively to type. So now, instead of hiding or slipping away in the opposite direction as the average man might have done, he ran straight down the corridor in the direction of the sound. His sandals made no more sound than the pads of a panther would have made; his eyes were slits, his lips unconsciously asnarl. Panic had momentarily touched his soul at the shock of that unexpected reverberation, and the red rage of the primitive that is wakened by threat of peril, always lurked close to the surface of the Cimmerian.

He emerged presently from the winding corridor into a small open court. Something glinting in the sun caught his eye. It was the gong, a great gold disk, hanging from a gold arm extending from the crumbling wall. A brass mallet lay near, but there was no sound or sight of humanity. The surrounding arches gaped emptily. Conan crouched inside the doorway for what seemed a long time. There was no sound or movement throughout the great palace. His patience exhausted at last, he glided around the curve of the court, peering into the arches, ready to leap either way like a flash of light, or to strike right or left as a cobra strikes.

He reached the gong, stared into the arch nearest it. He saw only a dim chamber, littered with the debris of decay. Beneath the gong the polished marble flags showed no footprint, but there was a scent in the air — a faintly fetid odor he could not classify; his nostrils dilated like those of a wild beast as he sought in vain to identify it.

He turned toward the arch — with appalling suddenness the seemingly solid flags splintered and gave way under his feet. Even as he fell, he spread wide his arms and caught the edges of the aperture that gaped beneath him. The edges crumbled off under his clutching fingers. Down into utter darkness he shot, into black icy water that gripped him and whirled him away with breathless speed.

2. A Goddess Awakens

The Cimmerian at first made no attempt to fight the current that was sweeping him through lightless night. He kept himself afloat, gripping between his teeth the sword, which he had not relinquished, even in his fall, and did not even seek to guess to what doom he was being borne. But suddenly a beam of light lanced the darkness ahead of him. He saw the surging, seething black surface of the water, in turmoil as if disturbed by some monster of the deep, and he saw the sheer stone walls of the channel curved up to a vault overhead. On each side ran a narrow ledge, just below the arching roof, but they were far out of his reach. At one point this roof had been broken, probably fallen in, and the light was streaming through the aperture. Beyond that shaft of light was utter blackness, and panic assailed the Cimmerian as he saw he would be swept on past that spot of light, and into the unknown blackness again.

Then he saw something else: bronze ladders extended from the ledges to the water's surface at regular intervals, and there was one just ahead of him. Instantly he struck out for it, fighting the current that would have held him to the middle of the stream. It dragged at him as with tangible, animate, slimy hands, but he buffeted the rushing surge with the strength of desperation and drew closer and closer inshore, fighting furiously for every inch. Now he was even with the ladder and with a fierce, gasping plunge he gripped the bottom rung and hung on, breathless.

A few seconds later he struggled up out of the seething water, trusting his weight dubiously to the corroded rungs. They sagged and bent, but they held, and he clambered up onto the narrow ledge which ran along the wall scarcely a man's length below the curving roof. The tall Cimmerian was forced to bend his head as he stood up. A heavy bronze door showed in the stone at a point even with the head of the ladder, but it did not give to Conan's efforts. He transferred his sword from his teeth to its scabbard, spitting blood — for the edge had cut his lips in that fierce fight with the river — and turned his attention to the broken roof.

He could reach his arms up through the crevice and grip the edge, and careful testing told him it would bear his weight. An instant later he had drawn himself up through the hole, and found himself in a wide chamber, in a state of extreme disrepair. Most of the roof had fallen in, as well as a great section of the floor, which was laid over the vault of a subterranean river. Broken arches opened into other chambers and corridors, and Conan believed he was still in the great palace. He wondered uneasily how many chambers in that palace had underground water directly under them, and when the ancient flags or tiles might give way again and precipitate him back into the current from which he had just crawled.

And he wondered just how much of an accident

that fall had been. Had those rotten flags simply chanced to give way beneath his weight, or was there a more sinister explanation? One thing at least was obvious: he was not the only living thing in that palace. That gong had not sounded of its own accord, whether the noise had been meant to lure him to his death, or not. The silence of the palace became suddenly sinister, fraught with crawling menace.

Could it be someone on the same mission as himself? A sudden thought occurred to him, at the memory of the mysterious Bît-Yakin. Was it not possible that this man had found the Teeth of Gwahlur in his long residence in Alkmeenon — that his servants had taken them with them when they departed? The possibility that he might be following a will-o'-the-wisp infuriated the Cimmerian.

Choosing a corridor which he believed led back toward the part of the palace he had first entered, he hurried along it, stepping gingerly as he thought of that black river that seethed and foamed somewhere below his feet.

His speculations recurrently revolved about the oracle chamber and its cryptic occupant. Somewhere in that vicinity must be the clue to the mystery of the treasure, if indeed it still remained in its immemorial hiding-place.

The great palace lay silent as ever, disturbed only by the swift passing of his sandaled feet. The chambers and halls he traversed were crumbling into ruin, but as he advanced the ravages of decay became less apparent. He wondered briefly for what purpose the ladders had been suspended from the ledges over the subterranean river, but dismissed the matter with a shrug. He was little interested in speculating over unremunerative problems of antiquity.

He was not sure just where the oracle chamber lay, from where he was, but presently he emerged into a corridor which led back into the great throne room under one of the arches. He had reached a decision; it was useless for him to wander aimlessly about the palace, seeking the hoard. He would conceal himself somewhere here, wait until the Keshani priests came, and then, after they had gone through the farce of consulting the oracle, he would follow them to the hiding-place of the gems, to which he was certain they would go. Perhaps they would take only a few of the jewels with them. He would content himself with the rest.

Drawn by a morbid fascination, he reentered the oracle chamber and stared down again at the motionless figure of the princess who was worshipped as a goddess, entranced by her frigid beauty. What cryptic secret was locked in that marvelously molded form?

He started violently. The breath sucked through his teeth, the short hairs prickled at the back of his scalp. The body still lay as he had first seen it, silent, motionless, in breast-plates of jeweled gold, gilded sandals and silken skirt. But now there was a subtle difference. The lissom limbs were not rigid, a peach-bloom touched the cheeks, the lips were red —

With a panicky curse Conan ripped out his sword. "Crom! She's alive!"

At his words the long dark lashes lifted; the eyes opened and gazed up at him inscrutably, dark, lustrous, mystical. He glared in frozen speechlessness.

She sat up with a supple ease, still holding his ensorcelled stare.

He licked his dry lips and found voice.

"You — are — are you Yelaya?" he stammered.

"I am Yelaya!" The voice was rich and musical, and he stared with new wonder. "Do not fear. I will not harm you if you do my bidding."

"How can a dead woman come to life after all these centuries?" he demanded, as if skeptical of what his senses told him. A curious gleam was beginning to smolder in his eyes.

She lifted her arms in a mystical gesture.

"I am a goddess. A thousand years ago there descended upon me the curse of the greater gods, the gods of darkness beyond the borders of light. The mortal in me died; the goddess in me could never die. Here I have lain for so many centuries, to awaken each night at sunset and hold my court as of yore, with specters drawn from the shadows of the past. Man, if you would not view that which will blast your soul forever, get hence quickly! I command you! Go!" The voice became imperious, and her slender arm lifted and pointed.

Conan, his eyes burning slits, slowly sheathed

his sword, but he did not obey her order. He stepped closer, as if impelled by a powerful fascination — without the slightest warning he grabbed her up in a bear-like grasp. She screamed a very ungoddess-like scream, and there was a sound of ripping silk, as with one ruthless wrench he tore off her skirt.

"Goddess! Ha!" His bark was full of angry contempt. He ignored the frantic writhings of his captive. "I thought it was strange that a princess of Alkmeenon would speak with a Corinthian accent! As soon as I'd gathered my wits I knew I'd seen you somewhere. You're Muriela, Zargheba's Corinthian dancing-girl. This crescent-shaped birthmark on your hip proves it. I saw it once when Zargheba was whipping you. Goddess! Bah!" He smacked the betraying hip contemptuously and resoundingly with his open hand, and the girl yelped piteously.

All her imperiousness had gone out of her. She was no longer a mystical figure of antiquity, but a terrified and humiliated dancing-girl, such as can be bought at almost any Shemitish marketplace. She lifted up her voice and wept unashamedly. Her captor glared down at her with angry triumph.

"Goddess! Ha! So you were one of the veiled women Zargheba brought to Keshia with him. Did you think you could fool me, you little idiot? A year ago I saw you in Akbitana with that swine, Zargheba, and I don't forget faces — or women's figures. I think I'll —"

Squirming about in his grasp she threw her

slender arms about his massive neck in an abandon of terror; tears coursed down her cheeks, and her sobs quivered with a note of hysteria.

"Oh, please don't hurt me! Don't! I had to do it! Zargheba brought me here to act as the oracle!"

"Why, you sacrilegious little hussy!" rumbled Conan. "Do you not fear the gods? Crom! Is there no honesty anywhere?"

"Oh, please!" she begged, quivering with abject fright. "I couldn't disobey Zargheba. Oh, what shall I do? I shall be cursed by these heathen gods!"

"What do you think the priests will do to you if they find out you're an impostor?" he demanded.

At the thought her legs refused to support her, and she collapsed in a shuddering heap, clasping Conan's knees and mingling incoherent pleas for mercy and protection with piteous protestations of her innocence of any malign intention. It was a vivid change from her pose as the ancient princess, but not surprizing. The fear that had nerved her then was now her undoing.

"Where is Zargheba?" he demanded. "Stop yammering, damn it, and answer me."

"Outside the palace," she whimpered, "watching for the priests."

"How many men with him?"

"None. We came alone."

"Ha!" It was much like the satisfied grunt of a hunting lion. "You must have left Keshia a few hours after I did. Did you climb the cliffs?"

She shook her head, too choked with tears to speak coherently. With an impatient imprecation he seized her slim shoulders and shook her until she gasped for breath.

"Will you quit that blubbering and answer me? How did you get into the valley?"

"Zargheba knew the secret way," she gasped. "The priest Gwarunga told him, and Thutmekri. On the south side of the valley there is a broad pool lying at the foot of the cliffs. There is a cave-mouth under the surface of the water that is not visible to the casual glance. We ducked under the water and entered it. The cave slopes up out of the water swiftly and leads through the cliffs. The opening on the side of the valley is masked by heavy thickets."

"I climbed the cliffs on the east side," he muttered. "Well, what then?"

"We came to the palace and Zargheba hid me among the trees while he went to look for the chamber of the oracle. I do not think he fully trusted Gwarunga. While he was gone I thought I heard a gong sound, but I was not sure. Presently Zargheba came and took me into the palace and brought me to this chamber, where the goddess Yelaya lay upon the dais. He stripped the body and clothed me in the garments and ornaments. Then he went forth to hide the body and watch for the priests. I have been afraid. When you entered I wanted to leap up and beg you to take me away from this place, but I feared Zargheba. When you discovered I was alive, I thought I could frighten you away."

"What were you to say as the oracle?" he asked.

"I was to bid the priests to take the Teeth of Gwahlur and give some of them to Thutmekri as a pledge, as he desired, and place the rest in the palace at Keshia. I was to tell them that an awful doom threatened Keshan if they did not agree to Thutmekri's proposals. And, oh yes, I was to tell them that you were to be skinned alive immediately."

"Thutmekri wanted the treasure where he — or the Zembabwans — could lay hand on it easily," muttered Conan, disregarding the remark concerning himself. "I'll carve his liver yet — Gorulga is a party to this swindle, of course?"

"No. He believes in his gods, and is incorruptible. He knows nothing about this. He will obey the oracle. It was all Thutmekri's plan. Knowing the Keshani would consult the oracle, he had Zargheba bring me with the embassy from Zembabwei, closely veiled and secluded."

"Well, I'm damned!" muttered Conan. "A priest who honestly believes in his oracle, and can not be bribed. Crom! I wonder if it was Zargheba who banged that gong. Did he know I was here? Could he have known about that rotten flagging? Where is he now, girl?"

"Hiding in a thicket of lotus trees, near the ancient avenue that leads from the south wall of the cliffs to the palace," she answered. Then she renewed her importunities. "Oh, Conan, have pity on me! I am afraid of this evil, ancient place. I know I have heard stealthy footfalls padding about me — Oh, Conan, take me away with you! Zargheba will kill me when I have served his purpose here — I know it! The priests, too, will kill me if they discover my deceit.

"He is a devil — he bought me from a slave-trader who stole me out of a caravan bound through southern Koth, and has made me the tool of his intrigues ever since. Take me away from him! You can not be as cruel as he. Don't leave me to be slain here! Please! Please!"

She was on her knees, clutching at Conan hysterically, her beautiful, tear-stained face upturned to him, her dark silken hair flowing in disorder over her white shoulders. Conan picked her up and set her on his knee.

"Listen to me. I'll protect you from Zargheba. The priests shall not know of your perfidy. But you've got to do as I tell you."

She faltered promises of explicit obedience, clasping his corded neck as if seeking security from the contact.

"Good. When the priests come, you'll act the part of Yelaya, as Zargheba planned — it'll be dark, and in the torchlight they'll never know the difference. But you'll say this to them: 'It is the will of the gods that the Stygian and his Shemitish dogs be driven from Keshan. They are thieves and traitors who plot to rob the gods. Let the Teeth of Gwahlur be placed in the care of the general Conan. Let him lead the armies of Keshan. He is beloved of the gods.'"

She shivered, with an expression of desperation, but acquiesced.

"But Zargheba?" she cried. "He'll kill me!"

"Don't worry about Zargheba," he grunted. "I'll take care of that dog. You do as I say. Here, put up your hair again. It's fallen all over your shoulders. And the gem's fallen out of it."

He replaced the great glowing gem himself, nodding approval.

"It's worth a roomful of slaves, itself alone. Here, put your skirt back on. It's torn down the side, but the priests will never notice it. Wipe your face. A goddess doesn't cry like a whipped schoolgirl. By Crom, you *do* look like Yelaya, face, hair, figure and all! If you act the goddess with the priests as well as you did with me, you'll fool them easily."

"I'll try," she shivered.

"Good; I'm going to find Zargheba."

At that she became panicky again.

"No! Don't leave me alone! This place is haunted!"

"There's nothing here to harm you," he assured her impatiently. "Nothing but Zargheba, and I'm going to look after him. I'll be back shortly. I'll be watching from close by in case anything goes wrong during the ceremony; but if you play your part properly, nothing will go wrong."

And turning, he hastened out of the oracle chamber; behind him Muriela squeaked wretchedly at his going.

Twilight had fallen. The great rooms and halls were shadowy and indistinct; copper friezes glinted dully through the dusk. Conan strode like a silent phantom through the great halls, with a sensation of being stared at from the shadowed recesses by invisible ghosts of the past. No wonder the girl was nervous amid such surroundings.

He glided down the marble steps like a slinking panther, sword in hand. Silence reigned over the valley, and above the rim of the cliffs, stars were blinking out. If the priests of Keshia had entered the valley there was not a sound, not a movement in the greenery to betray them. He made out the ancient broken-paved avenue, wandering away to the south, lost amid clustering masses of fronds and thick-leaved bushes. He followed it warily, hugging the edge of the paving where the shrubs massed their shadows thickly, until he saw ahead of him, dimly in the dusk, the clump of lotus-trees, the strange growth peculiar to the black lands of Kush. There, according to the girl, Zargheba should be lurking. Conan became stealth personified. A velvet-footed shadow, he melted into the thickets.

He approached the lotus grove by a circuitous movement, and scarcely the rustle of a leaf proclaimed his passing. At the edge of the trees he halted suddenly, crouched like a suspicious panther among the deep shrubs. Ahead of him, among the dense leaves, showed a pallid oval, dim in the uncertain light. It might have been one of the great white blossoms which shone thickly among the branches. But Conan knew that it was a man's face. And it was turned toward him. He shrank quickly deeper into the shadows. Had Zargheba seen him? The man was looking directly toward him. Seconds passed. That dim face had not moved. Conan could make out the dark tuft below that was the short black beard.

And suddenly Conan was aware of something unnatural. Zargheba, he knew, was not a tall man. Standing erect, his head would scarcely top the Cimmerian's shoulder; yet that face was on a level with Conan's own. Was the man standing on something? Conan bent and peered toward the ground below the spot where the face showed, but his vision was blocked by undergrowth and the thick boles of the trees. But he saw something else, and he stiffened. Through a slot in the underbrush he glimpsed the stem of the tree under which, apparently, Zargheba was standing. The face was directly in line with that tree. He should have seen below that face, not the tree-trunk, but Zargheba's body — but there was no body there.

Suddenly tenser than a tiger who stalks his prey, Conan glided deeper into the thicket, and a moment later drew aside a leafy branch and glared at the face that had not moved. Nor would it ever move again, of its own volition. He looked on Zargheba's severed head, suspended from the branch of the tree by its own long black hair.

3. The Return of the Oracle

Conan wheeled supplely, sweeping the shadows with a fiercely questing stare. There was no sign of the murdered man's body; only yonder the tall lush grass was trampled and broken down and the sward was dabbled darkly and wetly. Conan stood scarcely breathing as he strained his ears into the silence. The trees and bushes with their great pallid blossoms stood dark, still, and sinister, etched against the deepening dusk.

Primitive fears whispered at the back of Conan's mind. Was this the work of the priests of Keshan? If so, where were they? Was it Zargheba, after all, who had struck the gong? Again there rose the memory of Bît-Yakin and his mysterious servants. Bît-Yakin was dead, shriveled to a hulk of wrinkled leather and bound in his hollowed crypt to greet the rising sun forever. But the servants of Bît-Yakin were unaccounted for. *There was no proof they had ever left the valley.*

Conan thought of the girl, Muriela, alone and unguarded in that great shadowy palace. He wheeled and ran back down the shadowed avenue, and he ran as a suspicious panther runs, poised even in full stride to whirl right or left and strike death blows.

The palace loomed through the trees, and he saw something else — the glow of fire reflecting redly from the polished marble. He melted into the bushes that lined the broken street, glided through the dense growth and reached the edge of the open space before the portico. Voices reached him; torches bobbed and their flare shone on glossy ebon shoulders. The priests of Keshan had come.

They had not advanced up the wide, overgrown avenue as Zargheba had expected them to do. Obviously there was more than one secret way into the valley of Alkmeenon.

They were filing up the broad marble steps, holding their torches high. He saw Gorulga at the head of the parade, a profile chiseled out of copper, etched in the torch glare. The rest were acolytes, giant black men from whose skins the torches struck highlights. At the end of the procession there stalked a huge Negro with an unusually wicked cast of countenance, at the sight of whom Conan scowled. That was Gwarunga, whom Muriela had named as the man who had revealed the secret of the pool-entrance to Zargheba. Conan wondered how deeply the man was in the intrigues of the Stygian.

He hurried toward the portico, circling the open space to keep in the fringing shadows. They left no one to guard the entrance. The torches streamed steadily down the long dark hall. Before they reached the double-valved door at the other end, Conan had mounted the outer steps and was in the hall behind them. Slinking swiftly along the column-lined wall, he reached the great door as they crossed the huge throne-room, their torches driving back the shadows. They did not look back. In single file, their ostrich plumes nodding, their leopard-skin tunics contrasting curiously with the marble and arab-esqued metal of the ancient palace, they moved across the wide room and halted momentarily at the golden door to the left of the throne-dais.

Gorulga's voice boomed eerily and hollowly in the great empty space, framed in sonorous phrases unintelligible to the lurking listener; then the high priest thrust open the golden door and entered, bow-ing repeatedly from his waist, and behind him the torches sank and rose, showering flakes of flame, as the worshippers imitated their master. The gold door closed behind them, shutting out sound and sight, and Conan darted across the throne-chamber and into the alcove behind the throne. He made less sound than a wind blowing across the chamber.

Tiny beams of light streamed through the aper-tures in the wall, as he pried open the secret panel. Gliding into the niche, he peered through. Muriela sat upright on the dais, her arms folded, her head leaning back against the wall, within a few inches of his eyes. The delicate perfume of her foamy hair was in his nostrils. He could not see her face, of course, but her attitude was as if she gazed tranquilly into some far gulf of space, over and beyond the shaven heads of the black giants who knelt before her. Conan grinned with appreciation. "The little slut's an actress," he told himself. He knew she was shriv-eling with terror, but she showed no sign. In the uncertain flare of the torches she looked exactly like the goddess he had seen lying on that same dais, if one could imagine that goddess imbued with vibrant life.

Gorulga was booming forth some kind of a chant in an accent unfamiliar to Conan, and which was probably some invocation in the ancient tongue of Alkmeenon, handed down from generation to generation of high priests. It seemed interminable. Conan grew restless. The longer the thing lasted, the more terrific would be the strain on Muriela. If she snapped — he hitched his sword and dagger forward. He could not see the little trollop tortured and slain by black men.

But the chant — deep, low-pitched and indescribably ominous — came to a conclusion at last, and a shouted acclaim from the acolytes marked its period. Lifting his head and raising his arms toward the silent form on the dais, Gorulga cried in the deep, rich resonance that was the natural attribute of the Keshani priest: "Oh, great goddess, dweller with the great one of darkness, let thy heart be melted, thy lips opened for the ears of thy slave whose head is in the dust beneath thy feet! Speak, great goddess of the holy valley! Thou knowest the paths before us; the darkness that vexes us is as the light of the midday sun to thee. Shed the radiance of thy wisdom on the paths of thy servants! Tell us, oh mouthpiece of the gods: what is their will concerning Thutmekri the Stygian?"

The high-piled burnished mass of hair that caught

the torchlight in dull bronze gleams quivered slightly. A gusty sigh rose from the blacks, half in awe, half in fear. Muriela's voice came plainly to Conan's ears in the breathless silence, and it seemed cold, detached, impersonal, though he winced at the Corinthian accent.

"It is the will of the gods that the Stygian and his Shemitish dogs be driven from Keshan!" She was repeating his exact words. "They are thieves and traitors who plot to rob the gods. Let the Teeth of Gwahlur be placed in the care of the general Conan. Let him lead the armies of Keshan. He is beloved of the gods!"

There was a quiver in her voice as she ended, and Conan began to sweat, believing she was on the point of a hysterical collapse. But the blacks did not notice, any more than they identified the Corinthian accent, of which they knew nothing. They smote their palms softly together and a murmur of wonder and awe rose from them. Gorulga's eyes glittered fanatically in the torchlight.

"Yelaya has spoken!" he cried in an exalted voice. "It is the will of the gods! Long ago, in the days of our ancestors, they were made taboo and hidden at the command of the gods, who wrenched them from the awful jaws of Gwahlur the king of darkness, in the birth of the world. At the command of the gods the Teeth of Gwahlur were hidden; at their command they shall be brought forth again. Oh starborn goddess, give us your leave to go to the secret hiding-place of the Teeth to secure them for him whom the gods love!"

"You have my leave to go!" answered the false goddess, with an imperious gesture of dismissal that set Conan grinning again, and the priests backed out, ostrich plumes and torches rising and falling with the rhythm of their genuflections.

The gold door closed and with a moan, the goddess fell back limply on the dais. "Conan!" she whimpered faintly. "Conan!"

"Shhh!" he hissed through the apertures, and turning, glided from the niche and closed the panel. A glimpse past the jamb of the carven door showed him the torches receding across the great throne-room, but he was at the same time aware of a radiance that did not emanate from the torches. He was startled, but the solution presented itself instantly. An early moon had risen and its light slanted through the pierced dome which by some curious workmanship intensified the light. The shining dome of Alkmeenon was no fable, then. Perhaps its interior was of the curious whitely flaming crystal found only in the hills of the black countries. The light flooded the throne-room and seeped into the chambers immediately adjoining.

But as Conan made toward the door that led into the throne-room, he was brought around suddenly by a noise that seemed to emanate from the passage that led off from the alcove. He crouched at the mouth, staring into it, remembering the clangor of the gong that had echoed from it to lure him into a snare. The light from the dome filtered only a little way into that narrow corridor, and showed him only empty space. Yet he could have sworn that he had heard the furtive pad of a foot somewhere down it.

While he hesitated, he was electrified by a woman's strangled cry from behind him. Bounding through the door behind the throne, he saw an unexpected spectacle, in the crystal light.

The torches of the priests had vanished from the great hall outside — but one priest was still in the palace: Gwarunga. His wicked features were convulsed with fury, and he grasped the terrified Muriela by the throat, choking her efforts to scream and plead, shaking her brutally.

"Traitress!" Between his thick red lips his voice hissed like a cobra. "What game are you playing? Did not Zargheba tell you what to say? Aye, Thutmekri told me! Are you betraying your master, or is he betraying his friends through you? Slut! I'll twist off your false head — but first I'll —"

A widening of his captive's lovely eyes as she stared over his shoulder warned the huge black. He released her and wheeled, just as Conan's sword lashed down. The impact of the stroke knocked him headlong backward to the marble floor, where he lay twitching, blood oozing from a ragged gash in his scalp.

Conan started toward him to finish the job — for he knew that the black's sudden movement had caused the blade to strike flat — but Muriela threw her arms convulsively about him.

"I've done as you ordered!" she gasped hysterically. "Take me away! Oh, please take me away!"

"We can't go yet," he grunted. "I want to follow the priests and see where they get the jewels. There may be more loot hidden there. But you can go with me. Where's that gem you wore in your hair?"

"It must have fallen out on the dais," she stammered, feeling for it. "I was so frightened — when the priests left I ran out to find you, and this big brute had stayed behind, and he grabbed me —"

"Well, go get it while I dispose of this carcass," he commanded. "Go on! That gem is worth a fortune itself."

She hesitated, as if loath to return to that cryptic chamber; then, as he grasped Gwarunga's girdle and dragged him into the alcove, she turned and entered the oracle room.

Conan dumped the senseless black on the floor, and lifted his sword. The Cimmerian had lived too long in the wild places of the world to have any illusions about mercy. The only safe enemy was a headless enemy. But before he could strike, a startling scream checked the lifted blade. It came from the oracle chamber.

"Conan! Conan! *She's come back!*" The shriek ended in a gurgle and a scraping shuffle.

With an oath Conan dashed out of the alcove, across the throne dais and into the oracle chamber, almost before the sound had ceased. There he halted, glaring bewilderedly. To all appearances Muriela lay placidly on the dais, eyes closed as if in slumber.

"What in thunder are you doing?" he demanded acidly. "Is this any time to be playing jokes —"

His voice trailed away. His gaze ran along the ivory thigh molded in the close-fitting silk skirt. That skirt should gape from girdle to hem. He knew, because it had been his own hand that tore it, as he ruthlessly stripped the garment from the dancer's writhing body. But the skirt showed no rent. A single stride brought him to the dais and he laid his hand on the ivory body — snatched it away as if it had encountered hot iron instead of the cold immobility of death.

"Crom!" he muttered, his eyes suddenly slits of bale-fire. "It's not Muriela! It's Yelaya!"

He understood now that frantic scream that had burst from Muriela's lips when she entered the chamber. The goddess had returned. The body had been stripped by Zargheba to furnish the accouterments for the pretender. Yet now it was clad in silk and jewels as Conan had first seen it. A peculiar prickling made itself manifest among the short hairs at the base of Conan's scalp.

"Muriela!" he shouted suddenly. "*Muriela!* Where the devil are you?"

The walls threw back his voice mockingly. There was no entrance that he could see except the golden door, and none could have entered or departed through that without his knowledge. This much was indisputable: Yelaya had been replaced on the dais within the few minutes that had elapsed since Muriela had first left the chamber to be seized by Gwarunga; his ears were still tingling with the echoes of Muriela's scream, yet the Corinthian girl had vanished as if into thin air. There was but one explanation, if he rejected the darker speculation that suggested the supernatural — somewhere in the chamber there was a secret door. And even as the thought crossed his mind, he saw it.

In what had seemed a curtain of solid marble, a thin perpendicular crack showed and in the crack hung a wisp of silk. In an instant he was bending over it. That shred was from Muriela's torn skirt. The implication was unmistakable. It had been caught in the closing door and torn off as she was borne through the opening by whatever grim beings were her captors. The bit of clothing had prevented the door from fitting perfectly into its frame.

Thrusting his dagger-point into the crack, Conan exerted leverage with a corded forearm. The blade bent, but it was of unbreakable Akbitanan steel. The marble door opened. Conan's sword was lifted as he peered into the aperture beyond, but he saw no shape of menace. Light filtering into the oracle chamber revealed a short flight of steps cut out of marble. Pulling the door back to its fullest extent, he drove his dagger into a crack in the floor, propping it open. Then he went down the steps without hesitation. He saw nothing, heard nothing.

A dozen steps down, the stair ended in a narrow corridor which ran straight away into gloom.

He halted suddenly, posed like a statue at the foot of the stair, staring at the paintings which frescoed the walls, half-visible in the dim light which filtered down from above. The art was unmistakably Pelishtim; he had seen frescoes of identical characteristics on the walls of Asgalun. But the scenes depicted had no connection with anything Pelishtim, except for one human figure, frequently recurrent: a lean, white-bearded old man whose racial characteristics were unmistakable. They seemed to represent various sections of the palace above. Several scenes showed a chamber he recognized as the oracle chamber with the figure of Yelaya stretched upon the ivory dais and huge black men kneeling before it. And there behind the wall, in the niche, lurked the ancient Pelishtim. And there were other figures, too — figures that moved through the deserted palace, did the bidding of the Pelishtim, and dragged unnamable things out of the subterranean river. In the few seconds Conan stood frozen, hitherto unintelligible phrases in the parchment manuscript blazed in his brain with chilling clarity. The loose bits of the pattern clicked into place. The mystery of Bît-Yakin was a mystery no longer, nor the riddle of Bît-Yakin's servants.

Conan turned and peered into the darkness, an icy finger crawling along his spine. Then he went along the corridor, cat-footed, and without hesitation, moving deeper and deeper into the darkness as he drew farther away from the stair. The air hung heavy with the odor he had scented in the court of the gong.

Now in utter blackness he heard a sound ahead of him — the shuffle of bare feet, or the swish of loose garments against stone, he could not tell which. But an instant later his outstretched hand encountered a barrier which he identified as a massive door of carved metal. He pushed against it fruitlessly, and his sword-point sought vainly for a crack. It fitted into the sill and jambs as if molded there. He exerted all his strength, his feet straining against the floor, the veins knotting in his temples. It was useless; a charge of elephants would scarcely have shaken that titanic portal.

As he leaned there he caught a sound on the other side that his ears instantly identified — it was the creak of rusty iron, like a lever scraping in its slot. Instinctively action followed recognition so spontaneously that sound, impulse and action were practically simultaneous. And as his prodigious bound carried him backward, there was the rush of a great bulk from above, and a thunderous crash filled the tunnel with deafening vibrations. Bits of flying splinters struck him — a huge block of stone, he knew from the sound, dropped on the spot he had just quitted. An instant's slower thought or action and it would have crushed him like an ant.

Conan fell back. Somewhere on the other side of that metal door Muriela was a captive, if she still lived. But he could not pass that door, and if he remained in the tunnel another block might fall, and he might not be so lucky. It would do the girl no good for him to be crushed into a purple pulp. He could not continue his search in that direction. He must get above ground and look for some other avenue of approach.

He turned and hurried toward the stair, sighing as he emerged into comparative radiance. And as he set foot on the first step, the light was blotted out, and above him the marble door rushed shut with a resounding reverberation.

Something like panic seized the Cimmerian then, trapped in that black tunnel, and he wheeled on the stair, lifting his sword and glaring murderously into the darkness behind him, expecting a rush of ghoulish assailants. But there was no sound or movement down the tunnel. Did the men beyond the door — if they *were* men — believe that be had been disposed of by the fall of the stone from the roof, which had undoubtedly been released by some sort of machinery?

Then why had the door been shut above him? Abandoning speculation, Conan groped his way up the steps, his skin crawling in anticipation of a knife in his back at every stride, yearning to drown his semi-panic in a barbarous burst of bloodletting.

He thrust against the door at the top, and cursed soulfully to find that it did not give to his efforts. Then as he lifted his sword with his right hand to hew at the marble, his groping left encountered a metal bolt that evidently slipped into place at the closing of the door. In an instant he had drawn this bolt, and then the door gave to his shove. He bounded into the chamber like a slit-eyed, snarling incarnation of fury, ferociously desirous to come to grips with whatever enemy was hounding him.

The dagger was gone from the floor. The chamber was empty, and so was the dais. Yelaya had again vanished.

"By Crom!" muttered the Cimmerian. "Is she alive, after all?"

He strode out into the throne-room, baffled, and then, struck by a sudden thought, stepped behind the throne and peered into the alcove. There was blood on the smooth marble where he had cast down the senseless body of Gwarunga — that was all. The black man had vanished as completely as Yelaya.

4. The Teeth of Gwahlur

Baffled wrath confused the brain of Conan the Cimmerian. He knew no more how to go about searching for Muriela than he had known how to go about searching for the Teeth of Gwahlur. Only one thought occurred to him — to follow the priests. Perhaps at the hiding-place of the treasure some clue would be revealed to him. It was a slim chance, but better than wandering about aimlessly.

As he hurried through the great shadowy hall that led to the portico he half-expected the lurking shadows to come to life behind him with rending fangs and talons. But only the beat of his own rapid heart accompanied him into the moonlight that dappled the shimmering marble.

At the foot of the wide steps he cast about in the bright moonlight for some sign to show him the direction he must go. And he found it — petals scattered on the sward told where an arm or garment had brushed against a blossom-laden branch. Grass had been pressed down under heavy feet. Conan, who had tracked wolves in his native hills, found no insurmountable difficulty in following the trail of the Keshani priests.

It led away from the palace, through masses of exotic-scented shrubbery where great pale blossoms spread their shimmering petals, through verdant, tangled bushes that showered blooms at the touch, until he came at last to a great mass of rock that jutted like a titan's castle out from the cliffs at a point closest to the palace, which, however, was almost hidden from view by vine-interlaced trees. Evidently that babbling priest in Keshia had been mistaken when he said the Teeth were hidden in the palace. This trail had led him away from the place where Muriela had disappeared, but a belief was growing in Conan that each part of the valley was connected with that palace by subterranean passages.

Crouching in the deep velvet-black shadows of the bushes, he scrutinized the great jut of rock which stood out in bold relief in the moonlight. It was covered with strange, grotesque carvings, depicting men and animals, and half-bestial creatures that might have been gods or devils. The style of art differed so strikingly from that of the rest of the valley, that Conan wondered if it did not represent a different era and race, and was itself a relic of an age lost and forgotten at whatever immeasurably distant date the people of Alkmeenon had found and entered the haunted valley.

A great door stood open in the sheer curtain of the cliff, and a gigantic dragon's head was carved about it so that the open door was like the dragon's gaping mouth. The door itself was of carven bronze and looked to weigh several tons. There was no lock that he could see, but a series of bolts showing along the edge of the massive portal, as it stood open, told him that there was some system of locking and unlocking — a system doubtless known only to the priests of Keshan.

The trail showed that Gorulga and his henchmen had gone through that door. But Conan hesitated. To wait until they emerged would probably mean to see the door locked in his face, and he might not be able to solve the mystery of its unlocking. On the other hand, if he followed them in, they might emerge and lock him in the cavern.

Throwing caution to the winds, he glided through the great portal. Somewhere in the cavern were the priests, the Teeth of Gwahlur, and perhaps a clue to the fate of Muriela. Personal risks had never yet deterred him from any purpose.

Moonlight illumined, for a few yards, the wide tunnel in which he found himself. Somewhere ahead of him he saw a faint glow and heard the echo of a weird chanting. The priests were not so far ahead of him as he had thought. The tunnel debouched into a wide room before the moonlight played out, an empty cavern of no great dimensions, but with a lofty, vaulted roof, glowing with a phosphorescent encrustation, which, as Conan knew, was a common phenomenon in that part of the world. It made a ghostly half-light, in which he was able to see a bestial image squatting on a shrine, and the black mouths of six or seven tunnels leading off from the chamber. Down the widest of these — the one directly behind the squat image which looked toward the outer opening — he caught the gleam of torches wavering, whereas the phosphorescent glow was fixed, and heard the chanting increase in volume.

Down it he went recklessly, and was presently peering into a larger cavern than the one he had just left. There was no phosphorus here, but the light of the torches fell on a larger altar and a more obscene and repulsive god squatting toad-like upon it. Before this repugnant deity Gorulga and his ten acolytes knelt and beat their heads upon the ground, while chanting monotonously. Conan realized why their progress had been so slow. Evidently approaching the secret crypt of the Teeth was a complicated and elaborate ritual.

He was fidgeting in nervous impatience before

the chanting and bowing were over, but presently they rose and passed into the tunnel which opened behind the idol. Their torches bobbed away into the nighted vault, and he followed swiftly. There was not much danger of being discovered. He glided along the shadows like a creature of the night, and the black priests were completely engrossed in their ceremonial mummery. Apparently they had not even noticed the absence of Gwarunga.

Emerging into a cavern of huge proportions, about whose upward curving walls gallery-like ledges marched in tiers, they began their worship anew before an alter which was larger, and a god which was more disgusting, than any encountered thus far.

Conan crouched in the black mouth of the tunnel, staring at the walls reflecting the lurid glow of torches. He saw a carven stone stair winding up from tier to tier of the galleries; the roof was lost in darkness.

He started violently and the chanting broke off as the kneeling blacks flung up their heads. An inhuman voice boomed out high above them. They froze on their knees, their faces turned upward with a ghastly blue hue in the sudden glare of a weird light that burst blindingly up near the lofty roof, and then burned with a throbbing glow. That glare lighted a gallery and a cry went up from the high priest, echoed shudderingly by his acolytes. In the flash there had been briefly disclosed to them a slim white figure standing upright in a sheen of silk and a glint of jewel-crusted gold. Then the blaze smoldered to a throbbing, pulsing luminosity in which nothing was distinct, and that slim shape was but a shimmering blur of ivory.

"*Yelaya!*" screamed Gorulga, his brown features ashen. "Why have you followed us? What is your pleasure?"

That weird unhuman voice rolled down from the roof, re-echoing under that arching vault that magnified and altered it beyond recognition.

"Woe to the unbelievers! Woe to the false children of Keshia! Doom to them which deny their deity!"

A cry of horror went up from the priests. Gorulga looked like a shocked vulture in the glare of the torches.

"I do not understand," he stammered. "We are faithful. In the chamber of the oracle you told us —"

"Do not heed what you heard in the chamber of the oracle!" rolled that terrible voice, multiplied until it was as though a myriad voices thundered and muttered the same warning. "Beware of false prophets and false gods! A demon in my guise spoke to you in the palace, giving false prophecy. Now harken and obey, for only I am the true goddess, and I give you one chance to save yourselves from doom!

"Take the Teeth of Gwahlur from the crypt where they were placed so long ago. Alkmeenon is no longer holy, because it has been desecrated by blasphemers. Give the Teeth of Gwahlur into the hands of Thutmekri, the Stygian, to place in the sanctuary of Dagon and Derketo. Only this can save Keshan from the doom the demons of the night have plotted. Take the Teeth of Gwahlur and go; return instantly to Keshia; there give the jewels to Thutmekri, and seize the foreign devil Conan and flay him alive in the great square."

There was no hesitation in obeying. Chattering with fear the priests scrambled up and ran for the door that opened behind the bestial god. Gorulga led the flight. They jammed briefly in the doorway, yelping as wildly waving torches touched squirming black bodies; they plunged through, and the patter of their speeding feet dwindled down the tunnel.

Conan did not follow. He was consumed with a furious desire to learn the truth of this fantastic affair. Was that indeed Yelaya, as the cold sweat on the backs of his hands told him, or was it that little hussy Muriela, turned traitress after all? If it was —

Before the last torch had vanished down the black tunnel he was bounding vengefully up the stone stair. The blue glow was dying down, but he could still make out that the ivory figure stood motionless on the gallery. His blood ran cold as he approached it, but he did not hesitate. He came on with his sword lifted, and towered like a threat of death over the inscrutable shape.

"Yelaya!" he snarled. "Dead as she's been for a thousand years! *Ha!*"

From the dark mouth of a tunnel behind him a dark form lunged. But the sudden, deadly rush of unshod feet had reached the Cimmerian's quick ears.

He whirled like a cat and dodged the blow aimed murderously at his back. As the gleaming steel in the dark hand hissed past him, he struck back with the fury of a roused python, and the long straight blade impaled his assailant and stood out a foot and a half between his shoulders.

"So!" Conan tore his sword free as the victim sagged to the floor, gasping and gurgling. The man writhed briefly and stiffened. In the dying light Conan saw a black body and ebon countenance, hideous in the blue glare. He had killed Gwarunga.

Conan turned from the corpse to the goddess. Thongs about her knees and breast held her upright against a stone pillar, and her thick hair, fastened to the column, held her head up. At a few yards' distance these bonds were not visible in the uncertain light.

"He must have come to after I descended into the tunnel," muttered Conan. "He must have suspected I was down there. So he pulled out the dagger" — Conan stooped and wrenched the identical weapon from the stiffening fingers, glanced at it and replaced it in his own girdle — "and shut the door. Then he took Yelaya to befool his brother idiots. That was he shouting a while ago. You couldn't recognize his voice, under this echoing roof. And that bursting blue flame — I thought it looked familiar. It's a trick of the Stygian priests. Thutmekri must have given some of it to Gwarunga."

The man could easily have reached this cavern

ahead of his companions. Evidently familiar with the plan of the caverns by hearsay or by maps handed down in the priestcraft, he had entered the cave after the others, carrying the goddess, followed a circuitous route through the tunnels and chambers, and ensconced himself and his burden on the balcony while Gorulga and the other acolytes were engaged in their endless rituals.

The blue glare had faded, but now Conan was aware of another glow, emanating from the mouth of one of the corridors that opened on the ledge. Somewhere down that corridor there was another field of phosphorus, for he recognized the faint steady radiance. The corridor led in the direction the priests had taken, and he decided to follow it, rather than descend into the darkness of the great cavern below. Doubtless it connected with another gallery in some other chamber, which might be the destination of the priests. He hurried down it, the illumination growing stronger as he advanced, until he could make out the floor and the walls of the tunnel. Ahead of him and below he could hear the priests chanting again.

Abruptly a doorway in the left-hand wall was limned in the phosphorous glow, and to his ears came the sound of soft, hysterical sobbing. He wheeled, and glared through the door.

He was looking again into a chamber hewn out of solid rock, not a natural cavern like the others. The domed roof shone with the phosphorous light, and the walls were almost covered with arabesques of beaten gold.

Near the farther wall on a granite throne, staring forever toward the arched doorway, sat the monstrous and obscene Pteor, the god of the Pelishtim, wrought in brass, with his exaggerated attributes reflecting the grossness of his cult. And in his lap sprawled a limp white figure.

"Well, I'll be damned!" muttered Conan. He glanced suspiciously about the chamber, seeing no other entrance or evidence of occupation, and then advanced noiselessly and looked down at the girl whose slim shoulders shook with sobs of abject misery, her face sunk in her arms. From thick bands of gold on the idol's arms slim gold chains ran to smaller bands on her wrists. He laid a hand on her naked shoulder and she started convulsively, shrieked, and twisted her tear-stained face toward him.

"*Conan!*" She made a spasmodic effort to go into the usual clinch, but the chains hindered her. He cut through the soft gold as close to her wrists as he could, grunting: "You'll have to wear these bracelets until I can find a chisel or a file. Let go of me, damn it! You actresses are too damned emotional. What happened to you, anyway?"

"When I went back into the oracle chamber," she whimpered, "I saw the goddess lying on the dais as I'd first seen her. I called out to you and started to run to the door — then something grabbed me from behind. It clapped a hand over my mouth and carried me through a panel in the wall, and down some steps and along a dark hall. I didn't see what it was that had hold of me until we passed through a big metal door and came into a tunnel whose roof was alight, like this chamber.

"Oh, I nearly fainted when I saw! They are not humans! They are gray, hairy devils that walk like men and speak a gibberish no human could understand. They stood there and seemed to be waiting, and once I thought I heard somebody trying the door. Then one of the *things* pulled a metal lever in the wall and something crashed on the other side of the door.

"Then they carried me on and on through winding tunnels and up stone stairways into this chamber, where they chained me on the knees of this abominable idol, and then they went away. Oh, Conan, what are they?"

"Servants of Bît-Yakin," he grunted. "I found a manuscript that told me a number of things, and then stumbled upon some frescoes that told me the rest. Bît-Yakin was a Pelishtim who wandered into the valley with his servants after the people of Alkmeenon had deserted it. He found the body of Princess Yelaya, and discovered that the priests returned from time to time to make offerings to her, for even then she was worshipped as a goddess.

"He made an oracle of her, and he was the voice of the oracle, speaking from a niche he cut in the wall behind the ivory dais. The priests never suspected, never saw him or his servants, for they always hid themselves when the men came. Bît-Yakin lived and died here without ever being discovered by the priests. Crom knows how long he dwelt here, but it must have been for centuries. The wise men of the Pelishtim know how to increase the span of their lives for hundreds of years. I've seen some of them myself. Why he lived here alone, and why he played the part of oracle no ordinary human can guess, but I believe the oracle part was to keep the city inviolate and sacred, so he could remain undisturbed. He ate the food the priests brought as an offering to Yelaya, and his servants ate other things — I've always known there was a subterranean river flowing away from the lake where the people of the Puntish highlands throw their dead. That river runs under this palace. They have ladders hung over the water where they can hang and fish for the corpses that come floating through. Bît-Yakin recorded everything on parchment and painted walls.

"But he died at last, and his servants mummified him according to instructions he gave them before his death, and stuck him in a cave in the cliffs. The rest is easy to guess. His servants, who were even more nearly immortal than he, kept on dwelling here, but the next time a high priest came to consult the oracle, not having a master to restrain them, they tore him to pieces. So since then — until Gorulga — nobody came to talk to the oracle.

"It's obvious they've been renewing the garments and ornaments of the goddess, as they'd seen Bît-Yakin do. Doubtless there's a sealed chamber somewhere where the silks are kept from decay. They clothed the goddess and brought her back to the oracle room after Zargheba had stolen her. And, oh, by the way, they took off Zargheba's head and hung it up in a thicket."

She shivered, yet at the same time breathed a sigh of relief.

"He'll never whip me again."

"Not this side of Hell," agreed Conan. "But come on. Gwarunga ruined my chances with his stolen goddess. I'm going to follow the priests and take my chance of stealing the loot from them after they get it. And you stay close to me. I can't spend all my time looking for you."

"But the servants of Bît-Yakin!" she whispered fearfully.

"We'll have to take our chance," he grunted. "I don't know what's in their minds, but so far they haven't shown any disposition to come out and fight in the open. Come on."

Taking her wrist he led her out of the chamber and down the corridor. As they advanced they heard the chanting of the priests, and mingling with the sound the low sullen rushing of waters. The light grew stronger above them as they emerged on a high-pitched gallery of a great cavern and looked down on a scene weird and fantastic.

Above them gleamed the phosphorescent roof; a hundred feet below them stretched the smooth floor of the cavern. On the far side this floor was cut by a deep, narrow stream brimming its rocky channel. Rushing out of impenetrable gloom, it swirled across the cavern and was lost again in darkness. The visible surface reflected the radiance above; the dark seething waters glinted as if flecked with living jewels, frosty blue, lurid red, shimmering green, an ever-changing iridescence.

Conan and his companion stood upon one of the gallery-like ledges that banded the curve of the lofty wall, and from this ledge a natural bridge of stone soared in a breathtaking arch over the vast gulf of the cavern to join a much smaller ledge on the opposite side, across the river. Ten feet below it another, broader arch spanned the cave. At either end a carven stair joined the extremities of these flying arches.

Conan's gaze, following the curve of the arch that swept away from the ledge on which they stood, caught a glint of light that was not the lurid phosphorus of the cavern. On that small ledge opposite them there was an opening in the cave wall through which stars were glinting.

But his full attention was drawn to the scene beneath them. The priests had reached their destination. There in a sweeping angle of the cavern wall stood a stone altar, but there was no idol upon it. Whether there was one behind it, Conan could not ascertain, because some trick of the light, or the sweep of the wall, left the space behind the altar in total darkness.

The priests had stuck their torches into holes in the stone floor, forming a semicircle of fire in front of the altar at a distance of several yards. Then the priests themselves formed a semicircle inside the crescent of torches, and Gorulga, after lifting his arms aloft in invocation, bent to the altar and laid hands on it. It lifted and tilted backward on its hinder edge, like the lid of a chest, revealing a small crypt.

Extending a long arm into the recess, Gorulga brought up a small brass chest. Lowering the altar back into place, he set the chest on it, and threw back the lid. To the eager watchers on the high gallery it seemed as if the action had released a blaze of living fire which throbbed and quivered about the opened chest. Conan's heart leaped and his hand caught at his hilt. The Teeth of Gwahlur at last! The treasure that would make its possessor the richest man in the world! His breath came fast between his clenched teeth.

Then he was suddenly aware that a new element had entered into the light of the torches and of the phosphorescent roof, rendering both void. Darkness stole around the altar, except for that glowing spot of evil radiance cast by the Teeth of Gwahlur, and that grew and grew. The blacks froze into basaltic statues, their shadows streaming grotesquely and gigantically out behind them.

The altar was laved in the glow now, and the astounded features of Gorulga stood out in sharp relief. Then the mysterious space behind the altar swam into the widening illumination. And slowly with the crawling light, figures became visible, like shapes growing out of the night and silence.

At first they seemed like gray stone statues, those motionless shapes, hairy, man-like, yet hideously human; but their eyes were alive, cold sparks of gray icy fire. And as the weird glow lit their bestial countenances, Gorulga screamed and fell backward, throwing up his long arms in a gesture of frenzied horror.

But a longer arm shot across the altar and a misshapen hand locked on his throat. Screaming and fighting, the high priest was dragged back across the altar; a hammer-like fist smashed down, and Gorulga's cries were stilled. Limp and broken he sagged across the altar, his brains oozing from his crushed skull. And then the servants of Bît-Yakin surged like a bursting flood from Hell on the black priests who stood like horror-blasted images.

Then there was slaughter, grim and appalling.

Conan saw black bodies tossed like chaff in the inhuman hands of the slayers, against whose horrible strength and agility the daggers and swords of the priests were ineffective. He saw men lifted bodily and their heads cracked open against the stone altar. He saw a flaming torch, grasped in a monstrous hand, thrust inexorably down the gullet of an agonized wretch who writhed in vain against the arms that pinioned him. He saw a man torn in two pieces, as one might tear a chicken, and the bloody fragments hurled clear across the cavern. The massacre was as short and devastating as the rush of a hurricane. In a burst of red abysmal ferocity it was over, except for one wretch who fled screaming back the way the priests had come, pursued by a swarm of blood-dabbled shapes of horror which reached out their red-smeared hands for him. Fugitive and pursuers vanished down the black tunnel, and the screams of the human came back dwindling and confused by the distance.

Muriela was on her knees clutching Conan's legs; her face pressed against his knee and her eyes tightly shut. She was a quaking, quivering mold of abject terror. But Conan was galvanized. A quick glance across at the aperture where the stars shone, a glance down at the chest that still blazed open on the blood-smeared altar, and he saw and seized the desperate gamble.

"I'm going after that chest!" he grated. "Stay here!"

"Oh Mitra, no!" In an agony of fright she fell to the floor and caught at his sandals. "Don't! Don't! Don't leave me!"

"Lie still and keep your mouth shut!" he snapped, disengaging himself from her frantic clasp.

He disregarded the tortuous stair. He dropped from ledge to ledge with reckless haste. There was no sign of the monsters as his feet hit the floor. A few of the torches still flared in their sockets, the phosphorescent glow throbbed and quivered, and the river flowed with an almost articulate muttering, scintillant with undreamed radiances. The glow that had heralded the appearance of the servants had vanished with them. Only the light of the jewels in the brass chest shimmered and quivered.

He snatched the chest, noting its contents in one lustful glance — strange, curiously shapen stones that burned with an icy, non-terrestrial fire. He slammed the lid, thrust the chest under his arm, and ran back up the steps. He had no desire to encounter the hellish servants of Bît-Yakin. His glimpse of them in action had dispelled any illusion concerning their fighting ability. Why they had waited so long before striking at the invaders he was unable to say. What human could guess the motives or thoughts of these monstrosities? That they were possessed of craft and intelligence equal to humanity had been demonstrated. And there on the cavern floor lay crimson proof of their bestial ferocity.

The Corinthian girl still cowered on the gallery where he had left her. He caught her wrist and yanked her to her feet, grunting: "I guess it's time to go!"

Too bemused with terror to be fully aware of what was going on, the girl suffered herself to be led across the dizzy span. It was not until they were poised over the rushing water that she looked down, voiced a startled yelp and would have fallen but for Conan's massive arm about her. Growling an objurgation in her ear, he snatched her up under his free arm and swept her, in a flutter of limply waving arms and legs, across the arch and into the aperture that opened at the other end. Without bothering to set her on her feet, he hurried through the short tunnel into which this aperture opened. An instant later they emerged upon a narrow ledge on the outer side of the cliffs that circled the valley. Less than a hundred feet below them the jungle waved in the starlight.

Looking down, Conan vented a gusty sigh of relief. He believed that he could negotiate the descent, even though burdened with the jewels and the girl; although he doubted if even he, unburdened, could have ascended at that spot. He set the chest, still smeared with Gorulga's blood and clotted with his brains, on the ledge, and was about to remove his girdle in order to tie the box to his back, when he was galvanized by a sound behind him, a sound sinister and unmistakable.

"Stay here!" he snapped at the bewildered Corinthian girl. "Don't move!" And drawing his sword, he glided into the tunnel, glaring back into the cavern.

Halfway across the upper span he saw a gray deformed shape. One of the servants of Bît-Yakin was on his trail. There was no doubt that the brute had seen them and was following them. Conan did not hesitate. It might be easier to defend the mouth of the tunnel — but this fight must be finished quickly, before the other servants could return.

He ran out on the span, straight toward the oncoming monster. It was no ape, neither was it a man. It was some shambling horror spawned in the mysterious, nameless jungles of the south, where strange life teemed in the reeking rot without the dominance of man, and drums thundered in temples that had never known the tread of a human foot. How the ancient Pelishtim had gained lordship over them — and with it eternal exile from humanity — was a foul riddle about which Conan did not care to speculate, even if he had had opportunity.

Man and monster; they met at the highest arch of the span, where, a hundred feet below, rushed the furious black water. As the monstrous shape with its leprous gray body and the features of a carven, unhuman idol loomed over him, Conan struck as a wounded tiger strikes, with every ounce of thew and fury behind the blow. That stroke would have sheared a human body asunder; but the bones of the servant of Bît-Yakin were like tempered steel. Yet even tempered steel could not wholly have withstood that furious stroke. Ribs and shoulder-bone parted and blood spouted from the great gash.

There was no time for a second stroke. Before the Cimmerian could lift his blade again or spring clear, the sweep of a giant arm knocked him from the span as a fly is flicked from a wall. As he plunged downward the rush of the river was like a knell in his ears, but his twisting body fell halfway across the lower arch. He wavered there precariously for one blood-chilling instant, then his clutching fingers hooked over the farther edge, and he scrambled to safety, his sword still in his other hand.

As he sprang up, he saw the monster, spurting blood hideously, rush toward the cliff-end of the bridge, obviously intending to descend the stair that connected the arches and renew the feud. At the very ledge the brute paused in mid-flight — and Conan saw it too — Muriela, with the jewel chest under her arm, stood staring wildly in the mouth of the tunnel.

With a triumphant bellow the monster scooped her up under one arm, snatched the jewel chest with the other hand as she dropped it, and turning, lumbered back across the bridge. Conan cursed with passion and ran for the other side also. He doubted if he could climb the stair to the higher arch in time to catch the brute before it could plunge into the labyrinths of tunnels on the other side.

But the monster was slowing, like clockwork running down. Blood gushed from that terrible gash in his breast, and he lurched drunkenly from side to side. Suddenly he stumbled, reeled and toppled sidewise — pitched headlong from the arch and hurtled downward. Girl and jewel chest fell from his nerveless hands and Muriela's scream rang terribly above the snarl of the water below.

Conan was almost under the spot from which the creature had fallen. The monster struck the lower arch glancingly and shot off, but the writhing figure of the girl struck and clung, and the chest hit the edge of the span near her. One falling object struck on one side of Conan and one on the other. Either was within arm's length; for the fraction of a split second the chest teetered on the edge of the bridge, and Muriela clung by one arm, her face turned desperately toward Conan, her eyes dilated with the fear of death and her lips parted in a haunting cry of despair.

Conan did not hesitate, nor did he even glance toward the chest that held the wealth of an epoch. With a quickness that would have shamed the spring of a hungry jaguar, he swooped, grasped the girl's arm just as her fingers slipped from the smooth stone, and snatched her up on the span with one explosive heave. The chest toppled on over and struck the water ninety feet below, where the body of servant of Bît-Yakin had already vanished. A splash, a jetting flash of foam marked where the Teeth of Gwahlur disappeared forever from the sight of man.

Conan scarcely wasted a downward glance. He darted across the span and ran up the cliff stair like a cat, carrying the limp girl as if she had been an infant. A hideous ululation caused him to glance over his shoulder as he reached the higher arch, to see the other servants streaming back into the cavern below, blood dripping from their bared fangs. They raced up the stair that wound up from tier to tier, roaring vengefully; but he slung the girl unceremoniously over his shoulder, dashed through the tunnel and went down the cliffs like an ape himself, dropping and springing from hold to hold with breakneck recklessness. When the fierce countenances looked over the ledge of the aperture, it was to see the Cimmerian and the girl disappearing into the forest that surrounded the cliffs.

"Well," said Conan, setting the girl on her feet within the sheltering screen of branches, "we can take our time now. I don't think those brutes will follow us outside the valley. Anyway, I've got a horse tied at a water hole close by, if the lions haven't eaten him. Crom's devils! What are you crying about *now*?"

She covered her tear-stained face with her hands, and her slim shoulders shook with sobs.

"I lost the jewels for you," she wailed miserably. "It was my fault. If I'd obeyed you and stayed out on the ledge, that brute would never have seen me. You should have caught the gems and let me drown!"

"Yes, I suppose I should," he agreed. "But forget it. Never worry about what's past. And stop crying, will you? That's better. Come on."

"You mean you're going to keep me? Take me with you?" she asked hopefully.

"What else do you suppose I'd do with you?" He ran an approving glance over her figure and grinned at the torn skirt which revealed a generous expanse of tempting ivory-tinted curves. "I can use an actress like you. There's no use going back to Keshia. There's nothing in Keshan now that I want. We'll go to Punt. The people of Punt worship an ivory woman, and they wash gold out of the rivers in wicker baskets. I'll tell them that Keshan is intriguing with Thutmekri to enslave them — which is true — and that the gods have sent me to protect them — for about a houseful of gold. If I can manage to smuggle you into their temple to exchange places with their ivory goddess, we'll skin them out of their jaw teeth before we get through with them!"

BEYOND THE BLACK RIVER

Weird Tales: Part 1, May 1935; Part 2, June 1935

1. Conan Loses His Ax

The stillness of the forest trail was so primeval that the tread of a soft-booted foot was a startling disturbance. At least it seemed so to the ears of the wayfarer, though he was moving along the path with the caution that must be practiced by any man who ventures beyond Thunder River. He was a young man of medium height, with an open countenance and a mop of tousled tawny hair unconfined by cap or helmet. His garb was common enough for that country — a coarse tunic, belted at the waist, short leather breeches beneath, and soft buckskin boots that came short of the knee. A knife hilt jutted from one boot-top. The broad leather belt supported a short, heavy sword and a buckskin pouch. There was no perturbation in the wide eyes that scanned the green walls which fringed the trail. Though not tall, he was well built, and the arms that the short wide sleeves of the tunic left bare were thick with corded muscle.

He tramped imperturbably along, although the last settler's cabin lay miles behind him, and each step was carrying him nearer the grim peril that hung like a brooding shadow over the ancient forest.

He was not making as much noise as it seemed to him, though he well knew that the faint tread of his booted feet would be like a tocsin of alarm to the fierce ears that might be lurking in the treacherous green fastness. His careless attitude was not genuine; his eyes and ears were keenly alert, especially his ears, for no gaze could penetrate the leafy tangle for more than a few feet in either direction.

But it was instinct more than any warning by the external senses which brought him up suddenly, his hand on his hilt. He stood stock-still in the middle of the trail, unconsciously holding his breath, wondering what he had heard, and wondering if indeed he had heard anything. The silence seemed absolute. Not a squirrel chattered or bird chirped. Then his gaze fixed itself on a mass of bushes beside the trail a few yards ahead of him. There was no breeze, yet he had seen a branch quiver. The short hairs on his scalp prickled, and he stood for an instant undecided, certain that a move in either direction would bring death streaking at him from the bushes.

A heavy chopping crunch sounded behind the leaves. The bushes were shaken violently, and simultaneously with the sound, an arrow arched erratically from among them and vanished among the trees along the trail. The wayfarer glimpsed its flight as he sprang frantically to cover.

Crouching behind a thick stem, his sword quivering in his fingers, he saw the bushes part, and a tall figure stepped leisurely into the trail. The traveler stared in surprize. The stranger was clad like himself in regard to boots and breeks, though the latter were of silk instead of leather. But he wore a sleeveless hauberk of dark mesh-mail in place of a tunic, and a helmet perched on his black mane. That helmet held the other's gaze; it was without a crest, but adorned by short bull's horns. No civilized hand ever forged that headpiece. Nor was the face below it that of a civilized man: dark, scarred, with smoldering blue eyes, it was a face as untamed as the primordial forest which formed its background. The man held a broadsword in his right hand, and the edge was smeared with crimson.

"Come on out," he called, in an accent unfamiliar to the wayfarer. "All's safe now. There was only one of the dogs. Come on out."

The other emerged dubiously and stared at the stranger. He felt curiously helpless and futile as he gazed on the proportions of the forest man — the massive iron-clad breast and the arm that bore the reddened sword, burned dark by the sun and ridged and corded with muscles. He moved with the dangerous ease of a panther; he was too fiercely supple to be a product of civilization, even of that fringe of civilization which composed the outer frontiers.

Turning, he stepped back to the bushes and pulled them apart. Still not certain just what had happened, the wayfarer from the east advanced and stared down into the bushes. A man lay there, a short, dark, thickly-muscled man, naked except for a loincloth, and one hand still gripped a heavy black bow. The man had long black hair; that was about all the wayfarer could tell about his head, for his features were a mask of blood and brains. His skull had been split to the teeth.

"A Pict, by the gods!" exclaimed the wayfarer.

The burning blue eyes turned upon him.

"Are you surprized?"

"Why, they told me at Velitrium, and again at the settlers' cabins along the road, that these devils sometimes sneaked across the border, but I didn't expect to meet one this far in the interior."

"You're only four miles east of Black River," the stranger informed him. "They've been shot within a mile of Velitrium. No settler between Thunder River and Fort Tuscelan is really safe. I picked up this dog's trail three miles south of the fort this morning, and I've been following him ever since. I came up behind him just as he was drawing an arrow on you. Another instant and there'd have been a stranger in Hell. But I spoiled his aim for him."

The wayfarer was staring wide-eyed at the larger man, dumbfounded by the realization that the man had actually tracked down one of the forest-devils and slain him unsuspected. That implied woodsmanship of a quality undreamed, even for Conajohara.

"You are one of the fort's garrison?" he asked.

"I'm no soldier. I draw the pay and rations of an officer of the line, but I do my work in the woods. Valannus knows I'm of more use ranging along the river than cooped up in the fort."

Casually the slayer shoved the body deeper into the thickets with his foot, pulled the bushes together and turned away down the trail. The other followed him.

"My name is Balthus," he offered. "I was at Velitrium last night. I haven't decided whether I'll take up a hide of land, or enter fort-service."

"The best land near Thunder River is already taken," grunted the slayer. "Plenty of good land between Scalp Creek — you crossed it a few miles back — and the fort, but that's getting too devilish close to the river. The Picts steal over to burn and murder — as that one did. They don't always come singly. Some day they'll try to sweep the settlers out of Conajohara. And they may succeed — probably will succeed. This colonization business is mad, anyway. There's plenty of good land east of the Bossonian marches. If the Aquilonians would cut up some of the big estates of their barons, and plant wheat where now only deer are hunted, they wouldn't have to cross the border and take the land of the Picts away from them."

"That's queer talk from a man in the service of the Governor of Conajohara," objected Balthus.

"It's nothing to me," the other retorted. "I'm a mercenary. I sell my sword to the highest bidder. I never planted wheat and never will, so long as there are other harvests to be reaped with the sword. But you Hyborians have expanded as far as you'll be allowed to expand. You've crossed the marches, burned a few villages, exterminated a few clans and pushed back the frontier to Black River; but I doubt if you'll even be able to hold what you've conquered, and you'll never push the frontier any further westward. Your idiotic king doesn't understand conditions here. He won't send you enough reinforcements, and there are not enough settlers to withstand the shock of a concerted attack from across the river."

"But the Picts are divided into small clans," persisted Balthus. "They'll never unite. We can whip any single clan."

"Or any three or four clans," admitted the slayer. "But some day a man will rise and unite thirty or forty clans, just as was done among the Cimmerians, when the Gundermen tried to push the border northward, years ago. They tried to colonize the southern marches of Cimmeria: destroyed a few small clans, built a fort town, Venarium — you've heard the tale."

"So I have indeed," replied Balthus, wincing. The memory of that red disaster was a black blot in the chronicles of a proud and warlike people. "My uncle was at Venarium when the Cimmerians swarmed over the walls. He was one of the few who escaped that slaughter. I've heard him tell the tale, many a time. The barbarians swept out of the hills in a ravening horde, without warning, and stormed Venarium with such fury none could stand before them. Men, women and children were butchered. Venarium was reduced to a mass of charred ruins, as it is to this day. The Aquilonians were driven back across the marches, and have never since tried to colonize the Cimmerian country. But you speak of Venarium familiarly. Perhaps you were there?"

"I was," grunted the other. "I was one of the horde that swarmed over the walls. I hadn't yet seen fifteen snows, but already my name was repeated about the council fires."

Balthus involuntarily recoiled, staring. It seemed incredible that the man walking tranquilly at his side should have been one of those screeching, blood-mad devils that had poured over the walls of Venarium on that long-gone day to make her streets run crimson.

"Then you, too, are a barbarian!" he exclaimed involuntarily.

The other nodded, without taking offense.

"I am Conan, a Cimmerian."

"I've heard of you." Fresh interest quickened Balthus' gaze. No wonder the Pict had fallen victim to his own sort of subtlety. The Cimmerians were barbarians as ferocious as the Picts, and much more intelligent. Evidently Conan had spent much time among civilized men, though that contact had obviously not softened him, nor weakened any of his primitive instincts. Balthus' apprehension turned to admiration as he marked the easy catlike stride, the effortless silence with which the Cimmerian moved along the trail. The oiled links of his armor did not clink, and Balthus knew Conan could glide through the deepest thicket or most tangled copse as noiselessly as any naked Pict that ever lived.

"You're not a Gunderman?" It was more assertion than question.

Balthus shook his head. "I'm from the Tauran."

"I've seen good woodsmen from the Tauran. But the Bossonians have sheltered you Aquilonians from the outer wilderness for too many centuries. You need hardening."

That was true; the Bossonian marches, with their fortified villages filled with determined bowmen, had long served Aquilonia as a buffer against the outlying barbarians. Now among the settlers beyond Thunder River there was growing up a breed of forest-men capable of meeting the barbarians at their own game, but their numbers were still scanty. Most of the frontiersmen were like Balthus — more of the settler than the woodsman type.

The sun had not set, but it was no longer in sight, hidden as it was behind the dense forest wall. The shadows were lengthening, deepening back in the woods as the companions strode on down the trail.

"It will be dark before we reach the fort," commented Conan casually; then: "Listen!"

He stopped short, half-crouching, sword ready, transformed into a savage figure of suspicion and menace, poised to spring and rend. Balthus had heard it too — a wild scream that broke at its highest note. It was the cry of a man in dire fear or agony.

Conan was off in an instant, racing down the trail, each stride widening the distance between him and his straining companion. Balthus puffed a curse. Among the settlements of the Tauran he was accounted a good runner, but Conan was leaving him behind with maddening ease. Then Balthus forgot his exasperation as his ears were outraged by the most frightful cry he had ever heard. It was not human, this one; it was a demoniacal caterwauling of hideous triumph that seemed to exult over fallen humanity and find echo in black gulfs beyond human ken.

Balthus faltered in his stride, and clammy sweat beaded his flesh. But Conan did not hesitate; he darted around a bend in the trail and disappeared, and Balthus, panicky at finding himself alone with that awful scream still shuddering through the forest in grisly echoes, put on an extra burst of speed and plunged after him.

The Aquilonian slid to a stumbling halt, almost colliding with the Cimmerian who stood in the trail over a crumpled body. But Conan was not looking at the corpse which lay there in the crimson-soaked dust. He was glaring into the deep woods on either side of the trail.

Balthus muttered a horrified oath. It was the body of a man which lay there in the trail, a short, fat man, clad in the gilt-worked boots and (despite the heat) the ermine-trimmed tunic of a wealthy merchant. His fat, pale face was set in a stare of frozen horror; his thick throat had been slashed from ear to ear as if by a razor-sharp blade. The short sword still in its scabbard seemed to indicate that he had been struck down without a chance to fight for his life.

"A Pict?" Balthus whispered, as he turned to peer into the deepening shadows of the forest.

Conan shook his head and straightened to scowl down at the dead man.

"A forest devil. This is the fifth, by Crom!"

"What do you mean?"

"Did you ever hear of a Pictish wizard called Zogar Sag?"

Balthus shook his head uneasily.

"He dwells in Gwawela, the nearest village across the river. Three months ago he hid beside this road and stole a string of pack-mules from a pack-train bound for the fort — drugged their drivers, somehow. The mules belonged to this man" — Conan casually indicated the corpse with his foot — "Tiberias, a merchant of Velitrium. They were loaded with ale-kegs, and old Zogar stopped to guzzle before he got across the river. A woodsman named Soractus trailed him, and led Valannus and three soldiers to where he lay dead drunk in a thicket. At the importunities of Tiberias, Valannus threw Zogar Sag into a cell, which is the worst insult you can give a Pict. He managed to kill his guard and escape, and sent back word that he meant to kill Tiberias and the five men who captured him in a way that would make Aquilonians shudder for centuries to come.

"Well, Soractus and the soldiers are dead. Soractus was killed on the river, the soldiers in the very shadow of the fort. And now Tiberias is dead. No Pict killed any of them. Each victim — except Tiberias, as you see — lacked his head — which no doubt is now ornamenting the altar of Zogar Sag's particular god."

"How do you know they weren't killed by the Picts?' demanded Balthus.

Conan pointed to the corpse of the merchant.

"You think that was done with a knife or a sword? Look closer and you'll see that only a talon could have made a gash like that. The flesh is ripped, not cut."

"Perhaps a panther —" began Balthus, without conviction.

Conan shook his head impatiently.

"A man from the Tauran couldn't mistake the mark of a panther's claws. No. It's a forest devil summoned by Zogar Sag to carry out his revenge. Tiberias was a fool to start for Velitrium alone, and so close to dusk. But each one of the victims seemed to be smitten with madness just before doom overtook him. Look here; the signs are plain enough. Tiberias came riding along the trail on his mule, maybe with a bundle of choice otter pelts behind his saddle to sell in Velitrium, and the *thing* sprang on him from behind that bush. See where the branches are crushed down.

"Tiberias gave one scream, and then his throat was torn open and he was selling his otter skins in Hell. The mule ran away into the woods. Listen! Even now you can hear him thrashing about under the trees. The demon didn't have time to take Tiberias' head; it took fright as we came up."

"As *you* came up," amended Balthus. "It must not be a very terrible creature if it flees from one armed man. But how do you know it was not a Pict with some kind of a hook that rips instead of slicing? Did you see it?"

"Tiberias was an armed man," grunted Conan. "If Zogar Sag can bring demons to aid him, he can tell them which men to kill and which to let alone. No, I didn't see it. I only saw the bushes shake as it left the trail. But if you want further proof, look here!"

The slayer had stepped into the pool of blood in which the dead man sprawled. Under the bushes at the edge of the path there was a footprint, made in blood on the hard loam.

"Did a man make that?" demanded Conan.

Balthus felt his scalp prickle. Neither man nor any beast that he had ever seen could have left that strange, monstrous three-toed print, that was curiously combined of the bird and the reptile, yet a true type of neither. He spread his fingers above the print, careful not to touch it, and grunted explosively. He could not span the mark.

"What is it?" he whispered. "I never saw a beast that left a spoor like that."

"Nor any other sane man," answered Conan grimly. "It's a swamp demon — they're thick as bats in the swamps beyond Black River. You can hear them howling like damned souls when the wind blows strong from the south on hot nights."

"What shall we do?" asked the Aquilonian, peering uneasily into the deep blue shadows. The frozen fear on the dead countenance haunted him. He wondered what hideous head the wretch had seen thrust grinning from among the leaves to chill his blood with terror.

"No use to try to follow a demon," grunted Conan, drawing a short woodsman's ax from his girdle. "I tried tracking him after he killed Soractus. I lost his trail within a dozen steps. He might have grown himself wings and flown away, or sunk down through the earth to Hell. I don't know. I'm not going after the mule, either. It'll either wander back to the fort, or to some settler's cabin."

As he spoke, Conan was busy at the edge of the trail with his ax. With a few strokes he cut a pair of saplings nine or ten feet long, and denuded them of their branches. Then he cut a length from a serpent-like vine that crawled among the bushes nearby, and making one end fast to one of the poles, a couple of feet from the end, whipped the vine over the other sapling and interlaced it back and forth. In a few moments he had a crude but strong litter.

"The demon isn't going to get Tiberias' head if I can help it," he growled. "We'll carry the body into the fort. It isn't more than three miles. I never liked the fat fool, but we can't have Pictish devils making so cursed free with white men's heads."

The Picts were a white race, though swarthy, but the border men never spoke of them as such.

Balthus took the rear end of the litter, onto which Conan unceremoniously dumped the unfortunate merchant, and they moved on down the trail as swiftly as possible. Conan made no more noise laden with their grim burden than he had made when unencumbered. He had made a loop with the merchant's belt at the end of the poles, and was carrying his share of the load with one hand, while the other gripped his naked broadsword, and his restless gaze roved the sinister walls about them. The shadows were thickening. A darkening blue mist blurred the outlines of the foliage. The forest deepened in the twilight, became a blue haunt of mystery sheltering unguessed things.

They had covered more than a mile, and the muscles in Balthus' sturdy arms were beginning to ache a little, when a cry rang shuddering from the woods whose blue shadows were deepening into purple.

Conan started convulsively, and Balthus almost let go the poles.

"A woman!" cried the younger man. "Great Mitra, a woman cried out then!"

"A settler's wife straying in the woods," snarled Conan, setting down his end of the litter. "Looking for a cow, probably, and — stay here!"

He dived like a hunting wolf into the leafy wall. Balthus' hair bristled.

"Stay here alone with this corpse and a devil hiding in the woods?" he yelped. "I'm coming with you!"

And suiting action to words, he plunged after the Cimmerian. Conan glanced back at him, but made no objection, though he did not moderate his pace to accommodate the shorter legs of his companion. Balthus wasted his wind in swearing as the Cimmerian drew away from him again, like a phantom between the trees, and then Conan burst into a dim glade and halted crouching, lips snarling, sword lifted.

"What are we stopping for?" panted Balthus, dashing the sweat out of his eyes and gripping his short sword.

"That scream came from this glade, or nearby," answered Conan. "I don't mistake the location of sounds, even in the woods. But where —"

Abruptly the sound rang out again — *behind them*; in the direction of the trail they had just quitted. It rose piercingly and pitifully, the cry of a woman in frantic terror — and then, shockingly, it changed to a yell of mocking laughter that might have burst from the lips of a fiend of lower Hell.

"What in Mitra's name —" Balthus' face was a pale blur in the gloom.

With a scorching oath Conan wheeled and dashed back the way he had come, and the Aquilonian stumbled bewilderedly after him. He blundered into the Cimmerian as the latter stopped dead, and rebounded from his brawny shoulders as though from an iron statue. Gasping from the impact, he heard Conan's breath hiss through his teeth. The Cimmerian seemed frozen in his tracks.

Looking over his shoulder, Balthus felt his hair stand up stiffly. Something was moving through the deep bushes that fringed the trail — something that neither walked nor flew, but seemed to glide like a serpent. But it was not a serpent. Its outlines were indistinct, but it was taller than a man, and not very bulky. It gave off a glimmer of weird light, like a faint blue flame. Indeed, the eery fire was the only tangible thing about it. It might have been an embodied flame moving with reason and purpose through the blackening woods.

Conan snarled a savage curse and hurled his ax with ferocious will. But the thing glided on without altering its course. Indeed, it was only a few instants' fleeting glimpse they had of it — a tall, shadowy thing of misty flame floating through the thickets. Then it was gone, and the forest crouched in breathless stillness.

With a snarl Conan plunged through the intervening foliage and into the trail. His profanity, as Balthus floundered after him, was lurid and impassioned. The Cimmerian was standing over the litter on which lay the body of Tiberias. And that body no longer possessed a head.

"Tricked us with its damnable caterwauling!" raved Conan, swinging his great sword about his head in his wrath. "I might have known! I might have guessed a trick! Now there'll be five heads to decorate Zogar's altar."

"But what thing is it that can cry like a woman and laugh like a devil, and shines like witch-fire as it glides through the trees?" gasped Balthus, mopping the sweat from his pale face.

"A swamp devil," responded Conan morosely. "Grab those poles. We'll take in the body, anyway. At least our load's a bit lighter."

With which grim philosophy he gripped the leathery loop and stalked down the trail.

2. The Wizard of Gwawela

Fort Tuscelan stood on the eastern bank of Black River, the tides of which washed the foot of the stockade. The latter was of logs, as were all the buildings within, including the donjon (to dignify it by that appellation), in which were the governor's quarters, overlooking the stockade and the sullen river. Beyond that river lay a huge forest, which approached jungle-like density along the spongy shores. Men paced the runways along the log parapet day and night, watching that dense green wall. Seldom a menacing figure appeared, but the sentries knew that they too were watched, fiercely, hungrily, with the mercilessness of ancient hate. The forest beyond the river might seem desolate and vacant of life to the ignorant eye, but life teemed there, not alone of bird and beast and reptile, but also of men, the fiercest of all the hunting beasts.

There, at the fort, civilization ended. Fort Tuscelan was the last outpost of a civilized world; it represented the westernmost thrust of the dominant Hyborian races. Beyond the river the primitive still reigned in shadowy forests, brush-thatched huts where hung the grinning skulls of men, and mud-walled enclosures where fires flickered and drums rumbled, and spears were whetted in the hands of dark, silent men with tangled black hair and the eyes of serpents. Those eyes often glared through the bushes at the fort across the river. Once dark-skinned men had built their huts where that fort stood; yes, and their huts had risen where now stood the fields and log cabins of fair-haired settlers, back beyond Velitrium, that raw, turbulent frontier town on the banks of Thunder River, to the shores of that other river that bounds the Bossonian marches. Traders had come, and priests of Mitra who walked with bare feet and empty hands, and died horribly, most of them; but soldiers had followed, and men with axes in their hands and women and children in ox-drawn wains. Back to Thunder River, and still back, beyond Black River, the aborigines had been pushed, with slaughter and massacre. But the dark-skinned people did not forget that once Conajohara had been theirs.

The guard inside the eastern gate bawled a challenge. Through a barred aperture torchlight flickered, glinting on a steel headpiece and suspicious eyes beneath it.

"Open the gate," snorted Conan. "You see it's I, don't you?"

Military discipline put his teeth on edge.

The gate swung inward and Conan and his companion passed through. Balthus noted that the gate was ranked by a tower on each side, the summits of which rose above the stockade. He saw loopholes for arrows.

The guardsmen grunted as they saw the burden borne between the men. Their pikes jangled against each other as they thrust shut the gate, chin on shoulder, and Conan asked testily: "Have you never seen a headless body before?"

The faces of the soldiers were pallid in the torchlight.

"That's Tiberias," blurted one. "I recognize that fur-trimmed tunic. Valerius here owes me five lunas. I told him Tiberias had heard the loon call when he rode through the gate on his mule, with his glassy stare. I wagered he'd come back without his head."

Conan grunted enigmatically, motioned Balthus to ease the litter to the ground, and then strode off toward the governor's quarters, with the Aquilonian at his heels. The tousle-headed youth stared about him eagerly and curiously, noting the rows of barracks along the walls, the stables, the tiny merchants' stalls, the towering blockhouse, and the other buildings, with the open square in the middle where the soldiers drilled, and where, now, fires danced and men off duty lounged. These were now hurrying to join the morbid crowd gathered about the litter at the gate. The rangy figures of Aquilonian pikemen and forest runners mingled with the shorter, stockier forms of Bossonian archers.

He was not greatly surprized that the governor received them himself. Autocratic society with its rigid caste laws lay east of the marches. Valannus was still a young man, well knit, with a finely chiseled countenance already carved into sober cast by toil and responsibility.

"You left the fort before daybreak, I was told," he said to Conan. "I had begun to fear that the Picts had caught you at last."

"When they smoke my head the whole river will know it," grunted Conan. "They'll hear Pictish women wailing their dead as far as Velitrium — I was on a lone scout. I couldn't sleep. I kept hearing drums talking across the river."

"They talk each night," reminded the governor, his fine eyes shadowed, as he stared closely at Conan.

He had learned the unwisdom of discounting wild men's instincts.

"There was a difference last night," growled Conan. "There has been ever since Zogar Sag got back across the river."

"We should either have given him presents and sent him home, or else hanged him," sighed the governor. "You advised that, but —"

"But it's hard for you Hyborians to learn the ways of the outlands," said Conan. "Well, it can't be helped now, but there'll be no peace on the border so long as Zogar lives and remembers the cell he sweated in. I was following a warrior who slipped over to put a few white notches on his bow. After I split his head I fell in with this lad whose name is Balthus and who's come from the Tauran to help hold the frontier."

Valannus approvingly eyed the young man's frank countenance and strongly-knit frame.

"I'm glad to welcome you, young sir. I wish more of your people would come. We need men used to forest life. Many of our soldiers and some of our settlers are from the eastern provinces and know nothing of woodcraft, or even of agricultural life."

"Not many of that breed this side of Velitrium," grunted Conan. "That town's full of them, though. But listen, Valannus, we found Tiberias dead on the trail." And in a few words he related the grisly affair.

Valannus paled. "I did not know he had left the fort. He must have been mad!"

"He was," answered Conan. "Like the other four; each one, when his time came, went mad and rushed into the woods to meet his death like a hare running down the throat of a python. *Something* called to them from the deeps of the forest, something the men call a loon, for lack of a better name, but only the doomed ones could hear it. Zogar Sag has made a magic that Aquilonian civilization can't overcome."

To this thrust Valannus made no reply; he wiped his brow with a shaky hand.

"Do the soldiers know of this?"

"We left the body by the eastern gate."

"You should have concealed the fact, hidden the corpse somewhere in the woods. The soldiers are nervous enough already."

"They'd have found it out some way. If I'd hidden the body, it would have been returned to the fort as the corpse of Soractus was — tied up outside the gate for the men to find in the morning."

Valannus shuddered. Turning, he walked to a casement and stared silently out over the river, black and shiny under the glint of the stars. Beyond the river the jungle rose like an ebony wall. The distant screech of a panther broke the stillness. The night pressed in, blurring the sounds of the soldiers outside the blockhouse, dimming the fires. A wind whispered through the black branches, rippling the dusky water. On its wings came a low, rhythmic pulsing, sinister as the pad of a leopard's foot.

"After all," said Valannus, as if speaking his thoughts aloud, "what do we know — what does anyone know — of the things that jungle may hide? We have dim rumors of great swamps and rivers, and a forest that stretches on and on over everlasting plains and hills to end at last on the shores of the western ocean. But what things lie between this river and that ocean we dare not even guess. No white man has ever plunged deep into that fastness and returned alive to tell us what he found. We are wise in our civilized knowledge, but our knowledge extends just so far — to the western bank of that ancient river. Who knows what shapes earthly and unearthly may lurk beyond the dim circle of light our knowledge has cast?

"Who knows what gods are worshipped under the shadows of that heathen forest, or what devils crawl out of the black ooze of the swamps? Who can be sure that all the inhabitants of that black country are natural? Zogar Sag — a sage of the eastern cities would sneer at his primitive magic-making as the mummery of a fakir; yet he has driven mad and killed five men in a manner no man can explain. I wonder if he himself is wholly human."

"If I can get within ax-throwing distance of him I'll settle that question," growled Conan, helping himself to the governor's wine and pushing a glass toward Balthus, who took it hesitatingly, and with an uncertain glance toward Valannus.

The governor turned toward Conan and stared at him thoughtfully.

"The soldiers, who do not believe in ghosts or devils," he said, "are almost in a panic of fear. You, who believe in ghosts, ghouls, goblins, and all manner of uncanny things, do not seem to fear any of the things in which you believe."

"There's nothing in the universe cold steel won't cut," answered Conan. "I threw my ax at the demon, and he took no hurt, but I might have missed, in the dusk, or a branch deflected its flight. I'm not going out of my way looking for devils; but I wouldn't step out of my path to let one go by."

Valannus lifted his head and met Conan's gaze squarely.

"Conan, more depends on you than you realize. You know the weakness of this province — a slender wedge thrust into the untamed wilderness. You know that the lives of all the people west of the marches depend on this fort. Were it to fall, red axes would be splintering the gates of Velitrium before a horseman could cross the marches. His majesty, or his majesty's advisers, have ignored my plea that more troops be sent to hold the frontier. They know nothing of border conditions, and are averse to expending any more money in this direction. The fate of the frontier depends upon the men who now hold it.

"You know that most of the army which conquered Conajohara has been withdrawn. You know the force left me is inadequate, especially since that devil Zogar Sag managed to poison our water supply, and forty men died in one day. Many of the others are sick, or have been bitten by serpents or mauled by wild beasts which seem to swarm in increasing numbers in the vicinity of the fort. The soldiers believe Zogar's boast that he could summon the forest beasts to slay his enemies.

"I have three hundred pikemen, four hundred Bossonian archers, and perhaps fifty men who, like yourself, are skilled in woodcraft. They are worth ten times their number of soldiers, but there are so few of them. Frankly, Conan, my situation is becoming precarious. The soldiers whisper of desertion; they are low-spirited, believing Zogar Sag has loosed devils on us. They fear the black plague with which he threatened us — the terrible black death of the swamplands. When I see a sick soldier I sweat with fear of seeing him turn black and shrivel and die before my eyes.

"Conan, if the plague is loosed upon us, the soldiers will desert in a body! The border will be left unguarded and nothing will check the sweep of the dark-skinned hordes to the very gates of Velitrium — maybe beyond! If we can not hold the fort, how can they hold the town?

"Conan, Zogar Sag must die, if we are to hold Conajohara. You have penetrated the unknown deeper than any other man in the fort; you know where Gwawela stands, and something of the forest trails across the river. Will you take a band of men tonight and endeavor to kill or capture him? Oh, I know it's mad. There isn't more than one chance in a thousand that any of you will come back alive. But if we don't get him, it's death for us all. You can take as many men as you wish."

"A dozen men are better for a job like that than a regiment," answered Conan. "Five hundred men couldn't fight their way to Gwawela and back, but a dozen might slip in and out again. Let me pick my men. I don't want any soldiers."

"Let me go!" eagerly exclaimed Balthus. "I've hunted deer all my life on the Tauran."

"All right. Valannus, we'll eat at the stall where the foresters gather, and I'll pick my men. We'll start within an hour, drop down the river in a boat to a point below the village and then steal upon it through the woods. If we live, we should be back by daybreak."

3. The Crawlers in the Dark

The river was a vague trace between walls of ebony. The paddles that propelled the long boat creeping along in the dense shadow of the eastern bank dipped softly into the water, making no more noise than the beak of a heron. The broad shoulders of the man in front of Balthus were a blur in the dense gloom. He knew that not even the keen eyes of the man who knelt in the prow would discern anything more than a few feet ahead of them. Conan was feeling his way by instinct and an intensive familiarity with the river.

No one spoke. Balthus had had a good look at his companions in the fort before they slipped out of the stockade and down the bank into the waiting canoe. They were of a new breed growing up in the world on the raw edge of the frontier — men whom grim necessity had taught woodcraft. Aquilonians of the western provinces to a man, they had many points in common. They dressed alike — in buckskin boots, leathern breeks and deerskin shirts, with broad girdles that held axes and short swords; and they were all gaunt and scarred and hard-eyed; sinewy and taciturn.

They were wild men, of a sort, yet there was still a wide gulf between them and the Cimmerian. They were sons of civilization, reverted to a semi-barbarism. He was a barbarian of a thousand generations of barbarians. They had acquired stealth and craft, but he had been born to these things. He excelled them even in lithe economy of motion. They were wolves, but he was a tiger.

Balthus admired them and their leader and felt a pulse of pride that he was admitted into their company. He was proud that his paddle made no more noise than did theirs. In that respect at least he was their equal, though woodcraft learned in hunts on the Tauran could never equal that ground into the souls of men on the savage border.

Below the fort the river made a wide bend. The lights of the outpost were quickly lost, but the canoe held on its way for nearly a mile, avoiding snags and floating logs with almost uncanny precision.

Then a low grunt from their leader, and they swung its head about and glided toward the opposite shore. Emerging from the black shadows of the brush that fringed the bank and coming into the open of the midstream created a peculiar illusion of rash exposure. But the stars gave little light, and Balthus knew that unless one were watching for it, it would be all but impossible for the keenest eye to make out the shadowy shape of the canoe crossing the river.

They swung in under the overhanging bushes of the western shore and Balthus groped for and found a projecting root which he grasped. No word was spoken. All instructions had been given before the scouting-party left the fort. As silently as a great panther Conan slid over the side and vanished in the bushes. Equally noiseless, nine men followed him. To Balthus, grasping the root with his paddle across his knee, it seemed incredible that ten men should thus fade into the tangled forest without a sound.

He settled himself to wait. No word passed between him and the other man who had been left with him. Somewhere, a mile or so to the northwest, Zogar Sag's village stood girdled with thick woods. Balthus understood his orders; he and his companion were to wait for the return of the raiding-party. If

Conan and his men had not returned by the first tinge of dawn, they were to race back up the river to the fort and report that the forest had again taken its immemorial toll of the invading race. The silence was oppressive. No sound came from the black woods, invisible beyond the ebony masses that were the overhanging bushes. Balthus no longer heard the drums. They had been silent for hours. He kept blinking, unconsciously trying to see through the deep gloom. The dank night-smells of the river and the damp forest oppressed him. Somewhere, nearby, there was a sound as if a big fish had flopped and splashed the water. Balthus thought it must have leaped so close to the canoe that it had struck the side, for a slight quiver vibrated the craft. The boat's stern began to swing, slightly away from the shore. The man behind him must have let go of the projection he was gripping. Balthus twisted his head to hiss a warning, and could just make out the figure of his companion, a slightly blacker bulk in the blackness.

The man did not reply. Wondering if he had fallen asleep, Balthus reached out and grasped his shoulder. To his amazement, the man crumpled under his touch and slumped down in the canoe. Twisting his body half-about, Balthus groped for him, his heart shooting into his throat. His fumbling fingers slid over the man's throat — only the youth's convulsive clenching of his jaws choked back the cry that rose to his lips. His fingers encountered a gaping, oozing wound — his companion's throat had been cut from ear to ear.

In that instant of horror and panic, Balthus started up — and then a muscular arm out of the darkness locked fiercely about his throat, strangling his yell. The canoe rocked wildly. Balthus' knife was in his hand, though he did not remember jerking it out of his boot, and he stabbed fiercely and blindly. He felt the blade sink deep, and a fiendish yell rang in his ear, a yell that was horribly answered. The darkness seemed to come to life about him. A bestial clamor rose on all sides, and other arms grappled him. Borne under a mass of hurtling bodies the canoe rolled sidewise, but before he went under with it, something cracked against Balthus' head and the night was briefly illuminated by a blinding burst of fire before it gave way to a blackness where not even stars shone.

4. The Beasts of Zogar Sag

Fires dazzled Balthus again as he slowly recovered his senses. He blinked, shook his head. Their glare hurt his eyes. A confused medley of sound rose about him, growing more distinct as his senses cleared. He lifted his head and stared stupidly about him. Black figures hemmed him in, etched against crimson tongues of flame.

Memory and understanding came in a rush. He was bound upright to a post in an open space, ringed by fierce and terrible figures. Beyond that ring fires burned, tended by naked, dark-skinned women. Beyond the fires he saw huts of mud and wattle, thatched with brush. Beyond the huts there was a stockade with a broad gate. But he saw these things only incidentally. Even the cryptic dark women with their curious coiffures were noted by him only absently. His full attention was fixed in awful fascination on the men who stood glaring at him.

Short men, broad-shouldered, deep-chested, lean-hipped, they were naked except for scanty loincloths. The firelight brought out the play of their swelling muscles in bold relief. Their dark faces were immobile, but their narrow eyes glittered with the fire that burns in the eyes of a stalking tiger. Their tangled manes were bound back with bands of copper. Swords and axes were in their hands. Crude bandages banded the limbs of some, and smears of blood were dried on their dark skins. There had been fighting, recent and deadly.

His eyes wavered away from the steady glare of his captors, and he repressed a cry of horror. A few feet away there rose a low, hideous pyramid: it was built of gory human heads. Dead eyes glared glassily up at the black sky. Numbly he recognized the countenances which were turned toward him. They were the heads of the men who had followed Conan into the forest. He could not tell if the Cimmerian's head were among them. Only a few faces were visible to him. It looked to him as if there must be ten or eleven heads at least. A deadly sickness assailed him. He fought a desire to retch. Beyond the heads lay the bodies of half a dozen Picts, and he was aware of a fierce exultation at the sight. The forest runners had taken toll, at least.

Twisting his head away from the ghastly spectacle, he became aware that another post stood near him — a stake painted black as was the one to which he was bound. A man sagged in his bonds there, naked except for his leathern breeks, whom Balthus recognized as one of Conan's woodsmen. Blood trickled from his mouth, oozed sluggishly from a gash in his side. Lifting his head as he licked his livid lips, he muttered, making himself heard with difficulty above the fiendish clamor of the Picts: "So they got you, too!"

"Sneaked up in the water and cut the other fellow's throat," groaned Balthus. "We never heard them till they were on us. Mitra, how can anything move so silently?"

"They're devils," mumbled the frontiersman. "They must have been watching us from the time we left midstream. We walked into a trap. Arrows from all sides were ripping into us before we knew it. Most of us dropped at the first fire. Three or four broke through the bushes and came to hand-grips. But there were too many. Conan might have gotten away. I haven't seen his head. Been better for you and me if they'd killed us outright. I can't blame Conan. Ordinarily we'd have gotten to the village without being discovered. They don't keep spies on the riverbank as far down as we landed. We must have stumbled into a big party coming up the river from the south. Some devilment is up. Too many Picts here. These aren't all Gwaweli; men from the western tribes here and from up and down the river."

Balthus stared at the ferocious shapes. Little as he knew of Pictish ways, he was aware that the number of men clustered about them was out of proportion to the size of the village. There were not enough huts to have accommodated them all. Then he noticed that there was a difference in the barbaric tribal designs painted on their faces and breasts.

"Some kind of devilment," muttered the forest runner. "They might have gathered here to watch Zogar's magic-making. He'll make some rare magic with our carcasses. Well, a border-man doesn't expect to die in bed. But I wish we'd gone out along with the rest."

The wolfish howling of the Picts rose in volume and exultation, and from a movement in their ranks, an eager surging and crowding, Balthus deduced that someone of importance was coming. Twisting his head about, he saw that the stakes were set before a long building, larger than the other huts, decorated by human skulls dangling from the eaves. Through the door of that structure now danced a fantastic figure.

"Zogar!" muttered the woodsman, his bloody countenance set in wolfish lines as he unconsciously strained at his cords. Balthus saw a lean figure of middle height, almost hidden in ostrich plumes set on a harness of leather and copper. From amidst the plumes peered a hideous and malevolent face. The plumes puzzled Balthus. He knew their source lay half the width of a world to the south. They fluttered and rustled evilly as the shaman leaped and cavorted.

With fantastic bounds and prancings he entered the ring and whirled before his bound and silent captives. With another man it would have seemed ridiculous — a foolish savage prancing meaninglessly in a whirl of feathers. But that ferocious face glaring out from the billowing mass gave the scene a grim significance. No man with a face like that could seem ridiculous or like anything except the devil he was.

Suddenly he froze to statuesque stillness; the plumes rippled once and sank about him. The howling warriors fell silent. Zogar Sag stood erect and motionless, and he seemed to increase in height — to grow and expand. Balthus experienced the illusion that the Pict was towering above him, staring contemptuously down from a great height, though he knew the shaman was not as tall as himself. He shook off the illusion with difficulty.

The shaman was talking now, a harsh, guttural intonation that yet carried the hiss of a cobra. He thrust his head on his long neck toward the wounded man on the stake; his eyes shone red as blood in the firelight. The frontiersman spat full in his face.

With a fiendish howl Zogar bounded convulsively into the air, and the warriors gave tongue to a yell that shuddered up to the stars. They rushed toward the man on the stake, but the shaman beat them back. A snarled command sent men running to the gate. They hurled it open, turned and raced back to the circle. The ring of men split, divided with desperate haste to right and left. Balthus saw the women and naked children scurrying to the huts. They peeked out of doors and windows. A broad lane was left to the open gate, beyond which loomed the black forest, crowding sullenly in upon the clearing, unlighted by the fires.

A tense silence reigned as Zogar Sag turned toward the forest, raised on his tiptoes and sent a weird inhuman call shuddering out into the night. Somewhere, far out in the black forest, a deeper cry answered him. Balthus shuddered. From the timbre of that cry he knew it never came from a human throat. He remembered what Valannus had said — that Zogar boasted that he could summon wild beasts to do his bidding. The woodsman was livid beneath his mask of blood. He licked his lips spasmodically.

The village held its breath. Zogar Sag stood still as a statue, his plumes trembling faintly about him. But suddenly the gate was no longer empty.

A shuddering gasp swept over the village and men crowded hastily back, jamming one another between the huts. Balthus felt the short hair stir on his scalp. The creature that stood in the gate was like the embodiment of nightmare legend. Its color was of a curious pale quality which made it seem ghostly and unreal in the dim light. But there was nothing unreal about the low-hung savage head, and the great curved fangs that glistened in the firelight. On noiseless padded feet it approached like a phantom out of the past. It was a survival of an older, grimmer age, the ogre of many an ancient legend — a saber-tooth tiger. No Hyborian hunter had looked upon one of those primordial brutes for centuries. Immemorial myths lent the creatures a supernatural quality, induced by their ghostly color and their fiendish ferocity.

The beast that glided toward the men on the stakes was longer and heavier than a common, striped tiger, almost as bulky as a bear. Its shoulders and forelegs were so massive and mightily muscled as to give it a curiously top-heavy look, though its hindquarters were more powerful than that of a lion. Its jaws were massive, but its head was brutishly shaped. Its brain capacity was small. It had room for no instincts except those of destruction. It was a freak of carnivorous development, evolution run amuck in a horror of fangs and talons.

This was the monstrosity Zogar Sag had summoned out of the forest. Balthus no longer doubted the actuality of the shaman's magic. Only the black arts could establish a domination over that tiny-brained, mighty-thewed monster. Like a whisper at the back of his consciousness rose the vague memory of the name of an ancient god of darkness and primordial fear, to whom once both men and beasts bowed and whose children — men whispered — still lurked in dark corners of the world. New horror tinged the glare he fixed on Zogar Sag.

The monster moved past the heap of bodies and the pile of gory heads without appearing to notice them. He was no scavenger. He hunted only the living, in a life dedicated solely to slaughter. An awful hunger burned greenly in the wide, unwinking eyes; the hunger not alone of belly-emptiness, but of the lust of death-dealing. His gaping jaws slavered. The shaman stepped back; his hand waved toward the woodsman.

The great cat sank into a crouch, and Balthus numbly remembered tales of its appalling ferocity: of how it would spring upon an elephant and drive its sword-like fangs so deeply into the titan's skull that they could never be withdrawn, but would keep it nailed to its victim, to die by starvation. The shaman cried out shrilly, and with an ear-shattering roar the monster sprang.

Balthus had never dreamed of such a spring, such a hurtling of incarnated destruction embodied in that giant bulk of iron thews and ripping talons. Full on the woodsman's breast it struck, and the stake splintered and snapped at the base, crashing to the earth under the impact. Then the saber-tooth was gliding toward the gate, half-dragging, half-carrying a hideous crimson hulk that only faintly resembled a man. Balthus glared almost paralyzed, his brain refusing to credit what his eyes had seen.

In that leap the great beast had not only broken off the stake, it had ripped the mangled body of its victim from the post to which it was bound. The huge talons in that instant of contact had disemboweled and partially dismembered the man, and the giant fangs had torn away the whole top of his head, shearing through the skull as easily as through flesh. Stout rawhide thongs had given way like paper; where the thongs had held, flesh and bones had not. Balthus retched suddenly. He had hunted bears and panthers, but he had never dreamed the beast lived which could make such a red ruin of a human frame in the flicker of an instant.

The saber-tooth vanished through the gate, and a few moments later a deep roar sounded through the forest, receding in the distance. But the Picts still shrank back against the huts, and the shaman still stood facing the gate that was like a black opening to let in the night.

Cold sweat burst suddenly out on Balthus' skin. What new horror would come through that gate to make carrion-meat of *his* body? Sick panic assailed him and he strained futilely at his thongs. The night pressed in very black and horrible outside the fire-light. The fires themselves glowed lurid as the fires of Hell. He felt the eyes of the Picts upon him — hundreds of hungry, cruel eyes that reflected the lust of souls utterly without humanity as he knew it. They no longer seemed men; they were devils of this black jungle, as inhuman as the creatures to which the fiend in the nodding plumes screamed through the darkness.

Zogar sent another call shuddering through the night, and it was utterly unlike the first cry. There was a hideous sibilance in it — Balthus turned cold at the implication. If a serpent could hiss that loud, it would make just such a sound.

This time there was no answer — only a period of breathless silence in which the pound of Balthus' heart strangled him; and then there sounded a swishing outside the gate, a dry rustling that sent chills down Balthus' spine. Again the firelit gate held a hideous occupant.

Again Balthus recognized the monster from ancient legends. He saw and knew the ancient and evil serpent which swayed there, its wedge-shaped head, huge as that of a horse, as high as a tall man's head, and its palely gleaming barrel rippling out behind it. A forked tongue darted in and out, and the firelight glittered on bared fangs.

Balthus became incapable of emotion. The horror of his fate paralyzed him. That was the reptile that the ancients called Ghost Snake, the pale, abominable terror that of old glided into huts by night to devour whole families. Like the python it crushed its victim, but unlike other constrictors its fangs bore venom that carried madness and death. It too had long been considered extinct. But Valannus had spoken truly. No white man knew what shapes haunted the great forests beyond Black River.

It came on silently, rippling over the ground, its hideous head on the same level, its neck curving back slightly for the stroke. Balthus gazed with glazed, hypnotized stare into that loathsome gullet down which he would soon be engulfed, and he was aware of no sensation except a vague nausea.

And then something that glinted in the firelight streaked from the shadows of the huts, and the great reptile whipped about and went into instant convulsions. As in a dream Balthus saw a short throwing-spear transfixing the mighty neck, just below the gaping jaws; the shaft protruded from one side, the steel head from the other.

Knotting and looping hideously, the maddened reptile rolled into the circle of men who strove back from him. The spear had not severed its spine, but merely transfixed its great neck muscles. Its furiously lashing tail mowed down a dozen men and its jaws snapped convulsively, splashing others with venom that burned like liquid fire. Howling, cursing, screaming, frantic, they scattered before it, knocking each other down in their flight, trampling the fallen, bursting through the huts. The giant snake rolled into a fire, scattering sparks and brands, and the pain lashed it to more frenzied efforts. A hut wall buckled under the ram-like impact of its flailing tail, disgorging howling people.

Men stampeded through the fires, knocking the

logs right and left. The flames sprang up, then sank. A reddish dim glow was all that lighted that nightmare scene where the giant reptile whipped and rolled, and men clawed and shrieked in frantic flight.

Balthus felt something jerk at his wrists, and then, miraculously, he was free, and a strong hand dragged him behind the post. Dazedly he saw Conan, felt the forest man's iron grip on his arm.

There was blood on the Cimmerian's mail, dried blood on the sword in his right hand; he loomed dim and gigantic in the shadowy light.

"Come on! Before they get over their panic!"

Balthus felt the haft of an ax shoved into his hand. Zogar Sag had disappeared. Conan dragged Balthus after him until the youth's numb brain awoke, and his legs began to move of their own accord. Then Conan released him and ran into the building where the skulls hung. Balthus followed him. He got a glimpse of a grim stone altar, faintly lighted by the glow outside; five human heads grinned on that altar, and there was a grisly familiarity about the features of the freshest; it was the head of the merchant Tiberias. Behind the altar was an idol, dim, indistinct, bestial, yet vaguely manlike in outline. Then fresh horror choked Balthus as the shape heaved up suddenly with a rattle of chains, lifting long misshapen arms in the gloom.

Conan's sword flailed down, crunching through flesh and bone, and then the Cimmerian was dragging Balthus around the altar, past a huddled shaggy bulk on the floor, to a door at the back of the long hut. Through this they burst, out into the enclosure again. But a few yards beyond them loomed the stockade.

It was dark behind the altar-hut. The mad stampede of the Picts had not carried them in that direction. At the wall Conan halted, gripped Balthus and heaved him at arm's length into the air as he might have lifted a child. Balthus grasped the points of the upright logs set in the sun-dried mud and scrambled up on them, ignoring the havoc done his skin. He lowered a hand to the Cimmerian, when around a corner of the altar-hut sprang a fleeing Pict. He halted short, glimpsing the man on the wall in the faint glow of the fires. Conan hurled his ax with deadly aim, but the warrior's mouth was already open for a yell of warning, and it rang loud above the din, cut short as he dropped with a shattered skull.

Blinding terror had not submerged all ingrained instincts. As that wild yell rose above the clamor, there was an instant's lull, and then a hundred throats bayed ferocious answer and warriors came leaping to repel the attack presaged by the warning.

Conan leaped high, caught, not Balthus' hand but his arm near the shoulder, and swung himself up. Balthus set his teeth against the strain, and then the Cimmerian was on the wall beside him, and the fugitives dropped down on the other side.

5. The Children of Jhebbal Sag

"Which way is the river?" Balthus was confused.

"We don't dare try for the river now," grunted Conan. "The woods between the village and the river are swarming with warriors. Come on! We'll head in the last direction they'll expect us to go — west!"

Looking back as they entered the thick growth, Balthus beheld the wall dotted with black heads as the savages peered over. The Picts were bewildered. They had not gained the wall in time to see the fugitives take cover. They had rushed to the wall expecting to repel an attack in force. They had seen the body of the dead warrior. But no enemy was in sight.

Balthus realized that they did not yet know their prisoner had escaped. From other sounds he believed that the warriors, directed by the shrill voice of Zogar Sag, were destroying the wounded serpent with arrows. The monster was out of the shaman's control. A moment later the quality of the yells was altered. Screeches of rage rose in the night.

Conan laughed grimly. He was leading Balthus along a narrow trail that ran west under the black branches, stepping as swiftly and surely as if he trod a well-lighted thoroughfare. Balthus stumbled after him, guiding himself by feeling the dense wall on either hand.

"They'll be after us now. Zogar's discovered you're gone, and he knows my head wasn't in the pile before the altar-hut. The dog! If I'd had another spear I'd have thrown it through him before I struck the snake. Keep to the trail. They can't track us by torchlight, and there are a score of paths leading from the village. They'll follow those leading to the river first — throw a cordon of warriors for miles along the bank, expecting us to try to break through. We won't take to the woods until we have to. We can make better time on this trail. Now buckle down to it and run as you never ran before."

"They got over their panic cursed quick!" panted Balthus, complying with a fresh burst of speed.

"They're not afraid of anything, very long," grunted Conan.

For a space nothing was said between them. The fugitives devoted all their attention to covering distance. They were plunging deeper and deeper into the wilderness and getting farther away from civilization at every step, but Balthus did not question Conan's wisdom. The Cimmerian presently took time to grunt: "When we're far enough away from the village we'll swing back to the river in a big circle. No other village within miles of Gwawela. All the Picts are gathered in that vicinity. We'll circle wide around them. They can't track us until daylight. They'll pick up our path then, but before dawn we'll leave the trail and take to the woods."

They plunged on. The yells died out behind them. Balthus' breath was whistling through his teeth. He felt a pain in his side, and running became torture. He blundered against the bushes on each side of the trail. Conan pulled up suddenly, turned and stared back down the dim path.

Somewhere the moon was rising, a dim white glow amidst a tangle of branches.

"Shall we take to the woods?" panted Balthus.

"Give me your ax," murmured Conan softly. "Something is close behind us."

"Then we'd better leave the trail!" exclaimed Balthus.

Conan shook his head and drew his companion into a dense thicket. The moon rose higher, making a dim light in the path.

"We can't fight the whole tribe!" whispered Balthus.

"No human being could have found our trail so quickly, or followed us so swiftly," muttered Conan. "Keep silent."

There followed a tense silence in which Balthus felt that his heart could be heard pounding for miles away. Then abruptly, without a sound to announce its coming, a savage head appeared in the dim path. Balthus' heart jumped into his throat; at first glance he feared to look upon the awful head of the saber-tooth. But this head was smaller, more narrow; it was a leopard which stood there, snarling silently and glaring down the trail. What wind there was was blowing toward the hiding men, concealing their scent. The beast lowered his head and snuffed the trail, then moved forward uncertainly. A chill played down Balthus' spine. The brute was undoubtedly trailing them.

And it was suspicious. It lifted its head, its eyes glowing like balls of fire, and growled low in its throat. And at that instant Conan hurled the ax.

All the weight of arm and shoulder was behind the throw, and the ax was a streak of silver in the dim moon. Almost before he realized what had happened, Balthus saw the leopard rolling on the ground in its death-throes, the handle of the ax standing up from its head. The head of the weapon had split its narrow skull.

Conan bounded from the bushes, wrenched his ax free and dragged the limp body in among the trees, concealing it from the casual glance.

"Now let's go, and go fast!" he grunted, leading the way southward, away from the trail. "There'll be warriors coming after that cat. As soon as he got his wits back Zogar sent him after us. The Picts would follow him, but he'd leave them far behind. He'd circle the village until he hit our trail and then come after us like a streak. They couldn't keep up with him, but they'll have an idea as to our general direction. They'd follow, listening for his cry. Well, they won't hear that, but they'll find the blood on the trail, and look around and find the body in the brush. They'll pick up our spoor there, if they can. Walk with care."

He avoided clinging briars and low-hanging branches effortlessly, gliding between trees without touching the stems and always planting his feet in the places calculated to show least evidence of his passing; but with Balthus it was slower, more laborious work.

No sound came from behind them. They had covered more than a mile when Balthus said: "Does Zogar Sag catch leopard-cubs and train them for bloodhounds?"

Conan shook his head. "That was a leopard he called out of the woods."

"But," Balthus persisted, "if he can order the beasts to do his bidding, why doesn't he rouse them all and have them after us? The forest is full of leopards; why send only one after us?"

Conan did not reply for a space, and when he did it was with a curious reticence.

"He can't command all the animals. Only such as remember Jhebbal Sag."

"Jhebbal Sag?" Balthus repeated the ancient name hesitantly. He had never heard it spoken more than three or four times in his whole life.

"Once all living things worshipped him. That was long ago, when beasts and men spoke one language. Men have forgotten him; even the beasts forget. Only a few remember. The men who remember Jhebbal Sag and the beasts who remember are brothers and speak the same tongue."

Balthus did not reply; he had strained at a Pictish stake and seen the nighted jungle give up its fanged horrors at a shaman's call.

"Civilized men laugh," said Conan, "but not one can tell me how Zogar Sag can call pythons and tigers and leopards out of the wilderness and make them do his bidding. They would say it is a lie, if they dared. That's the way with civilized men. When they can't explain something by their half-baked science, they refuse to believe it."

The people on the Tauran were closer to the primitive than most Aquilonians; superstitions persisted, whose sources were lost in antiquity. And Balthus had seen that which still prickled his flesh. He could not refute the monstrous thing which Conan's words implied.

"I've heard that there's an ancient grove sacred to Jbebbal Sag somewhere in this forest," said Conan. "It don't know. I've never seen it. But more beasts *remember* in this country than any I've ever seen."

"Then others will be on our trail?"

"They are now," was Conan's disquieting answer. "Zogar would never leave our tracking to one beast alone."

"What are we to do, then?" asked Balthus uneasily, grasping his ax as he stared at the gloomy arches above him. His flesh crawled with the momentary expectation of ripping talons and fangs leaping from the shadows.

"Wait!"

Conan turned, squatted and with his knife began scratching a curious symbol in the mold. Stooping to look at it over his shoulder, Balthus felt a crawling of the flesh along his spine, he knew not why. He felt no wind against his face, but there was a rustling of leaves above them and a weird moaning swept ghostily through the branches. Conan glanced up inscrutably, then rose and stood staring somberly down at the symbol he had drawn.

"What is it?" whispered Balthus. It looked archaic and meaningless to him. He supposed that it was his ignorance of artistry which prevented his identifying it as one of the conventional designs of some prevailing culture. But had he been the most erudite artist in the world, he would have been no nearer the solution.

"I saw it carved in the rock of a cave no human had visited for a million years," muttered Conan, "in the uninhabited mountains beyond the Sea of Vilayet, half a world away from this spot. Later I saw a black witch-finder of Kush scratch it in the sand of a nameless river. He told me part of its meaning — it's sacred to Jhebbel Sag and the creatures which worship him. Watch!"

They drew back among the dense foliage some yards away and waited in tense silence. To the east drums muttered and somewhere to north and west other drums answered. Balthus shivered, though he knew long miles of black forest separated him from the grim beaters of those drums whose dull pulsing was a sinister overture that set the dark stage for bloody drama.

Balthus found himself holding his breath. Then with a slight shaking of the leaves, the bushes parted and a magnificent panther came into view. The moonlight dappling through the leaves shone on its glossy coat rippling with the play of the great muscles beneath it.

With its head held low it glided toward them. It was smelling out their trail. Then it halted as if frozen, its muzzle almost touching the symbol cut in the mold. For a long space it crouched motionless; it flattened its long body and laid its head on the ground before the mark. And Balthus felt the short hairs stir on his scalp. For the attitude of the great carnivore was one of awe and adoration.

Then the panther rose and backed away carefully, belly almost to the ground. With his hindquarters among the bushes he wheeled as if in sudden panic and was gone like a flash of dappled light.

Balthus mopped his brow with a trembling hand and glanced at Conan.

The barbarian's eyes were smoldering with fires that never lit the eyes of men bred to the ideas of civilization. In that instant he was all wild, and had forgotten the man at his side. In his burning gaze Balthus glimpsed and vaguely recognized pristine images and half-embodied memories, shadows from Life's dawn, forgotten and repudiated by sophisticated races — ancient, primeval fantasms unnamed and nameless.

Then the deeper fires were masked and Conan was silently leading the way deeper into the forest.

"We've no more to fear from the beasts," he said after a while, "but we've left a sign for men to read.

They won't follow our trail very easily, and until they find that symbol they won't know for sure we've turned south. Even then it won't be easy to smell us out without the beasts to aid them. But the woods south of the trail will be full of warriors looking for us. If we keep moving after daylight, we'll be sure to run into some of them. As soon as we find a good place we'll hide and wait until another night to swing back and make the river. We've got to warn Valannus, but it won't help him any if we get ourselves killed."

"Warn Valannus?"

"Hell, the woods along the river are swarming with Picts! That's why they got us. Zogar's brewing war-magic; no mere raid this time. He's done something no Pict has done in my memory — united as many as fifteen or sixteen clans. His magic did it; they'll follow a wizard farther than they will a war-chief. You saw the mob in the village; and there were hundreds hiding along the river bank that you didn't see. More coming, from the farther villages. He'll have at least three thousand fighting-men. I lay in the bushes and heard their talk as they went past. They mean to attack the fort; when, I don't know, but Zogar doesn't dare delay long. He's gathered them and whipped them into a frenzy. If he doesn't lead them into battle quickly, they'll fall to quarreling with one another. They're like blood-mad tigers.

"I don't know whether they can take the fort or

not. Anyway, we've got to get back across the river and give the warning. The settlers on the Velitrium road must either get into the fort or back to Velitrium. While the Picts are besieging the fort, war parties will range the road far to the east — might even cross Thunder River and raid the thickly settled country behind Velitrium."

As he talked he was leading the way deeper and deeper into the ancient wilderness. Presently he grunted with satisfaction. They had reached a spot where the underbrush was more scattered, and an outcropping of stone was visible, wandering off southward. Balthus felt more secure as they followed it. Not even a Pict could trail them over naked rock.

"How did you get away?" he asked presently.

Conan tapped his mail-shirt and helmet.

"If more borderers would wear harness there'd be fewer skulls hanging on the altar-huts. But most men make noise if they wear armor. They were waiting on each side of the path, without moving. And when a Pict stands motionless, the very beasts of the forest pass him without seeing him. They'd seen us crossing the river and got in their places. If they'd gone into ambush after we left the bank, I'd have had some hint of it. But they were waiting, and not even a leaf trembled. The Devil himself couldn't have suspected anything. The first suspicion I had was when I heard a shaft rasp against a bow as it was pulled back. I dropped and yelled for the men behind me to drop, but they were too slow, taken by surprize like that.

"Most of them fell at the first volley that raked us from both sides. Some of the arrows crossed the trail and struck Picts on the other side. I heard them howl." He grinned with vicious satisfaction. "Such of us as were left plunged into the woods and closed with them. When I saw the others were all down or taken, I broke through and outfooted the painted devils through the darkness. They were all around me. I ran and crawled and sneaked, and sometimes I lay on my belly under the bushes while they passed me on all sides.

"I tried for the shore and found it lined with them, waiting for just such a move. But I'd have cut my way through and taken a chance on swimming, only I heard the drums pounding in the village and knew they'd taken somebody alive.

"They were all so engrossed in Zogar's magic that I was able to climb the wall behind the altar-hut. There was a warrior supposed to be watching at that point, but he was squatting behind the hut and peering around the comer at the ceremony. I came up behind him and broke his neck with my hands before he knew what was happening. It was his spear I threw into the snake, and that's his ax you're carrying."

"But what was that — that thing you killed in the altar-hut?" asked Balthus, with a shiver at the memory of the dim-seen horror.

"One of Zogar's gods. One of Jhebbal's children that didn't remember and had to be kept chained to the altar. A bull ape. The Picts think they're sacred to the Hairy One who lives on the moon — the gorilla-god of Gullah.

"It's getting light. Here's a good place to hide until we see how close they're on our trail. Probably have to wait until night to break back to the river."

A low hill pitched upward, girdled and covered with thick trees and bushes. Near the crest Conan slid into a tangle of jutting rocks, crowned by dense bushes. Lying among them they could see the jungle below without being seen. It was a good place to hide or defend. Balthus did not believe that even a Pict could have trailed them over the rocky ground for the past four or five miles, but he was afraid of the beasts that obeyed Zogar Sag. His faith in the curious symbol wavered a little now. But Conan had dismissed the possibility of beasts tracking them.

A ghostly whiteness spread through the dense branches; the patches of sky visible altered in hue, grew from pink to blue. Balthus felt the gnawing of hunger, though he had slaked his thirst at a stream they had skirted. There was complete silence, except for an occasional chirp of a bird. The drums were no longer to be heard. Balthus' thoughts reverted to the grim scene before the altar-hut.

"Those were ostrich plumes Zogar Sag wore," he said. "I've seen them on the helmets of knights who rode from the East to visit the barons of the marches. There are no ostriches in this forest, are there?"

"They came from Kush," answered Conan. "West of here, many marches, lies the seashore. Ships from Zingara occasionally come and trade weapons and ornaments and wine to the coastal tribes for skins and copper ore and gold dust. Sometimes they trade ostrich plumes they got from the Stygians, who in turn got them from the black tribes of Kush, which lies south of Stygia. The Pictish shamans place great store by them. But there's much risk in such trade. The Picts are too likely to try to seize the ship. And the coast is dangerous to ships. I've sailed along it when I was with the pirates of the Barachan Isles, which lie southwest of Zingara."

Balthus looked at his companion with admiration.

"I knew you hadn't spent your life on this frontier. You've mentioned several far places. You've traveled widely?"

"I've roamed far; farther than any other man of my race ever wandered. I've seen all the great cities of the Hyborians, the Shemites, the Stygians and the Hyrkanians. I've roamed in the unknown countries south of the black kingdoms of Kush, and east of the Sea of Vilayet. I've been a mercenary captain, a corsair, a *kozak*, a penniless vagabond, a general — hell, I've been everything except a king, and I may be that, before I die." The fancy pleased him, and he grinned hardly. Then he shrugged his shoulders and stretched his mighty figure on the rocks. "This is as good a life as any. I don't know how long I'll stay on the frontier; a week, a month, a year. I have a roving foot. But it's as well on the border as anywhere."

Balthus set himself to watch the forest below them. Momentarily he expected to see fierce painted faces thrust through the leaves. But as the hours passed no stealthy footfall disturbed the brooding quiet. Balthus believed the Picts had missed their trail and given up the chase. Conan grew restless.

"We should have sighted parties scouring the woods for us. If they've quit the chase, it's because they're after bigger game. They may be gathering to cross the river and storm the fort."

"Would they come this far south if they lost the trail?"

"They've lost the trail, all right; otherwise they'd have been on our necks before now. Under ordinary circumstances they'd scour the woods for miles in every direction. Some of them should have passed within sight of this hill. They must be preparing to cross the river. We've got to take a chance and make for the river."

Creeping down the rocks Balthus felt his flesh crawl between his shoulders as he momentarily expected a withering blast of arrows from the green masses about them. He feared that the Picts had discovered them and were lying about in ambush. But Conan was convinced no enemies were near, and the Cimmerian was right.

"We're miles to the south of the village," grunted Conan. "We'll hit straight through for the river. I don't know how far down the river they've spread. We'll hope to hit it below them."

With haste that seemed reckless to Balthus, they hurried eastward. The woods seemed empty of life. Conan believed that all the Picts were gathered in the vicinity of Gwawela, if, indeed, they had not already crossed the river. He did not believe they would cross in the daytime, however.

"Some woodsman would be sure to see them and give the alarm. They'll cross above and below the fort, out of sight of the sentries. Then others will get in canoes and make straight across for the river wall. As soon as they attack, those hidden in the woods on the east shore will assail the fort from the other sides. They've tried that before, and got the guts shot and hacked out of them. But this time they've got enough men to make a real onslaught of it."

They pushed on without pausing, though Balthus gazed longingly at the squirrels flitting among the branches, which he could have brought down with a cast of his ax. With a sigh he drew up his broad belt. The everlasting silence and gloom of the primitive forest was beginning to depress him. He found himself thinking of the open groves and sun-dappled meadows of the Tauran, of the bluff cheer of his father's steep-thatched, diamond-paned house, of the fat cows browsing through the deep, lush grass, and the hearty fellowship of the brawny, bare-armed plowmen and herdsmen.

He felt lonely, in spite of his companion. Conan

was as much a part of this wilderness as Balthus was alien to it. The Cimmerian might have spent years among the great cities of the world; he might have walked with the rulers of civilization; he might even achieve his wild whim someday and rule as king of a civilized nation; stranger things had happened. But he was no less a barbarian. He was concerned only with the naked fundamentals of life. The warm intimacies of small, kindly things, the sentiments and delicious trivialities that make up so much of civilized men's lives were meaningless to him. A wolf was no less a wolf because a whim of chance caused him to run with the watchdogs. Bloodshed and violence and savagery were the natural elements of the life Conan knew; he could not, and would never, understand the little things that are so dear to civilized men and women.

The shadows were lengthening when they reached the river and peered through the masking bushes. They could see up and down the river for about a mile each way. The sullen stream lay bare and empty. Conan scowled across at the other shore.

"We've got to take another chance here. We've got to swim the river. We don't know whether they've crossed or not. The woods over there may be alive with them. We've got to risk it. We're about six miles south of Gwawela."

He wheeled and ducked as a bowstring twanged. Something like a white flash of light streaked through the bushes. Balthus knew it was an arrow.

Then with a tigerish bound Conan was through the bushes. Balthus caught the gleam of steel as he whirled his sword, and heard a death scream. The next instant he had broken through the bushes after the Cimmerian.

A Pict with a shattered skull lay facedown on the ground, his fingers spasmodically clawing at the grass. Half a dozen others were swarming about Conan, swords and axes lifted. They had cast away their bows, useless at such deadly close quarters. Their lower jaws were painted white, contrasting vividly with their dark faces, and the designs on their muscular breasts differed from any Balthus had ever seen.

One of them hurled his ax at Balthus and rushed after it with lifted knife. Balthus ducked and then caught the wrist that drove the knife licking at his throat. They went to the ground together, rolling over and over. The Pict was like a wild beast, his muscles hard as steel strings.

Balthus was striving to maintain his hold on the wild man's wrist and bring his own ax into play, but so fast and furious was the struggle that each attempt to strike was blocked. The Pict was wrenching furiously to free his knife hand, was clutching at Balthus' ax, and driving his knees at the youth's groin. Suddenly he attempted to shift his knife to his free hand, and in that instant Balthus, struggling up on one knee, split the painted head with a desperate blow of his ax.

He sprang up and glared wildly about for his companion, expecting to see him overwhelmed by numbers. Then he realized the full strength and ferocity of the Cimmerian. Conan bestrode two of his attackers, shorn half-asunder by that terrible broadsword. As Balthus looked he saw the Cimmerian beat down a thrusting shortsword, avoid the stroke of an ax with a catlike sidewise spring which brought him within arm's length of a squat savage stooping for a bow. Before the Pict could straighten, the red sword flailed down and clove him from shoulder to mid-breastbone, where the blade stuck. The remaining warriors rushed in, one from either side. Balthus hurled his ax with an accuracy that reduced the attackers to one, and Conan, abandoning his efforts to free his sword, wheeled and met the remaining Pict with his bare hands. The stocky warrior, a head shorter than his tall enemy, leaped in, striking with his ax, at the same time stabbing murderously with his knife. The knife broke on the Cimmerian's mail, and the ax checked in midair as Conan's fingers locked like iron on the descending arm. A bone snapped loudly, and Balthus saw the Pict wince and falter. The next instant he was swept off his feet, lifted high above the Cimmerian's head — he writhed in midair for an instant, kicking and thrashing, and then was dashed headlong to the earth with such force that he rebounded, and then lay still, his limp posture telling of splintered limbs and a broken spine.

"Come on!" Conan wrenched his sword free and snatched up an ax. "Grab a bow and a handful of arrows, and hurry! We've got to trust to our heels again. That yell was heard. They'll be here in no time. If we tried to swim now, they'd feather us with arrows before we reached midstream!"

6. Red Axes of the Border

Conan did not plunge deeply into the forest. A few hundred yards from the river, he altered his slanting course and ran parallel with it. Balthus recognized a grim determination not to be hunted away from the river which they must cross if they were to warn the men in the fort. Behind them rose more loudly the yells of the forest men. Balthus believed the Picts had reached the glade where the bodies of the slain men lay. Then further yells seemed to indicate that the savages were streaming into the woods in pursuit. They had left a trail any Pict could follow.

Conan increased his speed, and Balthus grimly set his teeth and kept on his heels, though he felt he might collapse any time. It seemed centuries since he had eaten last. He kept going more by an effort of will than anything else. His blood was pounding so furiously in his eardrums that he was not aware when the yells died out behind them.

Conan halted suddenly. Balthus leaned against a tree and panted.

"They've quit!" grunted the Cimmerian, scowling.

"Sneaking — up — on — us!" gasped Balthus.

Conan shook his head.

"A short chase like this they'd yell every step of the way. No. They've gone back. I thought I heard somebody yelling behind them a few seconds before the noise began to get dimmer. They've been recalled. And that's good for us, but damned bad for the men in the fort. It means the warriors are being summoned out of the woods for the attack. These men we ran into were warriors from a tribe down the river. They were undoubtedly headed for Gwawela to join in the assault on the fort. Damn it, we're farther away than ever, now. We've got to get across the river."

Turning east he hurried through the thickets with no attempt at concealment. Balthus followed him, for the first time feeling the sting of lacerations on his breast and shoulder where the Pict's savage teeth had scored him. He was pushing through the thick bushes that fringed the bank when Conan pulled him back. Then he heard a rhythmic splashing, and peering through the leaves, saw a dugout canoe coming up the river, its single occupant paddling hard against the current. He was a strongly built Pict with a white heron feather thrust in a copper band that confined his square-cut mane.

"That's a Gwawela man," muttered Conan. "Emissary from Zogar. White plume shows that.

He's carried a peace talk to the tribes down the river and now he's trying to get back and take a hand in the slaughter."

The lone ambassador was now almost even with their hiding-place, and suddenly Balthus almost jumped out of his skin. At his very ear had sounded the harsh gutturals of a Pict. Then he realized that Conan had called to the paddler in his own tongue. The man started, scanned the bushes and called back something, then cast a startled glance across the river, bent low and sent the canoe shooting in toward the western bank. Not understanding, Balthus saw Conan take from his hand the bow he had picked up in the glade, and notch an arrow.

The Pict had run his canoe in close to the shore, and staring up into the bushes, called out something. His answer came in the twang of the bowstring, the streaking flight of the arrow that sank to the feathers in his broad breast. With a choking gasp he slumped sidewise and rolled into the shallow water. In an instant Conan was down the bank and wading into the water to grasp the drifting canoe. Balthus stumbled after him and somewhat dazedly crawled into the canoe. Conan scrambled in, seized the paddle and sent the craft shooting toward the eastern shore. Balthus noted with envious admiration the play of the great muscles beneath the sun-burnt skin. The Cimmerian seemed an iron man, who never knew fatigue.

"What did you say to the Pict?" asked Balthus.

"Told him to pull into shore; said there was a white forest runner on the bank who was trying to get a shot at him."

"That doesn't seem fair," Balthus objected. "He thought a friend was speaking to him. You mimicked a Pict perfectly —"

"We needed his boat," grunted Conan, not pausing in his exertions. "Only way to lure him to the bank. Which is worse — to betray a Pict who'd enjoy skinning us both alive, or betray the men across the river whose lives depend on our getting over?"

Balthus mulled over this delicate ethical question for a moment, then shrugged his shoulder and asked: "How far are we from the fort?"

Conan pointed to a creek which flowed into Black River from the east, a few hundred yards below them.

"That's South Creek; it's ten miles from its mouth to the fort. It's the southern boundary of Conajohara. Marshes miles wide south of it. No danger of a raid from across them. Nine miles above the fort North Creek forms the other boundary. Marshes beyond that, too. That's why an attack must come from the west, across Black River. Conajohara's just like a spear, with a point nineteen miles wide, thrust into the Pictish wilderness."

"Why don't we keep to the canoe and make the trip by water?"

"Because, considering the current we've got to brace, and the bends in the river, we can go faster afoot. Besides, remember Gwawela is south of the fort; if the Picts are crossing the river we'd run right into them."

Dusk was gathering as they stepped upon the eastern bank. Without pause Conan pushed on northward, at a pace that made Balthus' sturdy legs ache.

"Valannus wanted a fort built at the mouths of North and South Creeks," grunted the Cimmerian. "Then the river could be patrolled constantly. But the Government wouldn't do it.

"Soft-bellied fools sitting on velvet cushions with naked girls offering them iced wine on their knees — I know the breed. They can't see any farther than their palace wall. Diplomacy — hell! They'd fight Picts with theories of territorial expansion. Valannus and men like him have to obey the orders of a set of damned fools. They'll never grab any more Pictish land, any more than they'll ever rebuild Venarium. The time may come when they'll see the barbarians swarming over the walls of the eastern cities!"

A week before, Balthus would have laughed at any such preposterous suggestion. Now he made no reply. He had seen the unconquerable ferocity of the men who dwelt beyond the frontiers.

He shivered, casting glances at the sullen river, just visible through the bushes, at the arches of the trees which crowded close to its banks. He kept remembering that the Picts might have crossed the river and be lying in ambush between them and the fort. It was fast growing dark.

A slight sound ahead of them jumped his heart into his throat, and Conan's sword gleamed in the air. He lowered it when a dog, a great, gaunt, scarred beast, slunk out of the bushes and stood staring at them.

"That dog belonged to a settler who tried to build his cabin on the bank of the river a few miles south of the fort," grunted Conan. "The Picts slipped over and killed him, of course, and burned his cabin. We found him dead among the embers, and the dog lying senseless among three Picts he'd killed. He was almost cut to pieces. We took him to the fort and dressed his wounds, but after he recovered he took to the woods and turned wild. — What now, Slasher, are you hunting the men who killed your master?"

The massive head swung from side to side and the eyes glowed greenly. He did not growl or bark. Silently as a phantom he slid in behind them.

"Let him come," muttered Conan. "He can smell the devils before we can see them."

Balthus smiled and laid his hand caressingly on the dog's head. The lips involuntarily writhed back to display the gleaming fangs; then the great beast bent his head sheepishly, and his tail moved with jerky uncertainty, as if the owner had almost forgotten the emotions of friendliness. Balthus mentally compared the great gaunt hard body with the fat sleek hounds tumbling vociferously over one another in his father's kennel yard. He sighed. The frontier was no less hard for beasts than for men. This dog had almost forgotten the meaning of kindness and friendliness.

Slasher glided ahead, and Conan let him take the lead. The last tinge of dusk faded into stark darkness. The miles fell away under their steady feet. Slasher seemed voiceless. Suddenly he halted, tense, ears lifted. An instant later the men heard it — a demoniac yelling up the river ahead of them, faint as a whisper.

Conan swore like a madman.

"They've attacked the fort! We're too late! Come on!"

He increased his pace, trusting to the dog to smell out ambushes ahead. In a flood of tense excitement, Balthus forgot his hunger and weariness. The yells grew louder as they advanced, and above the devilish screaming they could hear the deep shouts of the soldiers. Just as Balthus began to fear they would run into the savages who seemed to be howling just ahead of them, Conan swung away from the river in a wide semicircle that carried them to a low rise from which they could look over the forest. They saw the fort, lighted with torches thrust over the parapets on long poles. These cast a flickering, uncertain light over the clearing, and in that light they saw throngs of naked, painted figures along the fringe of the clearing. The river swarmed with canoes. The Picts had the fort completely surrounded.

An incessant hail of arrows rained against the stockade from the woods and the river. The deep twanging of the bowstrings rose above the howling. Yelling like wolves, several hundred naked warriors with axes in their hands ran from under the trees and raced toward the eastern gate. They were within a hundred and fifty yards of their objective when a withering blast of arrows from the wall littered the ground with corpses and sent the survivors fleeing back to the trees. The men in the canoes rushed their boats toward the river-wall, and were met by another shower of clothyard shafts and a volley from the small ballistae mounted on towers on that side of the stockade. Stones and logs whirled through the air and splintered and sank half a dozen canoes, killing their occupants, and the other boats drew back out of range. A deep roar of triumph rose from the walls of the fort, answered by bestial howling from all quarters.

"Shall we try to break through?" asked Balthus, trembling with eagerness.

Conan shook his head. He stood with his arms folded, his head slightly bent, a somber and brooding figure.

"The fort's doomed. The Picts are blood-mad, and won't stop until they're all killed. And there are too many of them for the men in the fort to kill. We couldn't break through, and if we did, we could do nothing but die with Valannus."

"There's nothing we can do but save our own hides, then?"

"Yes. We've got to warn the settlers. Do you

know why the Picts are not trying to burn the fort with fire-arrows? Because they don't want a flame that might warn the people to the east. They plan to stamp out the fort, and then sweep east before anyone knows of its fall. They may cross Thunder River and take Velitrium before the people know what's happened. At least they'll destroy every living thing between the fort and Thunder River.

"We've failed to warn the fort, and I see now it would have done no good if we had succeeded. The fort's too poorly manned. A few more charges and the Picts will be over the walls and breaking down the gates. But we can start the settlers toward Velitrium. Come on! We're outside the circle the Picts have thrown around the fort. We'll keep clear of it."

They swung out in a wide arc, hearing the rising and falling of the volume of the yells, marking each charge and repulse. The men in the fort were holding their own; but the shrieks of the Picts did not diminish in savagery. They vibrated with a timbre that held assurance of ultimate victory.

Before Balthus realized they were close to it, they broke into the road leading east.

"Now run!" grunted Conan. Balthus set his teeth. It was nineteen miles to Velitrium, a good five to Scalp Creek beyond which began the settlements. It seemed to the Aquilonian that they had been fighting and running for centuries. But the nervous excitement that rioted through his blood stimulated him to herculean efforts.

Slasher ran ahead of them, his head to the ground, snarling low, the first sound they had heard from him.

"Picts ahead of us!" snarled Conan, dropping to one knee and scanning the ground in the starlight. He shook his head, baffled. "I can't tell how many. Probably only a small party. Some that couldn't wait to take the fort. They've gone ahead to butcher the settlers in their beds! Come on!"

Ahead of them presently they saw a small blaze through the trees, and heard a wild and ferocious chanting. The trail bent there, and leaving it, they cut across the bend, through the thickets. A few moments later they were looking on a hideous sight. An ox-wain stood in the road piled with meager household furnishings; it was burning; the oxen lay near with their throats cut. A man and a woman lay in the road, stripped and mutilated. Five Picts were dancing about them with fantastic leaps and bounds, waving bloody axes; one of them brandished the woman's red-smeared gown.

At the sight a red haze swam before Balthus. Lifting his bow he lined the prancing figure, black against the fire, and loosed. The slayer leaped convulsively and fell dead with the arrow through his heart. Then the two white men and the dog were upon the startled survivors. Conan was animated merely by his fighting spirit and an old, old racial hate, but Balthus was afire with wrath.

He met the first Pict to oppose him with a ferocious swipe that split the painted skull, and sprang over his falling body to grapple with the others. But Conan had already killed one of the two he had chosen, and the leap of the Aquilonian was a second late. The warrior was down with the long sword through him even as Balthus' ax was lifted. Turning toward the remaining Pict, Balthus saw Slasher rise from his victim, his great jaws dripping blood.

Balthus said nothing as he looked down at the pitiful forms in the road beside the burning wain. Both were young, the woman little more than a girl. By some whim of chance the Picts had left her face unmarred, and even in the agonies of an awful death it was beautiful. But her soft young body had been hideously slashed with many knives — a mist clouded Balthus' eyes and he swallowed chokingly. The tragedy momentarily overcame him. He felt like falling upon the ground and weeping and biting the earth.

"Some young couple just hitting out on their own," Conan was saying as he wiped his sword unemotionally. "On their way to the fort when the Picts met them. Maybe the boy was going to enter the service; maybe take up land on the river. Well, that's what will happen to every man, woman and child this side of Thunder River if we don't get them into Velitrium in a hurry."

Balthus' knees trembled as he followed Conan. But there was no hint of weakness in the long easy stride of the Cimmerian. There was a kinship between him and the great gaunt brute that glided beside him. Slasher no longer growled with his head to the trail. The way was clear before them. The yelling on the river came faintly to them, but Balthus believed the fort was still holding. Conan halted suddenly, with an oath.

He showed Balthus a trail that led north from the road. It was an old trail, partly grown with new young growth, and this growth had recently been broken down. Balthus realized this fact more by feel than sight, though Conan seemed to see like a cat in the dark. The Cimmerian showed him where broad wagon tracks turned off the main trail, deeply indented in the forest mold.

"Settlers going to the licks after salt," he grunted. "They're at the edges of the marsh, about nine miles from here. Blast it! They'll be cut off and butchered to a man! Listen! One man can warn the people on the road. Go ahead and wake them up and herd them into Velitrium. I'll go and get the men gathering the salt. They'll be camped by the licks. We won't come back to the road. We'll head straight through the woods."

With no further comment Conan turned off the trail and hurried down the dim path, and Balthus, after staring after him for a few moments, set out along the road. The dog had remained with him, and glided softly at his heels. When Balthus had gone a few rods he heard the animal growl. Whirling, he glared back the way he had come, and was startled to see a vague ghostly glow vanishing into the forest in the direction Conan had taken. Slasher rumbled deep in his throat, his hackles stiff and his eyes balls of green fire. Balthus remembered the grim apparition that had taken the head of the merchant Tiberias not far from that spot, and he hesitated. The thing must be following Conan. But the giant Cimmerian had repeatedly demonstrated his ability to take care of himself, and Balthus felt his duty lay toward the helpless settlers who slumbered in the path of the red hurricane. The horror of the fiery phantom was overshadowed by the horror of those limp, violated bodies beside the burning ox-wain.

He hurried down the road, crossed Scalp Creek and came in sight of the first settler's cabin — a long, low structure of ax-hewn logs. In an instant he was pounding on the door. A sleepy voice inquired his pleasure.

"Get up! The Picts are over the river!"

That brought instant response. A low cry echoed his words and then the door was thrown open by a woman in a scanty shift. Her hair hung over her bare shoulders in disorder; she held a candle in one hand and an ax in the other. Her face was colorless, her eyes wide with terror.

"Come in!" she begged. "We'll hold the cabin."

"No. We must make for Velitrium. The fort can't hold them back. It may have fallen already. Don't stop to dress. Get your children and come on."

"But my man's gone with the others after salt!" she wailed, wringing her hands. Behind her peered three tousled youngsters, blinking and bewildered.

"Conan's gone after them. He'll fetch them through safe. We must hurry up the road to warn the other cabins."

Relief flooded her countenance.

"Mitra be thanked!" she cried. "If the Cimmerian's gone after them, they're safe if mortal man can save them!"

In a whirlwind of activity she snatched up the smallest child and herded the others through the door ahead of her. Balthus took the candle and ground it out under his heel. He listened an instant. No sound came up the dark road.

"Have you got a horse?"

"In the stable," she groaned. "Oh, hurry!"

He pushed her aside as she fumbled with shaking hands at the bars. He led the horse out and lifted the children on its back, telling them to hold to its mane and to one another. They stared at him seriously, making no outcry. The woman took the horse's halter and set out up the road. She still gripped her ax and Balthus knew that if cornered she would fight with the desperate courage of a she-panther.

He held behind, listening. He was oppressed by the belief that the fort had been stormed and taken; that the dark-skinned hordes were already streaming up the road toward Velitrium, drunken on slaughter and mad for blood. They would come with the speed of starving wolves.

Presently they saw another cabin looming ahead. The woman started to shriek a warning, but Balthus stopped her. He hurried to the door and knocked. A woman's voice answered him. He repeated his warning, and soon the cabin disgorged its occupants: an old woman, two young women and four children. Like the other woman's husband, their men had gone to the salt licks the day before, unsuspecting of any danger. One of the young women seemed dazed, the other prone to hysteria. But the old woman, a stern old veteran of the frontier, quieted them harshly; she helped Balthus get out the two horses that were stabled in a pen behind the cabin and put the children on them. Balthus urged that she herself mount with them, but she shook her head and made one of the younger women ride.

"She's with child," grunted the old woman. "I can walk — and fight, too, if it comes to that."

As they set out, one of the young women said: "A young couple passed along the road about dusk; we advised them to spend the night at our cabin, but they were anxious to make the fort tonight. Did — did —"

"They met the Picts," answered Balthus briefly, and the woman sobbed in horror.

They were scarcely out of sight of the cabin when some distance behind them quavered a long high-pitched yell.

"A wolf!" exclaimed one of the women.

"A painted wolf with an ax in his hand," muttered Balthus. "Go! Rouse the other settlers along the road and take them with you. I'll scout along behind."

Without a word the old woman herded her charges ahead of her. As they faded into the darkness, Balthus could see the pale ovals that were the faces of the children twisted back over their shoulders to stare toward him. He remembered his own people on the Tauran and a moment's giddy sickness swam over him. With momentary weakness he groaned and sank down in the road; his muscular arm fell over Slasher's massive neck and he felt the dog's warm moist tongue touch his face.

He lifted his head and grinned with a painful effort.

"Come on, boy," he mumbled, rising. "We've got work to do."

A red glow suddenly became evident through the trees. The Picts had fired the last hut. He grinned. How Zogar Sag would froth if he knew his warriors had let their destructive natures get the better of them. The fire would warn the people farther up the road. They would be awake and alert when the fugitives reached them. But his face grew grim. The women were traveling slowly, on foot and on the overloaded horses. The swift-footed Picts would run them down within a mile, unless — he took his position behind a tangle of fallen logs beside the trail. The road west of him was lighted by the burning cabin, and when the Picts came he saw them first — black furtive figures etched against the distant glare.

Drawing a shaft to the head, he loosed and one of the figures crumpled. The rest melted into the woods on either side of the road. Slasher whimpered with the killing lust beside him. Suddenly a figure appeared on the fringe of the trail, under the trees, and began gliding toward the fallen timbers. Balthus' bowstring twanged and the Pict yelped, staggered and fell into the shadows with the arrow through his thigh. Slasher cleared the timbers with a bound and leaped into the bushes. They were violently shaken and then the dog slunk back to Balthus' side, his jaws crimson.

No more appeared in the trail; Balthus began to fear they were stealing past his position through the woods, and when he heard a faint sound to his left he loosed blindly. He cursed as he heard the shaft splinter against a tree, but Slasher glided away as silently as a phantom, and presently Balthus heard a thrashing and a gurgling; then Slasher came like a ghost through the bushes, snuggling his great, crimson-stained head against Balthus' arm. Blood oozed from a gash in his shoulder, but the sounds in the wood had ceased forever.

The men lurking on the edges of the road evidently sensed the fate of their companion, and decided that an open charge was preferable to being dragged down in the dark by a devil-beast they could neither see nor hear. Perhaps they realized that only one man lay behind the logs. They came with a sudden rush, breaking cover from both sides of the trail. Three dropped with arrows through them — and the remaining pair hesitated. One turned and ran back down the road, but the other lunged over the breastwork, his eyes and teeth gleaming in the dim light, his ax lifted. Balthus' foot slipped as he sprang up, but the slip saved his life. The descending ax shaved a lock of hair from his head, and the Pict rolled down the logs from the force of his wasted blow. Before he could regain his feet Slasher tore his throat out.

Then followed a tense period of waiting, in which time Balthus wondered if the man who had fled had been the only survivor of the party. Obviously it had been a small band that had either left the fighting at the fort, or was scouting ahead of the main body. Each moment that passed increased the chances for safety of the women and children hurrying toward Velitrium.

Then without warning a shower of arrows whistled over his retreat. A wild howling rose from the woods along the trail. Either the survivor had gone after aid, or another party had joined the first. The burning cabin still smoldered, lending a little light. Then they were after him, gliding through the trees beside the trail. He shot three arrows and threw the bow away. As if sensing his plight, they came on, not yelling now, but in deadly silence except for a swift pad of many feet.

He fiercely hugged the head of the great dog

growling at his side, muttered: "All right, boy, give 'em hell!" and sprang to his feet, drawing his ax. Then the dark figures flooded over the breastworks and closed in a storm of flailing axes, stabbing knives and ripping fangs.

7. The Devil in the Fire

When Conan turned from the Velitrium road he expected a run of some nine miles and set himself to the task. But he had not gone four when he heard the sounds of a party of men ahead of him. From the noise they were making in their progress he knew they were not Picts. He hailed them.

"Who's there?" challenged a harsh voice. "Stand where you are until we know you, or you'll get an arrow through you."

"You couldn't hit an elephant in this darkness," answered Conan impatiently. "Come on, fool; it's I — Conan. The Picts are over the river."

"We suspected as much," answered the leader of the men, as they strode forward — tall, rangy men, stern-faced, with bows in their hands. "One of our party wounded an antelope and tracked it nearly to Black River. He heard them yelling down the river and ran back to our camp. We left the salt and the wagons, turned the oxen loose and came as swiftly as we could. If the Picts are besieging the fort, war-parties will be ranging up the road toward our cabins."

"Your families are safe," grunted Conan. "My

companion went ahead to take them to Velitrium. If we go back to the main road we may run into the whole horde. We'll strike southeast, through the timber. Go ahead. I'll scout behind."

A few moments later the whole band was hurrying southeastward. Conan followed more slowly, keeping just within earshot. He cursed the noise they were making; that many Picts or Cimmerians would have moved through the woods with no more noise than the wind makes as it blows through the black branches.

He had just crossed a small glade when he wheeled, answering the conviction of his primitive instincts that he was being followed. Standing motionless among the bushes he heard the sounds of the retreating settlers fade away. Then a voice called faintly back along the way he had come: "Conan! Conan! Wait for me, Conan!"

"Balthus!" he swore bewilderedly. Cautiously he called: "Here I am!"

"Wait for me, Conan!" the voice came more distinctly.

Conan moved out of the shadows, scowling. "What the devil are you doing here? — *Crom!*"

He half-crouched, the flesh prickling along his spine. It was not Balthus who was emerging from the other side of the glade. A weird glow burned through the trees. It moved toward him, shimmering weirdly — a green witch-fire that moved with purpose and intent.

It halted some feet away and Conan glared at it, trying to distinguish its fire-misted outlines. The quivering flame had a solid core; the flame was but a green garment that masked some animate and evil entity; but the Cimmerian was unable to make out its shape or likeness. Then, shockingly, a voice spoke to him from amidst the fiery column.

"Why do you stand like a sheep waiting for the butcher, Conan?"

The voice was human but carried strange vibrations that were not human.

"Sheep?" Conan's wrath got the best of his momentary awe. "Do you think I'm afraid of a dammed Pictish swamp-devil? A friend called me."

"I called in his voice," answered the other. "The men you follow belong to my brother; I would not rob his knife of their blood. But you are mine. O fool, you have come from the far gray hills of Cimmeria to meet your doom in the forests of Conajohara."

"You've had your chance at me before now," snorted Conan. "Why didn't you kill me then, if you could?"

"My brother had not painted a skull black for you and hurled it into the fire that burns forever on Gullah's black altar. He had not whispered your name to the black ghosts that haunt the uplands of the Dark Land. But a bat has flown over the Mountains of the Dead and drawn your image in blood on the white tiger's hide that hangs before the long hut where sleep the Four Brothers of the Night. The great serpents coil about their feet and the stars burn like fireflies in their hair."

"Why have the gods of darkness doomed me to death?" growled Conan.

Something — a hand, foot or talon, he could not tell which, thrust out from the fire and marked swiftly on the mold. A symbol blazed there, marked with fire, and faded, but not before he recognized it.

"You dared make the sign which only a priest of Jhebbal Sag dare make. Thunder rumbled through the black Mountain of the Dead and the altar-hut of Gullah was thrown down by a wind from the Gulf of Ghosts. The loon which is messenger to the Four Brothers of the Night flew swiftly and whispered your name in my ear. Your race is run. You are a dead man already. Your head will hang in the altar-hut of my brother. Your body will be eaten by the black-winged, sharp-beaked Children of Jhil."

"Who the devil is your brother?" demanded Conan. His sword was naked in his hand, and he was subtly loosening the ax in his belt.

"Zogar Sag; a child of Jhebbal Sag who still visits his sacred groves at times. A woman of Gwawela slept in a grove holy to Jhebbal Sag. Her babe was Zogar Sag. I too am a son of Jhebbal Sag, out of a fire-being from a far realm. Zogar Sag summoned me out of the Misty Lands. With incantations and sorcery and his own blood he materialized me in the flesh of his own planet. We are one, tied together by invisible threads. His thoughts are my thoughts; if he is struck, I am bruised. If I am cut, he bleeds. But I have talked enough. Soon your ghost will talk with the ghosts of the Dark Land, and they will tell you of the old gods which are not dead, but sleep in the outer abysses, and from time to time awake."

"I'd like to see what you look like," muttered Conan, working his ax free, "you who leave a track like a bird, who burn like a flame and yet speak with a human voice."

"You shall see," answered the voice from the flame. "See, and carry the knowledge with you into the Dark Land."

The flames leaped and sank, dwindling and dimming. A face began to take shadowy form. At first Conan thought it was Zogar Sag himself who stood wrapped in green fire. But the face was higher than his own, and there was a demoniac aspect about it — Conan had noted various abnormalities about Zogar Sag's features — an obliqueness of the eyes, a sharpness of the ears, a wolfish thinness of the lips: these peculiarities were exaggerated in the apparition which swayed before him. The eyes were red as coals of living fire.

More details came into view: a slender torso, covered with snaky scales, which was yet manlike in shape, with manlike arms, from the waist upward; below, long crane-like legs ended in splay, three-toed feet like those of some huge bird. Along the monstrous limbs the blue fire fluttered and ran. He saw it as through a glistening mist.

Then suddenly it was towering over him, though he had not seen it move toward him. A long arm, which for the first time he noticed was armed with curving, sickle-like talons, swung high and swept down at his neck. With a fierce cry he broke the spell and bounded aside, hurling his ax. The demon avoided the cast with an unbelievably quick movement of its narrow head and was on him again with a hissing rush of leaping flames.

But fear had fought for it when it slew its other victims, and Conan was not afraid. He knew that any being clothed in material flesh can be slain by material weapons, however grisly its form may be.

One flailing talon-armed limb knocked his helmet from his head. A little lower and it would have decapitated him. But fierce joy surged through him as his savagely driven sword sank deep in the monster's groin. He bounded backward from a flailing stroke, tearing his sword free as he leaped. The talons raked his breast, ripping through mail-links as if they had been cloth. But his return spring was like that of a starving wolf. He was inside the lashing arms and driving his sword deep in the monster's belly — felt the arms lock about him and the talons ripping the mail from his back as they sought his vitals — he was lapped and dazzled by blue flame that was chill as ice — then he had torn fiercely away from the weakening arms and his sword cut the air in a tremendous swipe.

The demon staggered and fell sprawling sidewise, its head hanging only by a shred of flesh. The fires that veiled it leaped fiercely upward, now red as gushing blood, hiding the figure from view. A scent of burning flesh filled Conan's nostrils. Shaking the blood and sweat from his eyes, he wheeled and ran staggering through the woods. Blood trickled down his limbs. Somewhere, miles to the south, he saw the faint glow of flames that might mark a burning cabin. Behind him, toward the road, rose a distant howling that spurred him to greater efforts.

8. Conajohara No More

There had been fighting on Thunder River; fierce fighting before the walls of Velitrium; ax and torch had been plied up and down the bank, and many a settler's cabin lay in ashes before the painted horde was rolled back.

A strange quiet followed the storm, in which people gathered and talked in hushed voices, and men with red-stained bandages drank their ale silently in the taverns along the riverbank.

There, to Conan the Cimmerian, moodily quaffing from a great wine-glass, came a gaunt forester with a bandage about his head and his arm in a sling. He was the one survivor of Fort Tuscelan.

"You went with the soldiers to the ruins of the fort?"

Conan nodded.

"I wasn't able," murmured the other. "There was no fighting?"

"The Picts had fallen back across Black River. Something must have broken their nerve, though only the devil who made them knows what."

The woodsman glanced at his bandaged arm and sighed.

"They say there were no bodies worth disposing of."

Conan shook his head. "Ashes. The Picts had piled them in the fort and set fire to the fort before they crossed the river. Their own dead and the men of Valannus."

"Valannus was killed among the last — in the hand-to-hand fighting when they broke the barriers. They tried to take him alive, but he made them kill him. They took ten of the rest of us prisoners when we were so weak from fighting we could fight no more. They butchered nine of us then and there. It was when Zogar Sag died that I got my chance to break free and run for it."

"Zogar Sag's dead?" ejaculated Conan.

"Aye. I saw him die. That's why the Picts didn't press the fight against Velitrium as fiercely as they did against the fort. It was strange. He took no wounds in battle. He was dancing among the slain, waving an ax with which he'd just brained the last of my comrades. He came at me, howling like a wolf — and then he staggered and dropped the ax, and began to reel in a circle screaming as I never heard a man or beast scream before. He fell between me and the fire they'd built to roast me, gagging and frothing at the mouth, and all at once he went rigid and the Picts shouted that he was dead. It was during the confusion that I slipped my cords and ran for the woods.

"I saw him lying in the firelight. No weapon had touched him. Yet there were red marks like the wounds of a sword in the groin, belly and neck — the last as if his head had been almost severed from his body. What do you make of that?"

Conan made no reply, and the forester, aware of the reticence of barbarians on certain matters, continued: "He lived by magic, and somehow, he died by magic. It was the mystery of his death that took the heart out of the Picts. Not a man who saw it was in the fighting before Velitrium. They hurried back across Black River. Those that struck Thunder River were warriors who had come on before Zogar Sag died. They were not enough to take the city by themselves.

"I came along the road, behind their main force, and I know none followed me from the fort. I sneaked through their lines and got into the town. You brought the settlers through all right, but their women and children got into Velitrium just ahead of those painted devils. If the youth Balthus and old Slasher hadn't held them up awhile, they'd have butchered every woman and child in Conajohara. I passed the place where Balthus and the dog made their last stand. They were lying amid a heap of dead

Picts — I counted seven, brained by his ax, or disemboweled by the dog's fangs, and there were others in the road with arrows sticking in them. Gods, what a fight that must have been!"

"He was a man," said Conan. "I drink to his shade, and to the shade of the dog, who knew no fear." He quaffed part of the wine, then emptied the rest upon the floor, with a curious heathen gesture, and smashed the goblet. "The heads of ten Picts shall pay for his, and seven heads for the dog, who was a better warrior than many a man."

And the forester, staring into the moody, smoldering blue eyes, knew the barbaric oath would be kept.

"They'll not rebuild the fort?"

"No; Conajohara is lost to Aquilonia. The frontier has been pushed back. Thunder River will be the new border."

The woodsman sighed and stared at his callused hand, worn from contact with ax-haft and sword-hilt. Conan reached his long arm for the wine-jug. The forester stared at him, comparing him with the men about them, the men who had died along the lost river, comparing him with those other wild men over that river. Conan did not seem aware of his gaze.

"Barbarism is the natural state of mankind," the borderer said, still staring somberly at the Cimmerian. "Civilization is unnatural. It is a whim of circumstance. And barbarism must always ultimately triumph."

THE CHALLENGE FROM BEYOND

by C.L. Moore, A. Merritt, H.P. Lovecraft, Robert E. Howard and Frank Belknap Long

Fantasy Magazine, September 1935

George Campbell opened sleep-fogged eyes upon darkness and lay gazing out of the tent flap upon the pale August night for some minutes before he roused enough even to wonder what had wakened him. There was in the keen, clear air of these Canadian woods a soporific as potent as any drug. Campbell lay quiet for a moment, sinking slowly back into the delicious borderlands of sleep, conscious of an exquisite weariness, an unaccustomed sense of muscles well used, and relaxed now into perfect ease. These were vacation's most delightful moments, after all — rest, after toil, in the clear, sweet forest night.

Luxuriously, as his mind sank backward into oblivion, he assured himself once more that three long months of freedom lay before him — freedom from cities and monotony, freedom from pedagogy and the University and students with no rudiments of interest in the geology he earned his daily bread by dinning into their obdurate ears. Freedom from —

Abruptly the delightful somnolence crashed about him. Somewhere outside the sound of tin shrieking across tin slashed into his peace. George Campbell sat up jerkily and reached for his flashlight. Then he laughed and put it down again, straining his eyes through the midnight gloom outside where among the tumbling cans of his supplies a dark anonymous little night beast was prowling. He stretched out a long arm and groped about among the rocks at the tent door for a missile. His fingers closed on a large stone, and he drew back his hand to throw.

But he never threw it. It was such a queer thing he had come upon in the dark. Square, crystal smooth, obviously artificial, with dull, rounded corners. The strangeness of its rock surfaces to his fingers was so remarkable that he reached again for the flashlight and turned its rays upon the thing he held.

All sleepiness left him as he saw what it was he had picked up in his idle groping. It was clear as rock crystal, this queer, smooth cube. Quartz unquestionably, but not in its usual hexagonal crystallized form. Somehow — he could not guess the method — it had been wrought into a perfect cube, about four inches in measurement over each worn face. For it was incredibly worn. The hard, hard crystal was rounded now until its corners were almost gone and the thing was beginning to assume the outlines of a sphere.

Ages and ages of wearing, years almost beyond counting, must have passed over this strange clear thing.

But the most curious thing of all was that shape he could make out dimly in the heart of the crystal. For imbedded in its center lay a little disc of a pale and nameless substance with characters incised deep upon its quartz-enclosed surface. Wedge-shaped characters, faintly reminiscent of cuneiform writing.

George Campbell wrinkled his brows and bent closer above the little enigma in his hands, puzzling helplessly. How could such a thing as this have imbedded in pure rock crystal? Remotely a memory floated through his mind of ancient legends that called quartz crystals ice which had frozen too hard to melt again. Ice — and wedge-shaped cuneiforms — yes, didn't that sort of writing originate among the Sumerians who came down from the north in history's remotest beginnings to settle in the primitive Mesopotamian valley? Then hard sense regained control and he laughed. Quartz, of course, was formed in the earliest of earth's geological periods, when there was nothing anywhere but heat and heaving rock. Ice had not come for tens of millions of years after this thing he held must have been formed.

And yet — that writing. Man-made, surely, although its characters were unfamiliar save in their faint hinting at cuneiform shapes. Or could there, in a Paleozoic world, have been things with a written language who might have graven these cryptic wedges upon the quartz-enveloped disc he held? Or — might a thing like this have fallen meteor-like out of space into the unformed rock of a still molten world? Could it —

Then he caught himself up sharply and felt his ears going hot at the luridness of his own imagination. The silence and the solitude and the queer thing in his hands were conspiring to play tricks with his common sense. He shrugged and laid the crystal down at the edge of his pallet, switching off the light. Perhaps morning and a clear head would bring him an answer to the questions that seemed so insoluble now.

But sleep did not come easily. For one thing, it seemed to him as he flashed off the light, that the little cube had shone for a moment as if with retained light before it faded into the surrounding dark. Or perhaps he was wrong. Perhaps it had been only his dazzled eyes that seemed to see the light forsake it reluctantly, glowing in the enigmatic deeps of the thing with queer persistence.

He lay there unquietly for a long while, turning the unanswered questions over and over in his mind. There was something about this crystal cube out of the unmeasured past, perhaps from the dawn of all history, that constituted a challenge that would not let him sleep.

He lay there it seemed to him for hours. It had been the lingering light, the luminescence that seemed so reluctant to die, which held his mind. It was as though something in the heart of the cube had awakened, stirred drowsily, become suddenly alert . . . and intent upon him.

Sheer fantasy, this. He stirred impatiently and flashed his light upon his watch. Close to one o'clock; three hours more before the dawn. The beam fell and was focused upon the warm crystal cube. He held it there closely, for minutes. He snapped it out, then watched.

There was no doubt about it now. As his eyes accustomed themselves to the darkness, he saw that the strange crystal was glimmering with tiny fugitive lights deep within it like threads of sapphire lightnings. They were at its center, and they seemed to him to come from the pale disc with its disturbing markings. And the disc itself was becoming larger. . . the markings shifting shapes . . . the cube was growing . . . was it illusion brought about by the tiny lightnings . . . .

He heard a sound. It was the very ghost of a sound, like the ghosts of harp strings being plucked with ghostly fingers. He bent closer. It came from the cube . . . .

There was squeaking in the underbrush, a flurry of bodies and an agonized wailing like a child in death throes and swiftly stilled. Some small tragedy of the wilderness, killer and prey. He stepped over to where it had been enacted, but could see nothing. He again snapped off the flash and looked toward his tent. Upon the ground was a pale blue glimmering. It was the cube. He stooped to pick it up; then obeying some obscure warning, drew back his hand.

And again, he saw, its glow was dying. The tiny sapphire lightnings flashing fitfully, withdrawing to the disc from which they had come. There was no sound from it.

He sat, watching the luminescence glow and fade, glow and fade, but steadily becoming dimmer. It came to him that two elements were necessary to produce the phenomenon. The electric ray itself, and his own fixed attention. His mind must travel along the ray, fix itself upon the cube's heart, if its beat were to wax, until . . . what?

He felt a chill of spirit, as though from contact with some alien thing. It was alien, he knew it; not of this earth. Not of earth's life. He conquered his shrinking, picked up the cube and took it into the tent. It was neither warm nor cold; except for its weight he would not have known he held it. He put it upon the table, keeping the torch turned from it; then stepped to the flap of the tent and closed it.

He went back to the table, drew up the camp chair, and turned the flash directly upon the cube, focusing it so far as he could upon its heart. He sent all his will, all his concentration, along it; focusing will and sight upon the disc as he had the light.

As though at command, the sapphire lightnings burned forth. They burst from the disc into the body of the crystal cube, then beat back, bathing the disc and the markings. Again these began to change, shifting, moving, advancing, and retreating in the blue gleaming. They were no longer writings, no longer cuneiform shapes. They were things . . . objects.

He heard the murmuring music, the plucked harp strings. Louder grew the sound and louder, and now all the body of the cube vibrated to their rhythm. The crystal walls were melting, growing misty as though formed of the mist of diamonds. And the disc itself was growing . . . the shapes shifting, dividing and multiplying as though some door had been opened and into it companies of phantasms were pouring. While brighter, more bright grew the pulsing light.

He felt swift panic, tried to withdraw sight and will, dropped the flash. The cube had no need now of the ray . . . and he could not withdraw . . . could not withdraw? Why, he himself was being sucked into that disc which was now a globe within which unnameable shapes danced to an alien music. And the lightnings had stilled and had become sapphire suns that bathed the globe with steady radiance.

There was no tent. There was only a vast curtain of sparkling mist behind which shone the globe . . . .

He felt himself drawn through that mist, sucked through it as if by a mighty wind, straight for the globe.

As the mist-blurred light of the sapphire suns grew more and more intense, the outlines of the globe ahead wavered and dissolved to a churning chaos. Its pallor and its motion and its music all blended themselves with the engulfing mist — bleaching it to a pale steel-colour and setting it undulantly in motion. And the sapphire suns, too, melted imperceptibly into the greying infinity of shapeless pulsation.

Meanwhile the sense of forward, outward motion grew intolerably, incredibly, cosmically swift. Every standard of speed known to earth seemed dwarfed, and Campbell knew that any such flight in physical reality would mean instant death to a human being. Even as it was — in this strange, hellish hypnosis or nightmare — the quasi-visual impression of meteor-like hurtling almost unhinged his mind. Though there were no real points of reference in the grey, pulsing, void, he felt that he was approaching and passing the speed of light itself. Finally his consciousness did go under — and merciful blackness swallowed everything.

It was very suddenly, and amidst the most impenetrable darkness, that thoughts and ideas again came to George Campbell. Of how many moments — or years — or eternities — had elapsed since his flight through the grey void, he could form no estimate. He knew only that he seemed to be at rest and without pain. Indeed, the absence of all physical sensation was the salient quality of his condition. It made even the blackness seem less solidly black — suggesting as it did that he was rather a disembodied intelligence in a state beyond physical senses, than a corporeal being with senses deprived of their accustomed objects of perception. He could think sharply and quickly — almost preternaturally so — yet could form no idea whatsoever of his situation.

Half by instinct, he realised that he was not in his own tent. True, he might have awaked there from a nightmare to a world equally black; yet he knew this was not so. There was no camp cot beneath him — he had no hands to feel the blankets and canvas surface and flashlight that ought to be around him — there was no sensation of cold in the air — no flap through which he could glimpse the pale night outside . . . something was wrong, dreadfully wrong.

He cast his mind backward and thought of the fluorescent cube which had hypnotised him — of that, and all which had followed. He had known that his mind was going, yet had been unable to draw back. At the last moment there had been a shocking, panic fear — a subconscious fear beyond even that caused by the sensation of daemonic flight. It had come from some vague flash or remote recollection — just what, he could not at once tell. Some cell-group in the back of his head had seemed to find a cloudily familiar quality in the cube — and that familiarity was fraught with dim terror. Now he tried to remember what the familiarity and the terror were.

Little by little it came to him. Once — long ago, in connection with his geological life-work — he had read of something like that cube. It had to do with those debatable and disquieting clay fragments called the Eltdown Shards, dug up from pre-carboniferous strata in southern England thirty years before. Their shape and markings were so queer that a few scholars hinted at artificiality, and made wild conjectures about them and their origin. They came, clearly, from a time when no human beings could exist on the globe — but their contours and figurings were damnably puzzling. That was how they got their name.

It was not, however, in the writings of any sober scientist that Campbell had seen that reference to a crystal, disc-holding globe. The source was far less reputable, and infinitely more vivid. About 1912 a deeply learned Sussex clergyman of occultist leanings — the Reverend Arthur Brooke Winters-Hall — had professed to identify the markings on the Eltdown Shards with some of the so-called "pre-human hieroglyphs" persistently cherished and esoterically handed down in certain mystical circles, and had published at his own expense what purported to be a "translation" of the primal and baffling "inscriptions" — a "translation" still quoted frequently and seriously by occult writers. In this "translation" — a surprisingly long brochure in view of the limited number of "shards" existing — had occurred the narrative, supposedly of pre-human authorship, containing the now frightening reference.

As the story went, there dwelt on a world — and eventually on countless other worlds — of outer space a mighty order of worm-like beings whose attainments and whose control of nature surpassed anything within the range of terrestrial imagination. They had mastered the art of interstellar travel early in their career, and had peopled every habitable planet in their own galaxy — killing off the races they found.

Beyond the limits of their own galaxy — which was not ours — they could not navigate in person; but in their quest for knowledge of all space and time they discovered a means of spanning certain trans-galactic gulfs with their minds. They devised peculiar objects — strangely energized cubes of a curious crystal containing hypnotic talismans and enclosed in space-resisting spherical envelopes of an unknown substance — which could be forcibly expelled beyond the limits of their universe, and which would respond to the attraction of cool solid matter only.

These, of which a few would necessarily land on various inhabited worlds in outside universes, formed the ether-bridges needed for mental communication. Atmospheric friction burned away the protecting envelope, leaving the cube exposed and subject to discovery by the intelligent minds of the world where it fell. By its very nature, the cube would attract and rivet attention. This, when coupled with the action of light, was sufficient to set its special properties working.

The mind that noticed the cube would be drawn into it by the power of the disc, and would be sent on a thread of obscure energy to the place whence the disc had come — the remote world of the worm-like space-explorers across stupendous galactic abysses. Received in one of the machines to which each cube was attuned, the captured mind would remain suspended without body or senses until examined by one of the dominant race. Then it would, by an obscure process of interchange, be pumped of all its contents. The investigator's mind would now occupy the strange machine while the captive mind occupied the interrogator's worm-like body. Then, in another interchange, the interrogator's mind would leap across boundless space to the captive's vacant and unconscious body on the trans-galactic world — animating the alien tenement as best it might, and exploring the alien world in the guise of one of its denizens.

When done with exploration, the adventurer would use the cube and its disc in accomplishing his return — and sometimes the captured mind would be restored safely to its own remote world. Not always, however, was the dominant race so kind. Sometimes, when a potentially important race capable of space travel was found, the worm-like folk would employ the cube to capture and annihilate minds by the thousands, and would extirpate the race for diplomatic reasons — using the exploring minds as agents of destruction.

In other cases sections of the worm-folk would permanently occupy a trans-galactic planet — destroying the captured minds and wiping out the remaining inhabitants preparatory to settling down in unfamiliar bodies. Never, however, could the parent civilization be quite duplicated in such a case; since the new planet would not contain all the materials necessary for the worm-race's arts. The cubes, for example, could be made only on the home planet.

Only a few of the numberless cubes sent forth ever found a landing and response on an inhabited world — since there was no such thing as *aiming* them at goals beyond sight or knowledge. Only three, ran the story, had ever landed on peopled worlds in our own particular universe. One of these had struck a planet near the galactic rim two thousand billion years ago, whilst another had lodged three billion years ago on a world near the centre of the galaxy. The third — and the only one ever known to have invaded the solar system — had reached our own earth 150,000,000 years ago.

It was with this latter that Dr. Winters-Hall's "translation" chiefly dealt. When the cube struck the earth, he wrote, the ruling terrestrial species was a huge, cone-shaped race surpassing all others before or since in mentality and achievements. This race was so advanced that it had actually sent minds abroad in both space *and time* to explore the cosmos, hence recognised something of what had happened when the cube fell from the sky and certain individuals had suffered mental change after gazing at it.

Realizing that the changed individuals represented invading minds, the race's leaders had them destroyed — even at the cost of leaving the displaced minds exiled in alien space. They had had experience with even stranger transitions. When, through a mental exploration of space and time, they formed a rough idea of what the cube was, they carefully hid the thing from light and sight, and guarded it as a menace. They did not wish to destroy a thing so rich in later experimental possibilities. Now and then some rash, unscrupulous adventurer would furtively gain access to it and sample its perilous powers despite the consequences — but all such cases were discovered, and safely and drastically dealt with.

Of this evil meddling the only bad result was that the worm-like outside race learned from the new exiles what had happened to their explorers on earth, and conceived a violent hatred of the planet and all its life-forms. They would have depopulated it if they could, and indeed sent additional cubes into space in the wild hope of striking it by accident in unguarded places — but that accident never came to pass.

The cone-shaped terrestrial beings kept the one existing cube in a special shrine as a relique and basis for experiments, till after aeons it was lost amidst the chaos of war and the destruction of the great polar city where it was guarded. When, fifty million years ago, the beings sent their minds ahead into the infinite future to avoid a nameless peril of inner earth, the whereabouts of the sinister cube from space were unknown.

This much, according to the learned occultist, the

Eltdown Shards had said. What now made the account so obscurely frightful to Campbell was the minute accuracy with which the alien cube had been described. Every detail tallied — dimensions, consistency, heiroglyphed central disc, hypnotic effects. As he thought the matter over and over amidst the darkness of his strange situation, he began to wonder whether his whole experience with the crystal cube — indeed, its very existence — were not a nightmare brought on by some freakish subconscious memory of this old bit of extravagant, charlatanic reading. If so, though, the nightmare must still be in force; since his present apparently bodiless state had nothing of normality in it.

Of the time consumed by this puzzled memory and reflection, Campbell could form no estimate. Everything about his state was so unreal that ordinary dimensions and measurements became meaningless. It seemed an eternity, but perhaps it was not really long before the sudden interruption came. What happened was as strange and inexplicable as the blackness it succeeded. There was a sensation — of the mind rather than of the body — and all at once Campbell felt his thoughts swept or sucked beyond his control in tumultuous and chaotic fashion.

Memories arose irresponsibly and irrelevantly. All that he knew — all his personal background, traditions, experiences, scholarship, dreams, ideas, and inspirations — welled up abruptly and simultaneously, with a dizzying speed and abundance which soon made him unable to keep track of any separate concept. The parade of all his mental contents became an avalanche, a cascade, a vortex. It was as horrible and vertiginous as his hypnotic flight through space when the crystal cube pulled him. Finally it sapped his consciousness and brought on fresh oblivion.

Another measureless blank — and then a slow trickle of sensation. This time it was physical, not mental. Sapphire light, and a low rumble of distant sound. There were tactile impressions — he could realize that he was lying at full length on something, though there was a baffling strangeness about the feel of his posture. He could not reconcile the pressure of the supporting surface with his own outlines — or with the outlines of the human form at all. He tried to move his arms, but found no definite response to the attempt. Instead, there were little, ineffectual nervous twitches all over the area which seemed to mark his body.

He tried to open his eyes more widely, but found himself unable to control their mechanism. The sapphire light came in a diffused, nebulous manner, and could nowhere be voluntarily focused into definiteness. Gradually, though, visual images began to trickle in curiously and indecisively. The limits and qualities of vision were not those which he was used to, but he could roughly correlate the sensation with what he had known as sight. As this sensation gained some degree of stability, Campbell realised that he must still be in the throes of nightmare.

He seemed to be in a room of considerable extent — of medium height, but with a large proportionate area. On every side — and he could apparently see all four sides at once — were high, narrowish slits which seemed to serve as combined doors and windows. There were singular low tables or pedestals, but no furniture of normal nature and proportions. Through the slits streamed floods of sapphire light, and beyond them could be mistily seen the sides and roofs of fantastic buildings like clustered cubes. On the walls — in the vertical panels between the slits — were strange markings of an oddly disquieting character. It was some time before Campbell understood why they disturbed him so — then he saw that they were, in repeated instances, precisely like some of the hieroglyphs on the crystal cube's disc.

The actual nightmare element, though, was something more than this. It began with the living thing which presently entered through one of the slits, advancing deliberately toward him and bearing a metal box of bizarre proportions and glassy, mirror-like surfaces. For this thing was nothing human — nothing of earth — nothing even of man's myths and dreams. It was a gigantic, pale-grey worm or centipede, as large around as a man and twice as long, with a disc-like, apparently eyeless, cilia-fringed head bearing a purple central orifice. It glided on its rear pairs of legs, with its fore part raised vertically — the legs, or at least two pairs of them, there serving as arms. Along its spinal ridge was a curious purple comb, and a fan-shaped tail of some grey membrane ended its grotesque bulk. There was a ring of flexible red spikes around its neck, and from the twistings of these came clicking, twanging sounds in measured, deliberate rhythms.

Here, indeed, was outre nightmare at its height — capricious fantasy at its apex. But even this vision of delirium was not what caused George Campbell to lapse a third time into unconsciousness. It took one more thing — one final, unbearable touch — to do that. As the nameless worm advanced with its glistening box, the reclining man caught in the mirror-like surface a glimpse of what should have been his own body. Yet — horribly verifying his disordered and unfamiliar sensations — it was not his own body at all that he saw reflected in the burnished metal. It was, instead, the loathsome, pale-grey bulk of one of the great centipedes.

From that final lap of senselessness, he emerged with a full understanding of his situation. His mind was imprisoned in the body of a frightful native of an alien planet, while, somewhere on the other side of the universe, his own body was housing the monster's personality.

He fought down an unreasoning horror. Judged from a cosmic standpoint, why should his metamorphosis horrify him? Life and consciousness were the only realities in the universe. *Form* was unimportant. His present body was hideous only according to terrestrial standards. Fear and revulsion were drowned in the excitement of titanic adventure.

What was his former body but a cloak, eventually to be cast off at death anyway? He had no sentimental illusions about the life from which he had been exiled. What had it ever given him save toil, poverty, continual frustration and repression? If this life before him offered no more, at least it offered no less. Intuition told him it offered more — much more.

With the honesty possible only when life is stripped to its naked fundamentals, he realized that he remembered with pleasure only the physical delights of his former life. But he had long ago exhausted all the physical possibilities contained in that earthly body. Earth held no new thrills. But in the possession of this new, alien body he felt promises of strange, exotic joys.

A lawless exultation rose in him. He was a man without a world, free of all conventions or inhibitions of Earth, or of this strange planet, free of every artificial restraint in the universe. He was a god! With grim amusement he thought of his body moving in earth's business and society, with all the while an alien monster staring out of the windows that were George Campbell's eyes on people who would flee if they knew.

Let him walk the earth slaying and destroying as

he would. Earth and its races no longer had any meaning to George Campbell. There he had been one of a billion nonentities, fixed in place by a mountainous accumulation of conventions, laws and manners, doomed to live and die in his sordid niche. But in one blind bound he had soared above the commonplace. This was not death, but re-birth — the birth of a full-grown mentality, with a new-found freedom that made little of physical captivity on Yekub.

He started. Yekub! It was the name of this planet, but how had he known? Then he knew, as he knew the name of him whose body he occupied — Tothe. Memory, deep grooved in Tothe's brain, was stirring in him — shadows of the knowledge Tothe had. Carved deep in the physical tissues of the brain, they spoke dimly as implanted instincts to George Campbell; and his human consciousness seized them and translated them to show him the way not only to safety and freedom, but to the power his soul, stripped to its primitive impulses, craved. Not as a slave would he dwell on Yekub, but as a king! Just as of old barbarians had sat on the throne of lordly empires.

For the first time he turned his attention to his surroundings. He still lay on the couch-like thing in the midst of that fantastic room, and the centipede man stood before him, holding the polished metal object, and clashing its neck-spikes. Thus it spoke to him, Campbell knew, and what it said he dimly understood, through the implanted thought processes of Tothe, just as he knew the creature was Yukth, supreme lord of science.

But Campbell gave no heed, for he had made his desperate plan, a plan so alien to the ways of Yekub that it was beyond Yukth's comprehension and caught him wholly unprepared. Yukth, like Campbell, saw the sharp-pointed metal shard on a nearby table, but to Yukth it was only a scientific implement. He did not even know it could be used as a weapon. Campbell's earthly mind supplied the knowledge and the action that followed, driving Tothe's body into movements no man of Yekub had ever made before.

Campbell snatched the pointed shard and struck, ripping savagely upward. Yukth reared and toppled, his entrails spilling on the floor. In an instant Campbell was streaking for a door. His speed was amazing, exhilarating, first fulfillment of the promise of novel physical sensations.

As he ran, guided wholly by the instinctive knowledge implanted in Tothe's physical reflexes, it was as if he were borne by a separate consciousness in his legs. Tothe's body was bearing him along a route it had traversed ten thousand times when animated by Tothe's mind.

Down a winding corridor he raced, up a twisted stair, through a carved door, and the same instincts that had brought him there told him he had found what he sought. He was in a circular room with a domed roof from which shone a livid blue light. A strange structure rose in the middle of the rainbow-hued floor, tier on tier, each of a separate, vivid color. The ultimate tier was a purple cone, from the apex of which a blue smoky mist drifted upward to a sphere that poised in mid-air — a sphere that shone like translucent ivory.

This, the deep-grooved memories of Tothe told Campbell, was the god of Yekub, though why the people of Yekub feared and worshipped it had been forgotten a million years. A worm-priest stood between him and the altar which no hand of flesh had ever touched. That it could be touched was a blasphemy that had never occurred to a man of Yekub. The worm-priest stood in frozen horror until Campbell's shard ripped the life out of him.

On his centipede-legs Campbell clambered the tiered altar, heedless of its sudden quiverings, heedless of the change that was taking place in the floating sphere, heedless of the smoke that now billowed out in blue clouds. He was drunk with the feel of power. He feared the superstitions of Yekub no more than he feared those of earth. With that globe in his hands he would be king of Yekub. The worm men would dare deny him nothing, when he held their god as hostage. He reached a hand for the ball — no longer ivory-hued, but red as blood. . . .

Out of the tent into the pale August night walked the body of George Campbell. It moved with a slow, wavering gait between the bodies of enormous trees, over a forest path strewed with sweet scented pine needles. The air was crisp and cold. The sky was an inverted bowl of frosted silver flecked with stardust, and far to the north the Aurora Borealis splashed streamers of fire.

The head of the walking man lolled hideously from side to side. From the corners of his lax mouth drooled thick threads of amber froth, which fluttered in the night breeze. He walked upright at first, as a man would walk, but gradually as the tent receded, his posture altered. His torso began almost imperceptibly to slant, and his limbs to shorten.

In a far-off world of outer space the centipede creature that was George Campbell clasped to its bosom a god whose lineaments were red as blood, and ran with insect-like quiverings across a rainbow-hued hall and out through massive portals into the bright glow of alien suns.

Weaving between the trees of earth in an attitude that suggested the awkward loping of a werebeast, the body of George Campbell was fulfilling a mindless destiny. Long, claw-tipped fingers dragged leaves from a carpet of odorous pine-needles as it moved toward a wide expanse of gleaming water.

In the far-off, extra-galactic world of the worm people, George Campbell moved between cyclopean blocks of black masonry down long, fern-planted avenues holding aloft the round red god.

There was a harsh animal cry in the underbrush near the gleaming lake on earth where the mind of a worm creature dwelt in a body swayed by instinct. Human teeth sank into soft animal fur, tore at black animal flesh. A little silver fox sank its fangs in frantic retaliation into a furry human wrist, and thrashed about in terror as its blood spurted. Slowly the body of George Campbell arose, its mouth splashed with fresh blood. With upper limbs swaying oddly it moved towards the waters of the lake.

As the veriform creature that was George Campbell crawled between the black blocks of stone thousands of worm-shapes prostrated themselves in the scintillating dust before it. A godlike power seemed to emanate from its weaving body as it moved with a slow, undulant motion toward a throne of spiritual empire transcending all the sovereignties of earth.

A trapper stumbling wearily through the dense woods of earth near the tent where the worm-creature dwelt in the body of George Campbell came to the gleaming waters of the lake and discerned something dark floating there. He had been lost in the woods all night, and weariness enveloped him like a leaden cloak in the pale morning light.

But the shape was a challenge that he could not ignore. Moving to the edge of the water he knelt in the soft mud and reached out toward the floating bulk. Slowly he pulled it to the shore.

Far off in outer space the worm-creature holding the glowing red god ascended a throne that gleamed like the constellation Cassiopeia under an alien vault of hyper-suns. The great deity that he held aloft energized his worm tenement, burning away in the white fire of a supermundane spirituality all animal dross.

On earth the trapper gazed with unutterable horror into the blackened and hairy face of the drowned man. It was a bestial face, repulsively anthropoid in contour, and from its twisted, distorted mouth black ichor poured.

George Campbell felt the round red god stir in his embrace. Vibrations flowed from it and as George Campbell sat enthroned, feeling the glow of empire in all his segments, Yekub's great deity spoke to him in accents that pulsed coolly through the corridors of his brain.

"He who sought your body in the abysses of Time will occupy an unresponsive tenement," said the red god. "No spawn of Yekub can control the body of a human.

"On all earth, living creatures rend one another, and feast with unutterable cruelty on their kith and kin. No worm-mind can control a bestial man-body when it yearns to raven. Only man-minds instinctively conditioned through the course of ten thousand generations can keep the human instincts in thrall. Your body will destroy itself on earth, seeking the blood of its animal kin, seeking the cool water where it can wallow at its ease. Seeking eventually destruction, for the death-instinct is more powerful in it than the instincts of life and it will destroy itself in seeking to return to the slime from which it sprang."

Thus spoke the round red god of Yekub in a far-off segment of the space-time continuum to George Campbell as the latter, with all human desire purged away, sat on a throne and ruled an empire of worms more wisely, kindly, and benevolently than any man of earth had ever ruled an empire of men.

SHADOWS IN ZAMBOULA

Weird Tales, November 1935

1. A Drum Begins

"Peril hides in the house of Aram Baksh!"

The speaker's voice quivered with earnestness and his lean, black-nailed fingers clawed at Conan's mightily-muscled arm as he croaked his warning. He was a wiry, sun-burnt man with a straggling black beard, and his ragged garments proclaimed him a nomad. He looked smaller and meaner than ever in contrast to the giant Cimmerian with his black brows, broad chest, and powerful limbs. They stood in a corner of the Sword-Makers' Bazar, and on either side of them flowed past the many-tongued, many-colored stream of the Zamboula streets, which is exotic, hybrid, flamboyant and clamorous.

Conan pulled his eyes back from following a bold-eyed, red-lipped Ghanara whose short slit skirt bared her brown thigh at each insolent step, and frowned down at his importunate companion.

"What do you mean by peril?" he demanded.

The desert man glanced furtively over his shoulder before replying, and lowered his voice.

"Who can say? But desert men and travelers *have* slept in the house of Aram Baksh, and never been seen or heard of again. What became of them? *He* swore they rose and went their way — and it is truth that no citizen of the city has ever disappeared from his house. But no one saw the travelers again, and men say that goods and equipment recognized as theirs have been seen in the bazars. If Aram did not sell them, after doing away with their owners, how came they there?"

"I have no goods," growled the Cimmerian, touching the shagreen-bound hilt of the broadsword that hung at his hip. "I have even sold my horse."

"But it is not always rich strangers who vanish by night from the house of Aram Baksh!" chattered the Zuagir. "Nay, poor desert men have slept there — because his score is less than that of the other taverns — and have been seen no more. Once a chief of the Zuagirs whose son had thus vanished complained to the satrap, Jungir Khan, who ordered the house searched by soldiers."

"And they found a cellar full of corpses?" asked Conan in good-humored derision.

"Nay! They found naught! And drove the chief from the city with threats and curses! But" — he drew closer to Conan and shivered — "something else was found! At the edge of the desert, beyond the houses, there is a clump of palm trees, and within that grove there is a pit. And within that pit have been found human bones, charred and blackened!

Not once, but many times!"

"Which proves what?" grunted the Cimmerian.

"Aram Baksh is a demon! Nay, in this accursed city which Stygians built and which Hyrkanians rule — where white, brown and black folk mingle together to produce hybrids of all unholy hues and breeds — who can tell who is a man, and who a demon in disguise? Aram Baksh is a demon in the form of a man! At night he assumes his true guise and carries his guests off into the desert where his fellow demons from the waste meet in conclave."

"Why does he always carry off strangers?" asked Conan skeptically.

"The people of the city would not suffer him to slay their people, but they care naught for the strangers who fall into his hands. Conan, you are of the West, and know not the secrets of this ancient land. But, since the beginning of happenings, the demons of the desert have worshipped Yog, the Lord of the Empty Abodes, with fire — fire that devours human victims.

"Be warned! You have dwelt for many moons in the tents of the Zuagirs, and you are our brother! Go not to the house of Aram Baksh!"

"Get out of sight!" Conan said suddenly. "Yonder comes a squad of the city-watch. If they see you they may remember a horse that was stolen from the satrap's stable —"

The Zuagir gasped, and moved convulsively. He ducked between a booth and a stone horse-trough, pausing only long enough to chatter: "Be warned, my brother! There are demons in the house of Aram Baksh!" Then he darted down a narrow alley and was gone.

Conan shifted his broad sword-belt to his liking, and calmly returned the searching stares directed at him by the squad of watchmen as they swung past. They eyed him curiously and suspiciously, for he was a man who stood out even in such a motley throng as crowded the winding streets of Zamboula. His blue eyes and alien features distinguished him from the Eastern swarms, and the straight sword at his hip added point to the racial difference.

The watchmen did not accost him, but swung on down the street, while the crowd opened a lane for them. They were Pelishtim, squat, hook-nosed, with blue-black beards sweeping their mailed breasts — mercenaries hired for work the ruling Turanians considered beneath themselves, and no less hated by the mongrel population for that reason.

Conan glanced at the sun, just beginning to dip behind the flat-topped houses on the western side of the bazar, and hitching once more at his belt, moved off in the direction of Aram Baksh's tavern.

With a hillman's stride he moved through the ever-shifting colors of the streets, where the ragged tunics of whining beggars brushed against the ermine-trimmed khalats of lordly merchants, and pearl-sewn satin of rich courtesans. Giant black slaves slouched along, jostling blue-bearded wanderers from the Shemitish cities, ragged nomads from the surrounding deserts, traders and adventurers from all the lands of the East.

The native population was no less heterogeneous. Here, centuries ago, the armies of Stygia had come, carving an empire out of the eastern desert. Zamboula was but a small trading-town then, lying amidst a ring of oases, and inhabited by descendants of nomads. The Stygians built it into a city and settled it with their own people, and with Shemite and Kushite slaves. The ceaseless caravans, threading the desert from east to west and back again, brought riches and more mingling of races. Then came the conquering Turanians, riding out of the East to thrust back the boundaries of Stygia, and now for a generation Zamboula had been Turan's westernmost outpost, ruled by a Turanian satrap.

The babel of a myriad of tongues smote on the Cimmerian's ears as the restless pattern of the Zamboula streets weaved about him — cleft now and then by a squad of clattering horsemen, the tall, supple warriors of Turan, with dark hawk-faces, clinking metal and curved swords. The throng scampered from under their horses' hoofs, for they were the lords of Zamboula. But tall, somber Stygians, standing back in the shadows, glowered darkly, remembering their ancient glories. The hybrid population cared little whether the king who controlled their destinies dwelt in dark Khemi or gleaming Aghrapur. Jungir Khan ruled Zamboula, and men whispered that Nafertari, the satrap's mistress, ruled Jungir Khan; but the people went their way, flaunting their myriad colors in the streets, bargaining, disputing, gambling, swilling, loving, as the people of Zamboula have done for all the centuries its towers and minarets have lifted over the sands of the Kharamun.

Bronze lanterns, carved with leering dragons, had been lighted in the streets before Conan reached the house of Aram Baksh. The tavern was the last occupied house on the street, which ran west. A wide garden, enclosed by a wall, where date-palms grew thick, separated it from the houses farther east. To the west of the inn stood another grove of palms, through which the street, now become a road, wound out into the desert. Across the road from the tavern stood a row of deserted huts, shaded by straggling palm trees, and occupied only by bats and jackals. As Conan came down the road he wondered why the beggars, so plentiful in Zamboula, had not appropriated these empty houses for sleeping-quarters. The lights ceased some distance behind him. Here were no lanterns, except the one hanging before the tavern gate: only the stars, the soft dust of the road underfoot, and the rustle of the palm-leaves in the desert breeze.

Aram's gate did not open upon the road, but upon the alley which ran between the tavern and the garden of the date-palms. Conan jerked lustily at the rope which depended from the bell beside the lantern, augmenting its clamor by hammering on the iron-bound teakwood gate with the hilt of his sword. A wicket opened in the gate and a black face peered through.

"Open, blast you," requested Conan. "I'm a guest. I've paid Aram for a room, and a room I'll have, by Crom!"

The black craned his neck to stare into the starlit road behind Conan; but he opened the gate without comment, closed it again behind the Cimmerian, locking it and bolting it. The wall was unusually high; but there were many thieves in Zamboula, and a house on the edge of the desert might have to be defended against a nocturnal nomad raid. Conan strode through a garden where great pale blossoms nodded in the starlight, and entered the taproom, where a Stygian with the shaven head of a student sat at a table brooding over nameless mysteries, and some nondescripts wrangled over a game of dice in a corner.

Aram Baksh came forward, walking softly, a portly man, with a black beard that swept his breast, a jutting hook-nose, and small black eyes which were never still.

"You wish food?" he asked. "Drink?"

"I ate a joint of beef and a loaf of bread in the *suk*," grunted Conan. "Bring me a tankard of Ghazan wine — I've got just enough left to pay for it." He tossed a copper coin on the wine-splashed board.

"You did not win at the gaming-tables?"

"How could I, with only a handful of silver to begin with? I paid you for the room this morning, because I knew I'd probably lose. I wanted to be sure I had a roof over my head tonight. I notice nobody sleeps in the streets in Zamboula. The very beggars hunt a niche they can barricade before dark. The city must be full of a particularly bloodthirsty brand of thieves."

He gulped the cheap wine with relish, and then followed Aram out of the taproom. Behind him the players halted their game to stare after him with a cryptic speculation in their eyes. They said nothing, but the Stygian laughed, a ghastly laugh of inhuman cynicism and mockery. The others lowered their eyes uneasily, avoiding one another's glance. The arts studied by a Stygian scholar are not calculated to make him share the feelings of a normal human being.

Conan followed Aram down a corridor lighted by copper lamps, and it did not please him to note his host's noiseless tread. Aram's feet were clad in soft slippers and the hallway was carpeted with thick Turanian rugs; but there was an unpleasant suggestion of stealthiness about the Zamboulan.

At the end of the winding corridor Aram halted at a door, across which a heavy iron bar rested in powerful metal brackets. This Aram lifted and showed the Cimmerian into a well-appointed chamber, the windows of which, Conan instantly noted, were small and strongly set with twisted bars of iron, tastefully gilded. There were rugs on the floor, a couch, after the Eastern fashion, and ornately carven stools. It was a much more elaborate chamber than Conan could have procured for the price nearer the center of the city — a fact that had first attracted him, when, that morning, he discovered how slim a purse his roisterings for the past few days had left him. He had ridden into Zamboula from the desert a week before.

Aram had lighted a bronze lamp, and he now called Conan's attention to the two doors. Both were provided with heavy bolts.

"You may sleep safely tonight, Cimmerian," said Aram, blinking over his bushy beard from the inner doorway.

Conan grunted and tossed his naked broadsword on the couch.

"Your bolts and bars are strong; but I always sleep with steel by my side."

Aram made no reply; he stood fingering his thick beard for a moment as he stared at the grim weapon. Then silently he withdrew, closing the door behind him. Conan shot the bolt into place, crossed the room, opened the opposite door and looked out. The room was on the side of the house that faced the road running west from the city. The door opened into a small court that was enclosed by a wall of its own. The end-walls, which shut it off from the rest of the tavern compound, were high and without entrances; but the wall that flanked the road was low, and there was no lock on the gate.

Conan stood for a moment in the door, the glow of the bronze lamp behind him, looking down the road to where it vanished among the dense palms. Their leaves rustled together in the faint breeze; beyond them lay the naked desert. Far up the street, in the other direction, lights gleamed and the noises of the city came faintly to him. Here was only starlight, the whispering of the palm-leaves, and beyond that low wall, the dust of the road and the deserted huts thrusting their flat roofs against the low stars. Somewhere beyond the palm groves a drum began.

The garbled warnings of the Zuagir returned to him, seeming somehow less fantastic than they had seemed in the crowded, sunlit streets. He wondered again at the riddle of those empty huts. Why did the beggars shun them? He turned back into the chamber, shut the door and bolted it.

The light began to flicker, and he investigated, swearing when he found the palm-oil in the lamp was almost exhausted. He started to shout for Aram, then shrugged his shoulders and blew out the light. In the soft darkness he stretched himself fully clad on the couch, his sinewy hand by instinct searching for and closing on the hilt of his broadsword. Glancing idly at the stars framed in the barred windows, with the murmur of the breeze through the palms in his ears, he sank into slumber with a vague consciousness of the muttering drum, out on the desert — the low rumble and mutter of a leather-covered drum, beaten with soft, rhythmic strokes of an open black hand. . . .

2. The Night Skulkers

It was the stealthy opening of a door which awakened the Cimmerian. He did not awake as civilized men do, drowsy and drugged and stupid. He awoke instantly, with a clear mind, recognizing the sound that had interrupted his sleep. Lying there tensely in the dark he saw the outer door slowly open. In a widening crack of starlit sky he saw framed a great black bulk, broad, stooping shoulders and a misshapen head blocked out against the stars.

Conan felt the skin crawl between his shoulders. He had bolted that door securely. How could it be opening now, save by supernatural agency? And how could a human being possess a head like that outlined against the stars? All the tales he had heard in the Zuagir tents of devils and goblins came back to bead his flesh with clammy sweat. Now the monster slid noiselessly into the room, with a crouching posture and a shambling gait; and a familiar scent assailed the Cimmerian's nostrils, but did not reassure him, since Zuagir legendry represented demons as smelling like that.

Noiselessly Conan coiled his long legs under him; his naked sword was in his right hand, and when he struck it was as suddenly and murderously as a tiger lunging out of the dark. Not even a demon could have avoided that catapulting charge. His sword met and clove through flesh and bone, and something went heavily to the floor with a strangling cry. Conan crouched in the dark above it, sword dripping in his hand. Devil or beast or man, the thing was dead there on the floor. He sensed death as any wild thing senses it. He glared through the half-open door into the starlit court beyond. The gate stood open, but the court was empty.

Conan shut the door but did not bolt it. Groping in the darkness he found the lamp and lighted it. There was enough oil in it to burn for a minute or so. An instant later he was bending over the figure that sprawled on the floor in a pool of blood.

It was a gigantic black man, naked but for a loincloth. One hand still grasped a knotty-headed bludgeon. The fellow's kinky wool was built up into hornlike spindles with twigs and dried mud. This barbaric coiffure had given the head its misshapen appearance in the starlight. Provided with a clue to the riddle, Conan pushed back the thick red lips, and grunted as he stared down at teeth filed to points.

He understood now the mystery of the strangers who had disappeared from the house of Aram Baksh; the riddle of the black drum thrumming out there beyond the palm groves, and of that pit of charred bones — that pit where strange meat might be roasted under the stars, while black beasts squatted about to glut a hideous hunger. The man on the floor was a cannibal slave from Darfar.

There were many of his kind in the city. Cannibalism was not tolerated openly in Zamboula. But Conan knew now why people locked themselves in so securely at night, and why even beggars shunned the open alleys and doorless ruins. He grunted in disgust as he visualized brutish black shadows skulking up and down the nighted streets, seeking human prey — and such men as Aram Baksh to open the doors to them. The innkeeper was not a demon; he was worse. The slaves from Darfar were notorious thieves; there was no doubt that some of their pilfered loot found its way into the hands of Aram Baksh. And in return he sold them human flesh.

Conan blew out the light, stepped to the door and opened it, and ran his hand over the ornaments on the outer side. One of them was movable and worked the bolt inside. The room was a trap to catch human prey like rabbits. But this time instead of a rabbit it had caught a saber-toothed tiger.

Conan returned to the other door, lifted the bolt and pressed against it. It was immovable and he remembered the bolt on the other side. Aram was taking no chances either with his victims or the men with whom he dealt. Buckling on his sword-belt, the Cimmerian strode out into the court, closing the door behind him. He had no intention of delaying the settlement of his reckoning with Aram Baksh. He wondered how many poor devils had been bludgeoned in their sleep and dragged out of that room and down the road that ran through the shadowed palm groves to the roasting-pit.

He halted in the court. The drum was still muttering, and he caught the reflection of a leaping red glare through the groves. Cannibalism was more than a perverted appetite with the black men of Darfar; it was an integral element of their ghastly cult. The black vultures were already in conclave. But whatever flesh filled their bellies that night, it would not be his.

To reach Aram Baksh he must climb one of the walls which separated the small enclosure from the main compound. They were high, meant to keep out the man-eaters; but Conan was no swamp-bred black man; his thews had been steeled in boyhood on the sheer cliffs of his native hills. He was standing at the foot of the nearer wall when a cry echoed under the trees.

In an instant Conan was crouching at the gate, glaring down the road. The sound had come from the shadows of the huts across the road. He heard a frantic choking and gurgling such as might result from a desperate attempt to shriek, with a black hand fastened over the victim's mouth. A close-knit clump of figures emerged from the shadows beyond the huts, and started down the road — three huge black men carrying a slender, struggling figure between them. Conan caught the glimmer of pale limbs writhing in the starlight, even as, with a convulsive wrench, the captive slipped from the grasp of the brutal fingers and came flying up the road, a supple young woman, naked as the day she was born. Conan saw her plainly before she ran out of the road and into the shadows between the huts. The blacks were at her heels, and back in the shadows the figures merged and an intolerable scream of anguish and horror rang out.

Stirred to red rage by the ghoulishness of the episode, Conan raced across the road.

Neither victim nor abductors were aware of his presence until the soft swish of the dust about his feet brought them about, and then he was almost upon them, coming with the gusty fury of a hill wind. Two of the blacks turned to meet him, lifting their bludgeons. But they failed to estimate properly the speed at which be was coming. One of them was down, disemboweled, before he could strike, and wheeling catlike, Conan evaded the stroke of the other's cudgel and lashed in a whistling counter-cut. The black's head flew into the air; the headless body took three staggering steps, spurting blood and clawing horribly at the air with groping hands, and then slumped to the dust.

The remaining cannibal gave back with a strangled yell, hurling his captive from him. She tripped and rolled in the dust, and the black fled in blind panic toward the city. Conan was at his heels. Fear winged the black feet, but before they reached the easternmost hut, he sensed death at his back, and bellowed like an ox in the slaughter-yards.

"Black dog of Hell!" Conan drove his sword

between the dusky shoulders with such vengeful fury that the broad blade stood out half its length from the black breast. With a choking cry the black stumbled headlong, and Conan braced his feet and dragged out his sword as his victim fell.

Only the breeze disturbed the leaves. Conan shook his head as a lion shakes its mane and growled his unsatiated blood-lust. But no more shapes slunk from the shadows, and before the huts the starlit road stretched empty. He whirled at the quick patter of feet behind him, but it was only the girl, rushing to throw herself on him and clasp his neck in a desperate grasp, frantic from terror of the abominable fate she had just escaped.

"Easy, girl," be grunted. "You're all right. How did they catch you?"

She sobbed something unintelligible. He forgot all about Aram Baksh as he scrutinized her by the light of the stars. She was white, though a very definite brunette, obviously one of Zamboula's many mixed-breeds. She was tall, with a slender, supple form, as he was in a good position to observe. Admiration burned in his fierce eyes as be looked down on her splendid bosom and her lithe limbs, which still quivered from fright and exertion. He passed an arm around her flexible waist and said, reassuringly: "Stop shaking, wench; you're safe enough."

His touch seemed to restore her shaken sanity. She tossed back her thick, glossy locks and cast a fearful glance over her shoulder, while she pressed closer to the Cimmerian as if seeking security in the contact.

"They caught me in the streets," she muttered, shuddering. "Lying in wait, beneath a dark arch — black men, like great, hulking apes! Set have mercy on me! I shall dream of it!"

"What were you doing out on the streets this time of night?" he inquired, fascinated by the satiny feel of her sleek skin under his questing fingers.

She raked back her hair and stared blankly up into his face. She did not seem aware of his caresses.

"My lover," she said. "My lover drove me into the streets. He went mad and tried to kill me. As I fled from him I was seized by those beasts."

"Beauty like yours might drive a man mad," quoth Conan, running his fingers experimentally through her glossy tresses.

She shook her head, like one emerging from a daze. She no longer trembled, and her voice was steady.

"It was the spite of a priest — of Totrasmek, the high priest of Hanuman, who desires me for himself — the dog!"

"No need to curse him for that," grinned Conan. "The old hyena has better taste than I thought."

She ignored the bluff compliment. She was regaining her poise swiftly.

"My lover is a — a young Turanian soldier. To spite me, Totrasmek gave him a drug that drove him mad. Tonight he snatched up a sword and came at me to slay me in his madness, but I fled from him into the streets. The Negroes seized me and brought me to this — *what was that?*"

Conan had already moved. Soundlessly as a shadow he drew her behind the nearest hut, beneath the straggling palms. They stood in tense stillness, while the low mutterings both had heard grew louder until voices were distinguishable. A group of Negroes, some nine or ten, were coming along the road from the direction of the city. The girl clutched Conan's arm and he felt the terrified quivering of her supple body against his.

Now they could understand the gutturals of the black men.

"Our brothers are already assembled at the pit," said one. "We have had no luck. I hope they have enough for us."

"Aram promised us a man," muttered another, and Conan mentally promised Aram something.

"Aram keeps his word," grunted yet another. "Many a man we have taken from his tavern. But we pay him well. I myself have given him ten bales of silk I stole from my master. It was good silk, by Set!"

The blacks shuffled past, bare splay feet scuffing up the dust, and their voices dwindled down the road.

"Well for us those corpses are lying behind these huts," muttered Conan. "If they look in Aram's death-room they'll find another. Let's begone."

"Yes, let us hasten!" begged the girl, almost hysterical again. "My lover is wandering somewhere in the streets alone. The Negroes may take him."

"A devil of a custom this is!" growled Conan, as he led the way toward the city, paralleling the road but keeping behind the huts and straggling trees. "Why don't the citizens clean out these black dogs?"

"They are valuable slaves," murmured the girl. "There are so many of them they might revolt if they were denied the flesh for which they lust. The people of Zamboula know they skulk the streets at night, and all are careful to remain within locked doors, except when something unforeseen happens, as it did to me. The blacks prey on anything they catch, but they seldom catch anybody but strangers. The people of Zamboula are not concerned with the strangers that pass through the city.

"Such men as Aram Baksh sell these strangers to the blacks. He would not dare attempt such a thing with a citizen."

Conan spat in disgust, and a moment later led his companion out into the road which was becoming a street, with still, unlighted houses on each side. Slinking in the shadows was not congenial to his nature.

"Where do you want to go?" he asked. The girl did not seem to object to his arm about her waist.

"To my house, to rouse my servants," she answered. "To bid them search for my lover. I do not wish the city — the priests — anyone — to know of his madness. He — he is a young officer with a promising future. Perhaps we can drive this madness from him if we can find him."

"If *we* find him?" rumbled Conan. "What makes you think I want to spend the night scouring the streets for a lunatic?"

She cast a quick glance into his face, and properly interpreted the gleam in his blue eyes. Any woman could have known that he would follow her wherever she led — for a while, at least. But being a woman, she concealed her knowledge of that fact.

"Please," she began with a hint of tears in her voice, "I have no one else to ask for help — you have been kind —"

"All right!" he grunted. "All right! What's the young reprobate's name?"

"Why — Alafdhal. I am Zabibi, a dancing-girl. I have danced often before the satrap, Jungir Khan, and his mistress Nafertari, and before all the lords and royal ladies of Zamboula. Totrasmek desired me, and because I repulsed him, he made me the innocent tool of his vengeance against Alafdhal. I asked a love potion of Totrasmek, not suspecting the depth of his guile and hate. He gave me a drug to mix with my lover's wine, and he swore that when Alafdhal drank it, he would love me even more madly than ever, and grant my every wish. I mixed the drug secretly with my lover's wine. But having drunk, my lover went raving mad and things came about as I have told you. Curse Totrasmek, the hybrid snake — ahhh!"

She caught his arm convulsively, and both

stopped short. They had come into a district of shops and stalls, all deserted and unlighted, for the hour was late. They were passing an alley, and in its mouth a man was standing motionless and silent. His head was lowered, but Conan caught the weird gleam of eery eyes regarding them unblinkingly. His skin crawled, not with fear of the sword in the man's hand, but because of the uncanny suggestion of his posture and silence. They suggested madness. Conan pushed the girl aside and drew his sword.

"Don't kill him!" she begged. "In the name of Set, do not slay him! You are strong — overpower him!"

"We'll see," he muttered, grasping his sword in his right hand and clenching his left into a mallet-like fist.

He took a wary step toward the alley — and with a horrible moaning laugh the Turanian charged. As he came he swung his sword, rising on his toes as he put all the power of his body behind the blows. Sparks flashed blue as Conan parried the blade, and the next instant the madman was stretched senseless in the dust from a thundering buffet of Conan's left fist.

The girl ran forward.

"'Oh, he is not — he is not —"

Conan bent swiftly, turned the man on his side and ran quick fingers ever him.

"He's not hurt much," he grunted. "Bleeding at the nose, but anybody's likely to do that, after a clout on the jaw. He'll come to after a bit, and maybe his mind will be right. In the meantime I'll tie his wrists with his sword-belt — so. Now where do you want me to take him?"

"Wait!" She knelt beside the senseless figure, seized the bound hands and scanned them avidly. Then, shaking her head as if in baffled disappointment, she rose. She came close to the giant Cimmerian, and laid her slender hands on his arching breast. Her dark eyes, like wet black jewels in the starlight, gazed up into his.

"You are a man! Help me! Totrasmek must die! Slay him for me!"

"And put my neck into a Turanian noose?" he grunted.

"Nay!" The slender arms, strong as pliant steel, were around his corded neck. Her supple body throbbed against his. "The Hyrkanians have no love for Totrasmek. The priests of Set fear him. He is a mongrel, who rules men by fear and superstition. I worship Set, and the Turanians bow to Erlik, but Totrasmek sacrifices to Hanuman the accursed! The Turanian lords fear his black arts and his power over the hybrid population, and they hate him. Even Jungir Khan and his mistress Nafertari fear and hate him. If he were slain in his temple at night, they would not seek his slayer very closely."

"And what of his magic?" rumbled the Cimmerian.

"You are a fighting-man," she answered. "To risk your life is part of your profession."

"For a price," he admitted.

"There will be a price!" she breathed, rising on tiptoes, to gaze into his eyes.

The nearness of her vibrant body drove a flame through his veins. The perfume of her breath mounted to his brain. But as his arms closed about her supple figure she avoided them with a lithe movement, saying: "Wait! First serve me in this matter."

"Name your price." He spoke with some difficulty.

"Pick up my lover," she directed, and the Cimmerian stooped and swung the tall form easily to his broad shoulder. At the moment he felt as if he could have toppled over Jungir Khan's palace with equal ease. The girl murmured an endearment to the unconscious man, and there was no hypocrisy in her attitude. She obviously loved Alafdhal sincerely. Whatever business arrangement she made with Conan would have no bearing on her relationship with Alafdhal. Women are more practical about these things than men.

"Follow me!" She hurried along the street, while the Cimmerian strode easily after her, in no way discomforted by his limp burden. He kept a wary eye out for black shadows skulking under arches, but saw nothing suspicious. Doubtless the men of Darfar were all gathered at the roasting-pit. The girl turned down a narrow side street, and presently knocked cautiously at an arched door.

Almost instantly a wicket opened in the upper

panel, and a black face glanced out. She bent close to the opening, whispering swiftly. Bolts creaked in their sockets, and the door opened. A giant black man stood framed against the soft glow of a copper lamp. A quick glance showed Conan the man was not from Darfar. His teeth were unfiled and his kinky hair was cropped close to his skull. He was from the Wadai.

At a word from Zabibi, Conan gave the limp body into the black's arms, and saw the young officer laid on a velvet divan. He showed no signs of returning consciousness. The blow that had rendered him senseless might have felled an ox. Zabibi bent over him for an instant, her fingers nervously twining and twisting. Then she straightened and beckoned the Cimmerian.

The door closed softly, the locks clicked behind them, and the closing wicket shut off the glow of the lamps. In the starlight of the street Zabibi took Conan's hand. Her own hand trembled a little.

"You will not fail me?"

He shook his maned head, massive against the stars.

"Then follow me to Hanuman's shrine, and the gods have mercy on our souls!"

Along the silent streets they moved like phantoms of antiquity. They went in silence. Perhaps the girl was thinking of her lover lying senseless on the divan under the copper lamps; or was shrinking with fear of what lay ahead of them in the demon-haunted shrine of Hanuman. The barbarian was thinking only of the woman moving so supplely beside him. The perfume of her scented hair was in his nostrils, the sensuous aura of her presence filled his brain and left room for no other thoughts.

Once they heard the clank of brass-shod feet, and drew into the shadows of a gloomy arch while a squad of Pelishtim watchmen swung past. There were fifteen of them; they marched in close formation, pikes at the ready, and the rearmost men had their broad brass shields slung on their backs, to protect them from a knife-stroke from behind. The skulking menace of the black man-eaters was a threat even to armed men.

As soon as the clang of their sandals had receded up the street, Conan and the girl emerged from their hiding-place and hurried on. A few moments later they saw the squat, flat-topped edifice they sought looming ahead of them.

The temple of Hanuman stood alone in the midst of a broad square, which lay silent and deserted beneath the stars. A marble wall surrounded the shrine, with a broad opening directly before the portico. This opening had no gate or any sort of barrier.

"Why don't the blacks seek their prey here?" muttered Conan. "There's nothing to keep them out of the temple."

He could feet the trembling of Zabibi's body as she pressed close to him.

"They fear Totrasmek, as all in Zamboula fear

him, even Jungir Khan and Nafertari. Come! Come quickly, before my courage flows from me like water!"

The girl's fear was evident, but she did not falter. Conan drew his sword and strode ahead of her as they advanced through the open gateway. He knew the hideous habits of the priests of the East, and was aware that an invader of Hanuman's shrine might expect to encounter almost any sort of nightmare horror. He knew there was a good chance that neither he nor the girl would ever leave the shrine alive, but he had risked his life too many times before to devote much thought to that consideration.

They entered a court paved with marble which gleamed whitely in the starlight. A short flight of broad marble steps led up to the pillared portico. The great bronze doors stood wide open as they had stood for centuries. But no worshippers burnt incense within. In the day men and women might come timidly into the shrine and place offerings to the ape-god on the black altar. At night the people shunned the temple of Hanuman as hares shun the lair of the serpent.

Burning censers bathed the interior in a soft weird glow that created an illusion of unreality. Near the rear wall, behind the black stone altar, sat the god with his gaze fixed forever on the open door, through which for centuries his victims had come, dragged by chains of roses. A faint groove ran from the sill to the altar, and when Conan's foot felt it, he stepped away as quickly as if he had trodden upon a snake. That groove had been worn by the faltering feet of the multitude of those who had died screaming on that grim altar.

Bestial in the uncertain light, Hanuman leered with his carven mask. He sat, not as an ape would crouch, but cross-legged as a man would sit, but his aspect was no less simian for that reason. He was carved from black marble, but his eyes were rubies, which glowed red and lustful as the coals of Hell's deepest pits. His great hands lay upon his lap, palms upward, taloned fingers spread and grasping. In the gross emphasis of his attributes, in the leer of his satyr-countenance, was reflected the abominable cynicism of the degenerate cult which deified him.

The girt moved around the image, making toward the back wall, and when her sleek flank brushed against a carven knee, she shrank aside and shuddered as if a reptile had touched her. There was a space of several feet between the broad back of the idol and the marble wall with its frieze of gold leaves. On either hand, flanking the idol, an ivory door under a gold arch was set in the wall.

"Those doors open into each end of a hairpin shaped corridor," she said hurriedly. "Once I was in the interior of the shrine — once!" She shivered and twitched her slim shoulders at a memory both terrifying and obscene. "The corridor is bent like a horseshoe, with each horn opening into this room. Totrasmek's chambers are enclosed within the curve of the corridor and open into it. But there is a secret door in this wall which opens directly into an inner chamber —"

She began to run her bands over the smooth surface, where no crack or crevice showed. Conan stood beside her, sword in hand, glancing warily about him. The silence, the emptiness of the shrine, with imagination picturing what might lie behind that wall, made him feel like a wild beast nosing a trap.

"Ah!" The girl had found a hidden spring at last; a square opening gaped blackly in the wall. Then: "Set!" she screamed, and even as Conan leaped toward her, he saw that a great misshapen hand had fastened itself in her hair. She was snatched off her feet and jerked headfirst through the opening. Conan, grabbing ineffectually at her, felt his fingers slip from a naked limb, and in an instant she had vanished and the wall showed blank as before. Only from beyond it came briefly the muffled sounds of a struggle, a scream, faintly heard, and a low laugh that made Conan's blood congeal in his veins.

3. Black Hands Gripping

With an oath the Cimmerian smote the wall a terrific blow with the pommel of his sword, and the marble cracked and chipped. But the hidden door did not give way, and reason told him that doubtless it had been bolted on the other side of the wall. Turning, he sprang across the chamber to one of the ivory doors.

He lifted his sword to shatter the panels, but on a venture tried the door first with his left hand. It swung open easily, and he glared into a long corridor that curved away into dimness under the weird light of censers similar to those in the shrine. A heavy gold bolt showed on the jamb of the door, and he touched it lightly with his fingertips. The faint warmness of the metal could have been detected only by a man whose faculties were akin to those of a wolf. That bolt had been touched — and therefore drawn — within the last few seconds. The affair was taking on more and more of the aspect of a baited trap. He might have known Totrasmek would know when anyone entered the temple.

To enter the corridor would undoubtedly be to walk into whatever trap the priest had set for him. But Conan did not hesitate. Somewhere in that dim-lit interior Zabibi was a captive, and, from what he knew of the characteristics of Hanuman's priests, he was sure that she needed help badly. Conan stalked into the corridor with a pantherish tread, poised to strike right or left.

On his left, ivory, arched doors opened into the corridor, and he tried each in turn. All were locked. He had gone perhaps seventy-five feet when the corridor bent sharply to the left, describing the curve the girl had mentioned. A door opened into this curve, and it gave under his hand.

He was looking into a broad, square chamber, somewhat more clearly lighted than the corridor. Its walls were of white marble, the floor of ivory, the ceiling of fretted silver. He saw divans of rich satin, gold-worked footstools of ivory, a disk-shaped table of some massive, metal-like substance. On one of the divans a man was reclining, looking toward the door. He laughed as he met the Cimmerian's startled glare.

This man was naked except for a loincloth and high-strapped sandals. He was brown-skinned, with close-cropped black hair and restless black eyes that set off a broad, arrogant face. In girth and breadth he was enormous, with huge limbs on which the great muscles swelled and rippled at each slightest movement. His hands were the largest Conan had ever seen. The assurance of gigantic physical strength colored his every action and inflection.

"Why not enter, barbarian?" he called mockingly, with an exaggerated gesture of invitation.

Conan's eyes began to smolder ominously, but he trod warily into the chamber, his sword ready.

"Who the devil are you?" he growled.

"I am Baal-pteor," the man answered. "Once, long ago and in another land, I had another name. But this is a good name, and why Totrasmek gave it to me, any temple wench can tell you."

"So you're his dog!" grunted Conan. "Well, curse your brown hide, Baal-pteor, where's the wench you jerked through the wall?"

"My master entertains her!" laughed Baal-pteor. "Listen!"

From beyond a door opposite the one by which

Conan had entered there sounded a woman's scream, faint and muffled in the distance.

"Blast your soul!" Conan took a stride toward the door, then wheeled with his skin tingling. Baal-pteor was laughing at him, and that laugh was edged with menace that made the hackles rise on Conan's neck and sent a red wave of murder-lust driving across his vision.

He started toward Baal-pteor, the knuckles on his sword-hand showing white. With a swift motion the brown man threw something at him — a shining crystal sphere that glistened in the weird light.

Conan dodged instinctively, but, miraculously, the globe stopped short in midair, a few feet from his face. It did not fall to the floor. It hung suspended, as if by invisible filaments, some five feet above the floor. And as he glared in amazement, it began to rotate with growing speed. And as it revolved it grew, expanded, became nebulous. It filled the chamber. It enveloped him. It blotted out furniture, walls, the smiling countenance of Baal-pteor. He was lost in the midst of a blinding bluish blur of whirling speed. Terrific winds screamed past Conan, tugging, tearing at him, striving to wrench him from his feet, to drag him into the vortex that spun madly before him.

With a choking cry Conan lurched backward, reeled, felt the solid wall against his back. At the contact the illusion ceased to be. The whirling, titanic sphere vanished like a bursting bubble.

Conan reeled upright in the silver-ceilinged room,

with a gray mist coiling about his feet, and saw Baal-pteor lolling on the divan, shaking with silent laughter.

"Son of a slut!" Conan lunged at him. But the mist swirled up from the floor, blotting out that giant brown form. Groping in a rolling cloud that blinded him, Conan felt a rending sensation of dislocation — and then room and mist and brown man were gone together. He was standing alone among the high reeds of a marshy fen, and a buffalo was lunging at him, head down. He leaped aside from the ripping scimitar-curved horns, and drove his sword in behind the foreleg, through ribs and heart. And then it was not a buffalo dying there in the mud, but the brown-skinned Baal-pteor. With a curse, Conan struck off his head; and the head soared from the ground and snapped beast-like tusks into his throat. For all his mighty strength he could not tear it loose — he was choking — strangling; then there was a rush and roar through space, the dislocating shock of an immeasurable impact, and he was back in the chamber with Baal-pteor, whose head was once more set firmly on his shoulders, and who laughed silently at him from the divan.

"Mesmerism!" muttered Conan, crouching and digging his toes hard against the marble.

His eyes blazed. This brown dog was playing with him, making sport of him! But this mummery, this child's play of mists and shadows of thought, it could not harm him. He had but to leap and strike and the brown acolyte would be a mangled corpse under his heel. This time he would not be fooled by shadows of illusion — but he was.

A blood-curdling snarl sounded behind him, and he wheeled and struck in a flash at the panther crouching to spring on him from the metal-colored table. Even as he struck, the apparition vanished and his blade clashed deafeningly on the adamantine surface. Instantly he sensed something abnormal. The blade stuck to the table! He wrenched at it savagely. It did not give. This was no mesmeristic trick. The table was a giant magnet. He gripped the hilt with both hands, when a voice at his shoulder brought him about, to face the brown man, who had at last risen from the divan.

Slightly taller than Conan, and much heavier, Baal-pteor loomed before him, a daunting image of muscular development. His mighty arms were unnaturally long, and his great hands opened and closed, twitching convulsively. Conan released the hilt of his imprisoned sword and fell silent, watching his enemy through slitted lids.

"Your head, Cimmerian!" taunted Baal-pteor. "I shall take it with my bare hands, twisting it from your shoulders as the head of a fowl is twisted! Thus the sons of Kosala offer sacrifice to Yajur. Barbarian, you look upon a strangler of Yota-pong. I was chosen by the priests of Yajur in my infancy, and throughout childhood, boyhood and youth I was trained in the art of slaying with the naked hands —

for only thus are the sacrifices enacted. Yajur loves blood, and we waste not a drop from the victim's veins. When I was a child they gave me infants to throttle; when I was a boy I strangled young girls; as a youth, women, old men and young boys. Not until I reached my full manhood was I given a strong man to slay on the altar of Yota-pong.

"For years I offered the sacrifices to Yajur. Hundreds of necks have snapped between these fingers —" he worked them before the Cimmerian's angry eyes.

"Why I fled from Yota-pong to become Totrasmek's servant is no concern of yours. In a moment you will be beyond curiosity. The priests of Kosala, the stranglers of Yajur, are strong beyond the belief of men. And I was stronger than any. With my hands, barbarian, I shall break your neck!"

And like the stroke of twin cobras, the great hands closed on Conan's throat. The Cimmerian made no attempt to dodge or fend them away, but his own hands darted to the Kosalan's bull-neck. Baal-pteor's black eyes widened as he felt the thick cords of muscles that protected the barbarian's throat. With a snarl he exerted his inhuman strength, and knots and lumps and ropes of thews rose along his massive arms. And then a choking gasp burst from him as Conan's fingers locked on his throat. For an instant they stood there like statues, their faces masks of effort, veins beginning to stand out purply on their temples. Conan's thin lips drew back from his teeth in a grinning snarl. Baal-pteor's eyes were distended; in them grew an awful surprize and the glimmer of fear. Both men stood motionless as images, except for the expanding of their muscles on rigid arms and braced legs, but strength beyond common conception was warring there — strength that might have uprooted trees and crushed the skulls of bullocks.

The wind whistled suddenly from between Baal-pteor's parted teeth. His face was growing purple. Fear flooded his eyes. His thews seemed ready to burst from his arms and shoulders, yet the muscles of the Cimmerian's thick neck did not give; they felt like masses of woven iron cords under his desperate fingers. But his own flesh was giving way under the iron fingers of the Cimmerian which ground deeper and deeper into the yielding throat-muscles, crushing them in upon jugular and windpipe.

The statuesque immobility of the group gave way to sudden, frenzied motion, as the Kosalan began to wrench and heave, seeking to throw himself backward. He let go of Conan's throat and grasped his wrists, trying to tear away those inexorable fingers.

With a sudden lunge Conan bore him backward until the small of his back crashed against the table. And still farther over its edge Conan bent him, back and back, until his spine was ready to snap.

Conan's low laugh was merciless as the ring of steel.

"You fool!" he all but whispered. "I think you

never saw a man from the West before. Did you deem yourself strong, because you were able to twist the heads off civilized folk, poor weaklings with muscles like rotten string? Hell! Break the neck of a wild Cimmerian bull before you call yourself strong. I did that, before I was a full-grown man — like this!"

And with a savage wrench he twisted Baal-pteor's head around until the ghastly face leered over the left shoulder, and the vertebra snapped like a rotten branch.

Conan hurled the flopping corpse to the floor, turned to the sword again and gripped the hilt with both hands, bracing his feet against the floor. Blood trickled down his broad breast from the wounds Baal-pteor's fingernails had torn in the skin of his neck. His black hair was damp, sweat ran down his face, and his chest heaved. For all his vocal scorn of Baal-pteor's strength, he had almost met his match in the inhuman Kosalan. But without pausing to catch his breath, he exerted all his strength in a mighty wrench that tore the sword from the magnet where it clung.

Another instant and he had pushed open the door from behind which the scream had sounded, and was looking down a long straight corridor, lined with ivory doors. The other end was masked by a rich velvet curtain, and from beyond that curtain came the devilish strains of such music as Conan had never heard, not even in nightmares. It made the short hairs bristle on the back of his neck. Mingled with it was the panting, hysterical sobbing of a woman. Grasping his sword firmly, he glided down the corridor.

4. Dance, Girl, Dance!

When Zabibi was jerked headfirst through the aperture which opened in the wall behind the idol, her first, dizzy, disconnected thought was that her time had come. She instinctively shut her eyes and waited for the blow to fall. But instead she felt herself dumped unceremoniously onto the smooth marble floor, which bruised her knees and hip. Opening her eyes she stared fearfully around her, just as a muffled impact sounded from beyond the wall. She saw a brown-skinned giant in a loincloth standing over her, and, across the chamber into which she had come, a man sat on a divan, with his back to a rich black velvet curtain, a broad, fleshy man, with fat white hands and snaky eyes. And her flesh crawled, for this man was Totrasmek, the priest of Hanuman, who for years had spun his slimy webs of power throughout the city of Zamboula.

"The barbarian seeks to batter his way through the wall," said Totrasmek sardonically, "but the bolt will hold."

The girl saw that a heavy golden bolt had been shot across the hidden door, which was plainly discernible from this side of the wall. The bolt and its sockets would have resisted the charge of an elephant.

"Go open one of the doors for him, Baal-pteor," ordered Totrasmek. "Slay him in the square chamber at the other end of the corridor."

The Kosalan salaamed and departed by the way of a door in the side wall of the chamber. Zabibi rose, staring fearfully at the priest, whose eyes ran avidly over her splendid figure. To this she was indifferent. A dancer of Zamboula was accustomed to nakedness. But the cruelty in his eyes started her limbs to quivering.

"Again you come to me in my retreat, beautiful one," he purred with cynical hypocrisy. "It is an unexpected honor. You seemed to enjoy your former visit so little, that I dared not hope for you to repeat it. Yet I did all in my power to provide you with an interesting experience."

For a Zamboula dancer to blush would be an impossibility, but a smolder of anger mingled with the fear in Zabibi's dilated eyes.

"Fat pig! You know I did not come here for love of you."

"No," laughed Totrasmek, "you came like a fool, creeping through the night with a stupid barbarian to cut my throat. Why should you seek my life?"

"You know why!" she cried, knowing the futility of trying to dissemble.

"You are thinking of your lover," he laughed. "The fact that you are here seeking my life shows that he quaffed the drug I gave you. Well, did you not ask for it? And did I not send what you asked for, out of the love I bear you?"

"I asked you for a drug that would make him slumber harmlessly for a few hours," she said bitterly. "And you — you sent your servant with a drug that drove him mad! I was a fool ever to trust you. I might have known your protestations of friendship were lies, to disguise your hate and spite."

"Why did you wish your lover to sleep?" he retorted. "So you could steal from him the only thing he would never give you — the ring with the jewel men call the Star of Khorala — the star stolen from the queen of Ophir, who would pay a roomful of gold for its return. He would not give it to you willingly, because he knew that it holds a magic which, when properly controlled, will enslave the hearts of any of the opposite sex. You wished to steal it from him, fearing that his magicians would discover the key to that magic and he would forget you in his conquests of the queens of the world. You would sell it back to the queen of Ophir, who understands its power and would use it to enslave men, as she did before it was stolen."

"And why did *you* want it?" she demanded sulkily.

"To understand its powers. It would increase the power of my arts."

"Well," she snapped, "you have it now!"

"*I* have the Star of Khorala? Nay, you err."

"Why bother to lie?" she retorted bitterly. "He had it on his finger when he drove me into the streets.

He did not have it when I found him again. Your servant must have been watching the house, and have taken it from him, after I escaped him. To the devil with it! I want my lover back sane and whole. You have the ring; you have punished us both. Why do you not restore his mind to him? Can you?"

"I could," he assured her, in evident enjoyment of her distress. He drew a phial from among his robes. "This contains the juice of the golden lotus. If your lover drank it he would be sane again. Yes, I will be merciful. You have both thwarted and flouted me, not once but many times; he has constantly opposed my wishes. But I will be merciful. Come and take the phial from my hand."

She stared at Totrasmek, trembling with eagerness to seize it, but fearing it was but some cruel jest. She advanced timidly, with a hand extended, and he laughed heartlessly and drew back out of her reach. Even as her lips parted to curse him, some instinct snatched her eyes upward. From the gilded ceiling four jade-hued vessels were falling. She dodged, but they did not strike her. They crashed to the floor about her, forming the four corners of a square. And she screamed, and screamed again. For out of each ruin reared the hooded head of a cobra, and one struck at her bare leg. Her convulsive movement to evade it brought her within reach of the one on the other side and again she had to shift like lightning to avoid the flash of its hideous head.

She was caught in a frightful trap. All four serpents were swaying and striking at foot, ankle, calf, knee, thigh, hip, whatever portion of her voluptuous body chanced to be nearest to them, and she could not spring over them or pass between them to safety. She could only whirl and spring aside and twist her body to avoid the strokes, and each time she moved to dodge one snake, the motion brought her within range of another, so that she had to keep shifting with the speed of light. She could move only a short space in any direction, and the fearful hooded crests were menacing her every second. Only a dancer of Zamboula could have lived in that grisly square.

She became, herself, a blur of bewildering motion. The heads missed her by hair's breadths, but they missed, as she pitted her twinkling feet, flickering limbs and perfect eye against the blinding speed of the scaly demons her enemy had conjured out of thin air.

Somewhere a thin whining music struck up, mingling with the hissing of the serpents, like an evil night-wind blowing through the empty sockets of a skull. Even in the flying speed of her urgent haste she realized that the darting of the serpents was no longer at random. They obeyed the grisly piping of the eery music. They struck with a horrible rhythm, and perforce her swaying, writhing, spinning body attuned itself to their rhythm. Her frantic motions melted into the measures of a dance compared to which the most obscene tarantella of Zamora would have seemed sane and restrained. Sick with shame and terror Zabibi heard the hateful mirth of her merciless tormenter.

"The Dance of the Cobras, my lovely one!" laughed Totrasmek. "So maidens danced in the sacrifice to Hanuman centuries ago — but never with such beauty and suppleness. Dance, girl, dance! How long can you avoid the fangs of the Poison People? Minutes? Hours? You will weary at last. Your swift, sure feet will stumble, your legs falter, your hips slow in their rotations. Then the fangs will begin to sink deep into your ivory flesh —"

Behind him the curtain shook as if struck by a gust of wind, and Totrasmek screamed. His eyes dilated and his hands caught convulsively at the length of bright steel which jutted suddenly from his breast.

The music broke off short. The girl swayed dizzily in her dance, crying out in dreadful anticipation of the flickering fangs — and then only four wisps of harmless blue smoke curled up from the floor about her, as Totrasmek sprawled headlong from the divan.

Conan came from behind the curtain, wiping his broad blade. Looking through the hangings he had seen the girl dancing desperately between four swaying spirals of smoke, but he had guessed that their appearance was very different to her. He knew he had killed Totrasmek.

Zabibi sank down on the floor, panting, but even as Conan started toward her, she staggered up again, though her legs trembled with exhaustion.

"The phial!" she gasped. "The phial!"

Totrasmek still grasped it in his stiffening hand. Ruthlessly she tore it from his locked fingers, and then began frantically to ransack his garments.

"What the devil are you looking for?" Conan demanded.

"A ring — he stole it from Alafdhal. He must have, while my lover walked in madness through the streets. Set's devils!"

She had convinced herself that it was not on the person of Totrasmek. She began to cast about the chamber, tearing up divan-covers and hangings, and upsetting vessels.

She paused and raked a damp lock of hair out of her eyes.

"I forgot Baal-pteor!"

"He's in Hell with his neck broken," Conan assured her.

She expressed vindictive gratification at the news, but an instant later swore expressively.

"We can't stay here. It's not many hours until dawn. Lesser priests are likely to visit the temple at any hour of the night, and if we're discovered here with his corpse, the people will tear us to pieces. The Turanians could not save us."

She lifted the bolt on the secret door, and a few moments later they were in the streets and hurrying away from the silent square where brooded the age-old shrine of Hanuman.

In a winding street a short distance away Conan

halted and checked his companion with a heavy hand on her naked shoulder.

"Don't forget there was a price —"

"I have not forgotten!" She twisted free. "But we must go to — to Alafdhal first!"

A few minutes later the black slave let them through the wicket door. The young Turanian lay upon the divan, his arms and legs bound with heavy velvet ropes. His eyes were open, but they were like those of a mad dog, and foam was thick on his lips. Zabibi shuddered.

"Force his jaws open!" she commanded, and Conan's iron fingers accomplished the task.

Zabibi emptied the phial down the maniac's gullet. The effect was like magic. Instantly he became quiet. The glare faded from his eyes; he stared up at the girl in a puzzled way, but with recognition and intelligence. Then he fell into a normal slumber.

"When he awakes he will be quite sane," she whispered, motioning to the silent slave.

With a deep bow be gave into her hands a small leathern bag, and drew about her shoulders a silken cloak. Her manner had subtly changed when she beckoned Conan to follow her out of the chamber.

In an arch that opened on the street, she turned to him, drawing herself up with a new regality.

"I must now tell you the truth," she said. "I am not Zabibi. I am Nafertari. And *he* is not Alafdhal, a poor captain of the guardsmen. He is Jungir Khan, satrap of Zamboula."

Conan made no comment; his scarred dark countenance was immobile.

"I lied to you because I dared not divulge the truth to anyone," she said. "We were alone when Jungir Khan went mad. None knew of it but myself. Had it been known that the satrap of Zamboula was a madman, there would have been instant revolt and rioting, even as Totrasmek planned, who plotted our destruction.

"You see now how impossible is the reward, for which you hoped. The satrap's mistress is not — cannot be for you. But you shall not go unrewarded. Here is a sack of gold."

She gave him the bag she had received from the slave.

"Go, now, and when the sun is up come to the palace. I will have Jungir Khan make you captain of his guard. But you will take your orders from me, secretly. Your first duty will be to march a squad to the shrine of Hanuman, ostensibly to search for clues of the priest's slayer; in reality to search for the Star of Khorala. It must be hidden there somewhere. When you find it, bring it to me. You have my leave to go now."

He nodded, still silent, and strode away. The girl, watching the swing of his broad shoulders, was piqued to note that there was nothing in his bearing to show that he was in any way chagrined or abashed.

When he had rounded a corner, he glanced back,

and then changed his direction and quickened his pace. A few moments later he was in the quarter of the city containing the Horse Market. There he smote on a door until from the window above a bearded head was thrust to demand the reason for the disturbance.

"A horse," demanded Conan. "The swiftest steed you have."

"I open no gates at this time of night," mumbled the horse-trader.

Conan rattled his coins.

"Dog's son knave! Don't you see I'm white, and alone? Come down, before I smash your door!"

Presently, on a bay stallion, Conan was riding toward the house of Aram Baksh.

He turned off the road into the alley that lay between the tavern compound and the date-palm garden, but he did not pause at the gate. He rode on to the northeast corner of the wall, then turned and rode along the north wall, to halt within a few paces of the northwest angle. No trees grew near the wall, but there were some low bushes. To one of these he tied his horse, and was about to climb into the saddle again, when he heard a low muttering of voices beyond the corner of the wall.

Drawing his foot from the stirrup he stole to the angle and peered around it. Three men were moving down the road toward the palm groves, and from their slouching gait he knew they were Negroes. They halted at his low call, bunching themselves as he strode toward them, his sword in his hand. Their eyes gleamed whitely in the starlight. Their brutish lust shone in their ebony faces, but they knew their three cudgels could not prevail against his sword, just as he knew it.

"Where are you going?" he challenged.

"To bid our brothers put out the fire in the pit beyond the groves," was the sullen, guttural reply. "Aram Baksh promised us a man, but he lied. We found one of our brothers dead in the trap-chamber. We go hungry this night."

"I think not," smiled Conan. "Aram Baksh will give you a man. Do you see that door?"

He pointed to a small, iron-bound portal set in the midst of the western wall.

"Wait there. Aram Baksh will give you a man."

Backing warily away until he was out of reach of a sudden bludgeon blow, he turned and melted around the northwest angle of the wall. Reaching his horse he paused to ascertain that the blacks were not sneaking after him, and then he climbed into the saddle and stood upright on it, quieting the uneasy steed with a low word. He reached up, grasped the coping of the wall and drew himself up and over. There he studied the grounds for an instant. The tavern was built in the southwest corner of the enclosure, the remaining space of which was occupied by groves and gardens. He saw no one in the grounds. The tavern was dark and silent, and he knew all the doors and windows were barred and bolted.

Conan knew that Aram Baksh slept in a chamber that opened into a cypress-bordered path that led to the door in the western wall. Like a shadow he glided among the trees and a few moments later he rapped lightly on the chamber door.

"What is it?" asked a rumbling voice within.

"Aram Baksh!" hissed Conan. "The blacks are stealing over the wall!"

Almost instantly the door opened, framing the tavern-keeper, naked but for his shirt, with a dagger in his hand.

He craned his neck to stare into the Cimmerian's face.

"What tale is this — *you!*"

Conan's vengeful fingers strangled the yell in his throat. They went to the floor together and Conan wrenched the dagger from his enemy's hand. The blade glinted in the starlight, and blood spurted. Aram Baksh made hideous noises, gasping and gagging on a mouthful of blood. Conan dragged him to his feet and again the dagger slashed, and most of the curly beard fell to the floor.

Still gripping his captive's throat — for a man can scream incoherently even with his tongue slit — Conan dragged him out of the dark chamber and down the cypress-shadowed path, to the iron-bound door in the outer wall. With one hand he lifted the bolt and threw the door open, disclosing the three shadowy figures which waited like black vultures outside. Into their eager arms Conan thrust the innkeeper.

A horrible, blood-choked scream rose from the Zamboulan's throat, but there was no response from the silent tavern. The people there were used to screams outside the wall. Aram Baksh fought like a wild man, his distended eyes turned frantically on the Cimmerian's face. He found no mercy there. Conan was thinking of the scores of wretches who owed their bloody doom to this man's greed.

In glee the Negroes dragged him down the road, mocking his frenzied gibberings. How could they recognize Aram Baksh in this half-naked, blood-stained figure, with the grotesquely shorn beard and unintelligible babblings? The sounds of the struggle came back to Conan, standing beside the gate, even after the clump of figures had vanished among the palms.

Closing the door behind him, Conan returned to his horse, mounted and turned westward, toward the open desert, swinging wide to skirt the sinister belt of palm groves. As he rode, he drew from his belt a ring in which gleamed a jewel that snared the starlight in a shimmering iridescence. He held it up to admire it, turning it this way and that. The compact bag of gold pieces clinked gently at his saddle-bow, like a promise of the greater riches to come.

"I wonder what she'd say if she knew I recognized her as Nafertari and him as Jungir Khan the instant I saw them," he mused. "I knew the Star of Khorala, too. There'll be a fine scene if she ever guesses that I slipped it off his finger while I was tying him with his sword belt. But they'll never catch me, with the start I'm getting."

He glanced back at the shadowy palm groves, among which a red glare was mounting. A chanting rose to the night, vibrating with savage exultation. And another sound mingled with it, a mad, incoherent screaming, a frenzied gibbering in which no words could be distinguished. The noise followed Conan as he rode westward beneath the paling stars.